D1459513

Shadow Girls

CAROL BIRCH is the award-winning writer of fourteen novels, including *Jamrach's Menagerie*, which was shortlisted for the Man Booker Prize in 2011. Her first novel, *Life in the Palace*, won the David Higham Award for Fiction (Best First Novel of the Year), and her second novel, *The Fog Line*, won the Geoffrey Faber Memorial Prize. Born in Manchester, she now lives in Lancaster.

Also by Carol Birch

Life in the Palace
The Fog Line
The Unmaking
Songs of the West
Little Sister
Come Back, Paddy Riley
Turn Again Home
In a Certain Light
The Naming of Eliza Quinn
Scapegallows
Jamrach's Menagerie
Orphans of the Carnival
Cold Boy's Wood

Shadow Girls

Carol Birch

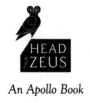

An Apollo Book

Head of Zeus Ltd
5–8 Hardwick Street
London EC1R 4RG
WWW.HEADOFZEUS.COM

For Jan

Part One

Penumbra

WE WERE THREE ROWS OF GIRLS in grey pleated skirts and green V-necked jumpers bearing the gold crest and the school motto: Veritas et Constantia. Music, Friday morning. I was in the middle row with Pamela. Her deep voice hovered above the girly highness, in tune but out of sync with all the rest – not that she cared, she'd belt it out even if she sounded like a crow. I only mouthed the words because I couldn't hold a tune to save my life. My voice was hopeless.

In front of us, front row centre, Sylvia Rose, star singer. Nothing nice about her but the name.

Mr Phelps stopped playing, held up his hands, swivelled round on his stool to face us. 'Some of you are going down when you should be going up,' he said.

'Sounds painful,' said Dotty Spawl and a titter ran through us, but he wasn't in the mood – poor thing with his high white face. 'Now, come on, look,' he said sadly, 'I know it's Friday and everyone's tired but at least *try* and make the effort. You *know* this,' and turned back to the old Broadwood, preparing to play, hair flopping in brown strings over his brow. He was young and thin and male, a rare thing in our school. 'Now let's go,' he said.

We'd sung it a hundred times. That tired old piano. Dum diddle *um* da dum dum, *dum* diddle *um* da – supposed to sound like the waves of the sea.

And we're off!

O-o-o-o-o-o-or the ocean flies a merry fae—

Thirty-six voices. And though I was behind her, all I could hear was that way that Sylvia sang that set my teeth on edge, unnatural, like dressage with horses. The way her mouth put itself through those smug distorted articulations. The way her throat clicked on the hard *g* at the end of *rolling* in *rolling sea*. She knew we were laughing at her.

as she passes all the blue waves say—

Well, she asks for it.

Marianina, do not roam
Whither, whither is thy home
Come and turn us into foam

And the music went tripping along.

At the end of the lesson I got a dirty look from Mr Phelps. Everyone was mucking about, not just me, but it was me he looked at. Mr Phelps was OK. Pamela's voice was in full mimic mode. *Co-o-me, oh co-o-me*, she sang pompously, *and turn us into foam*, mouth all over the place, conducting with her arms. Sylvia was up ahead of us pretending to take no notice.

'Ssh,' I said, 'stop it, stop it,' hoping Mr Phelps would hear.

Pamela laughed and stopped, and we walked along the

corridor with our books clutched tight against our chests, mine completely flat, hers enormous. The knot of her tie was always too small and looked as if it was strangling her. It was lunchtime.

We didn't have school dinners. We were supposed to take our packed lunches into the dining hall and eat in the packed lunch section, but we always took our sandwiches up to the greenhouse on the roof. The corridors teemed. Staff swept the floors with their black gowns and every height and corner of the place was stuffed with the smell of meat pie, hot pastry, gravy. The building was old, with lofty ceilings and high windows, wide corridors and walls of shiny brown tiles, five stacked layers of them with a staircase at either end going from top to bottom, and at each mid-landing the light streaming in through arched windows frosted at the bottom so you couldn't look out. You reached the greenhouse up a narrow wooden stair from the top floor where the science labs were, out of bounds unless you had special permission, but no one ever went there at lunchtime. All you had to do was get past Tasker and Tufton, Chemistry and Physics, standing apart from the herd like scary old bulls on the top floor. We were good at sneaking.

We loved the greenhouse. So quiet after all the downstairs jumble, so nice to eat your sandwiches looking up at the sky. The roof was a fantasia of turrets and chimneys, with skylights and sheds, all kinds of strange things. From where we sat on our bench we could look straight out at the big central turret, a flat-topped grey slate pyramid crowned with iron spikes. Our school was a long building of red brick and yellow sandstone right in the middle of the city.

The streets all around teemed with traffic but it was far away. It wasn't much of a greenhouse, just a small, earthy-smelling, wooden-floored space with shelves on either side and a couple of benches to sit on and a small stepladder to the door leading onto the roof, which sometimes was locked but more often was not. I don't think I ever heard anyone say the roof itself was out of bounds, but I suppose it must have been. Anyhow, you could push hard against the stiffness of the old door and get out. The sky made you dizzy up there. Once we actually ate our sandwiches sitting right next to the wall that overlooked the playground, and once next to the plinth under the big turret.

It was too cold to go out today. Inside was musty and warm. Pamela lit a cigarette and opened a window slightly to blow the smoke through. She smoked the way my mum and dad did, second nature. I didn't smoke, it made me feel sick.

'I don't mind her being posh,' Pamela said, 'it's the way she looks down her nose.'

'I know.' First time I saw Sylvia, eleven years old, all of us new, standing next to my desk doing nothing in particular, just looking down into it – she comes by, says in that snotty voice, 'What are you looking at?' Her face frowning at me, not meeting my eyes. All sharp bones, even her face with its witchy chin and pointy nose and long upper lip, snooty eyebrows arching up into her forehead.

'What do you mean?' I said. 'I'm not looking at anything.'

'Why are you looking in my desk?'

'It's *my* desk.'

Sylvia realised she'd made a mistake and blushed. 'Sorry,'

she said and off she marched as if she was in the right anyway. That's how she was.

'Good voice though,' I said.

'Oh aye, she's got a good voice. Got to give the girl something.'

'She can go really high and low.'

Pamela gave a pig snort.

The few plants were a bit straggly. This was not hyacinth season, when all the little first-formers brought their bulbs out of the darkness and the whole place was full of the gorgeous scent. This was getting on for the tail end of the year. Two months to Christmas and Mocks coming up. Horrors. The light was subdued by the shadow of the turret. Hardly afternoon and the sky was darkening.

'That big black cloud,' I said.

'Gonna pour.'

This was where we came to tell scary stories. I still hated going upstairs to the toilet in the old house where my grandparents lived, so why on earth I loved scary stories I don't know. Pamela was full of them. That one, that one time, the one where I nearly fell down the stairs, I never had a tingle down the back of my neck and to my heels as I had that time descending the wooden steps after—

'James?'

'Yes, Madame?'

'James?'

'Yes, Madame? Madame, may I ask one thing?'

'Yes, James?'

'Madame—?'

'Yes, James?'
'Madame—?'
'Yes, James?'
'Madame—'
AAAAAAAAAAAAAAARGHHH

—for God's sake, the way she screamed! Curdled the blood in your spine.

'Whose daft idea was it to choose *Caesar and Cleopatra* for the play?' said Pamela, inhaling.

'Frith.'

'Stupid. There's only two female roles.' She blew the last smoky mouthful out of the window and ground the dog-end viciously into the wood at the back of the bench.

'Hope it's better than *She Stoops to Conquer.*'

'Ach!' she gagged.

The bell rang.

English with Miss Swett, *Macbeth*, then triple Games. We were bunking off from that, me because I was rubbish at anything and everything to do with sports apart from dodging the ball, she because though she could've demolished a hockey team with one charge she hated stripping off and running round a stupid field in the freezing cold and it took her ages getting home from the Games field and she didn't see the point. Anyway, we liked going round town. We'd been bunking off for so long now that it would be noticed if we suddenly turned up. Best not to rock the boat. In our classroom Dotty was sticking out her huge breasts as she put her hair up, Shanna was plaiting Linda's hair, Gail Turnbull was talking about how spotty her boyfriend's back was. The light was harsh and pressing. Shanna poked me between the shoulder blades. 'You bunking off?' she said.

'Of course.'

'One of these days.' She smashed the spine of her exercise book down along its length with the side of her fist. I was jealous of Shanna's hair, a natural riot of thick black curls.

'Live dangerously,' said Pamela.

'Yup,' said Sheila Simpson, 'till the excrement hits the proverbial.'

Miss Swett came in the open door and walked to the teacher's desk on stumpy black heels, dropped her books and files on it and let them fall sideways. 'Afternoon, girls,' she said. Miss Swett was young and trim with short dark hair.

'Afternoon, Miss Swett.' We'd got used to her name by now.

'Tell me, someone,' she said, half-turned to the blackboard, chalk in hand, 'where did we leave off last time?'

'Sheesh!' said Dotty Spawl. She was always saying that. She said, 'Sheesh!' and Sheila said, 'Heavens to Murgatroyd!' about fifty times a day, and I can tell you, it was trying.

'Anyone?'

'The murderers killed Lady Macduff and the little boy,' said Sheila.

'They did indeed, Sheila. But we went further than that, didn't we?'

Linda put her hand up. 'Macduff wants revenge. They were in England getting up an army.'

'That's right. A bit more, please.'

'It was Malcolm and Macduff. Macduff took it very hard.'

'Well, you would, wouldn't you,' said Sheila and a laugh went round.

'I don't think he took it that badly really.' Gail from the back row. 'That was me, I'd've been screaming blue murder.'

'Well, what do you think about that?' Miss Swett was writing on the board: Act V, Scene 1. 'Would it have been more effective, do you think, if we'd seen Macduff break down and shout and scream or fall on the floor?'

'No,' I said.

'Can you tell us why, Sally?'

'Well, people don't necessarily behave like that, do they? I mean, it's like if you're in shock. You might look normal, you might not say anything, but all it means is that you just can't take it in. I thought it was really sad, when he said, "What, all my pretty ones?" very quietly, and then he said it again a bit later as if he couldn't believe it. I think he did.'

'That's right.' Miss Swett sat down and dragged a book from the collapsed pile. 'And that's why Shakespeare's such a powerful playwright. He sees the complexity in the way people behave.'

Pamela poked me in the side. 'You're right, you know,' she said.

'Act V, Scene 1,' said Miss Swett.

We opened our books. Pamela slightly raised the lid of her desk and slipped one hand in the gap to scrabble about inside.

'We'll carry on with the read-through. Now this is a small scene but it's a very important one.'

'Out, damned spot!' said Sheila, splaying her hand.

'Thank you, Sheila. I'm sure you've all remembered this bit.' We'd had the whole thing on the radio over three lessons. Next was Lady Macbeth. Miss Swett looked around at us all. 'Sheila,' she said, 'will you be Lady Macbeth?'

Sheila pulled a face.

'OK. Doctor? Any volunteers?'

'I'll do it.'

'Good, thank you, Susan. Gentlewoman? Gentlewoman? Pamela, put your desk lid down.'

Pamela looked up, surprised. The underside of her desk lid was papered with cut-offs from *Disc* and *Pop Weekly* – Stones, Beatles, the Walker Brothers. She closed it but not before she'd sneaked out a crumpled package with the remains of her cold toast and laid it on her knee. No one wanted to be Gentlewoman.

'Sally,' Miss Swett said, 'you're the Gentlewoman.'

We were terrible actors, sitting there at our desks reading from the page. I don't know who was worse. Me and Susan Grech speaking the words with minimal inflection, Susan stumbling over *perturbation*, me at one point trying to put in a bit of expression but hearing my voice sound stupid as it left my mouth just the way it did when I sang. So I gave up and just read the words. Enter Lady Macbeth. Sheila, bending her high sweaty forehead over the book. 'Yet here's a spot,' she said as if she was cleaning the kitchen. And all the damned spot and murky hell and the smell of the blood and – Oh, oh, oh! – all that – the three of us just reading the words.

'Can you put a bit more into it?' Miss Swett asked without much hope.

I got the easiest part. Sheila sighed loudly behind me when she finished her bit. Susan had the final speech, plod plod plod, and I got the last line:

'Good night, good doctor.'

We were awful. After I said, 'Good night, good doctor', Pamela gave me a gormless-face look and drawled, 'Night-night!', in an idiot nasal whisper, and it was so stupid it made me laugh and I couldn't stop.

'All right, all right,' Miss Swett said, 'yes yes yes yes yes, it's all very funny, ha ha. Now settle down.'

The trouble with me was, when I got going, I couldn't stop.

'Now,' Miss Swett said, 'if you had to put it in one word, what is that scene about?'

Pamela ripped off a piece of toast, leaving her finger marks in it, handed it sideways to me underneath the desk. 'I think you deserve this,' she said under her breath, 'after that brilliant performance.'

'Guilt,' said Sylvia Rose.

'Guilt indeed,' said Miss Swett.

The basement was tiled and dim and stretched into shadows at either end. Mysterious doors on one side were never opened and always kept locked. On the other side a high partition of painted wood and frosted glass concealed the toilet block with its long row of face-to-face sinks all down the middle of the room. At either end of the corridor there

was a cloakroom, each one dark and spooky, but ours was
the worst. We used to be in the other one down at the far
end – it was bigger and more impersonal and much more
crowded – but now we were higher up the school we had
the little cloakroom in the dark end, and it was creepy as
hell. We had our own toilets but not enough sinks for us all
and you could smell the toilets. I once saw a pair of pale
bare feet walking rapidly along the whole length of the
toilet row, below the line of the partition, but no one came
out at the other end. Instead of going to look, I clamped
my teeth together, goggled at the dark air and flew from
that place with the devils of hell nipping the nape of my
neck.

We hung about in the cloakroom trying to look as if we
were getting ready for the Games field like everyone else.
Pamela spent ages washing her hands at one of the basins,
the back of her yellow blouse pulled out of her waistband
and bunching up at the back. Me, deeply absorbed in
packing my school bag just so, cutting out all eye contact
with the others, silly strident voices spouting nonsense –
Sheila: Rose! Rose! Lend me your nose! – Dotty, back to her:
Rose! Rose! Give me your toes! Then a double cascading
cackle. Just anything stupid that came into their heads and
out of their mouths. The sound of Sylvia blowing her nose.
She cleared her nose about fifty times a day and carried
a fancy initialled handkerchief in the breast pocket of her
blouse for the purpose. She was always sniffy. I thought it
was funny for someone with such a good voice to be always
sniffy, but having no voice myself, who was I to say? From
the corner of our eyes we watched them go, tired stoic girls

trooping with gym pumps sticking out of drawstring bags slung on their shoulders. Not for a million pounds would I have gone with them. The buses, the blabber blabber, the horrible knowledge that you were crap at what was coming next. Never. Bloody Sylvia, of course, taking forever, looking back once and seeing us there, giving us one of her weird scowls, a face you could punch, looking down on us, immaculate hat straight and smart on her plain brown hair, feet in sensible shoes with newly polished round brown toes, bag with embossed initials in gold – S.F.R. – a bag that did not hang from one shoulder but sat straight across her back with its straps symmetrical.

The buses left from the back of the school, across the yard. When everyone had gone and it was all quiet we went the front way, moving quickly. If we didn't get to the end of Portland Street in about two minutes, we might meet the bus as it turned out of Sackville Street and then, as Pamela said, we'd really be bucked and fuggered. First, though, we had to get across the park in full view of the staff room and Miss Demery's room. Upstairs, out the door, brisk and confident, looking as if we should. The park was small, really not much more than a green square with paths and flower beds shaped like orange segments, past the bench where sometimes Rob Callan sat waiting for me after school. We had dental appointments. Of course we did. Sorry, I was in a rush this morning and I left the note on the table, I'll bring it in tomorrow. Sorry, sorry.

You'd never really know if you'd been seen till the next day, but once we were out we didn't care. Town was busy, traffic revving and wheezing, people waiting at bus stops or walking head down into the gritty wind. Our route to Piccadilly was complicated and brought us out near Victoria's statue. It was good to be out and about, not to be feeling carsick on the bus as it jerked through broken-winded traffic, not to be watching goosebumps prickle on your forearm as you changed into your gym kit, not to be listening to the constant girly babble-and-snigger, not to be watery-eyed on the edge of a field feeling pointless. We ran across at the lights and carried on running straight down into the toilets, where we took off our hats and ties in front of the long mirror, stuffed them in our bags, hitched up our skirts and rolled them over at the waist to make them shorter. I took the elastic bands out of my hair and fluffed it up. A thick-bodied woman in an overall was sweeping the floor. Pamela got a block of mascara out of her bag and wet the brush under a tap. She was quite fastidious and never spat on it.

'I'm going to get my hair cut really short,' she said, loading the brush and stroking the brush against her eyelashes.

'It's short already,' I said.

'No, a pixie cut. I don't like this.'

'You'd suit a pixie cut.'

'I don't care, I'm going to get it done anyway,' she said as if someone was telling her not to. Her eyes were getting spiky. 'You know, like Audrey Hepburn.'

'That's not a pixie cut. She puts it up. You'd suit a pixie cut, though, you've got thick hair. Mine would just lie down flat if I got one.'

'I don't know,' she said. 'You've got a nice little face. I think you could get away with it.' Sometimes she was positively motherly.

'I'd never dare cut all my hair off,' I said, looking at my boring brown hair.

The woman in the overall was nearer than before. She had a cigarette sticking out of one corner of her mouth, and the ash was spilling down her front. 'No school, girls?' she said in a throaty voice.

'Got the dentist,' said Pamela. 'I've got a wisdom tooth.'

'Both of you?'

'Yeah, she has to look after me. I pass out sometimes at the dentist's, I get really nervous.'

We smiled and she smiled along with us knowingly. Pamela clipped the mascara box shut, dropped it in her bag and got out a ten pack of Number Eights. 'Can I have a light, love?' she said. The woman handed over a still glowing stub and wandered away with her brush. Pamela sucked hard, lit up, flicked the stub into the sink and ran the tap on it and up we went into noisy daylight. Queen Victoria was all white with droppings. Not much was blooming in the gardens but the fountain was going and there were a few people on the benches. Buses lined up, some two abreast, all round the square.

It was cold so we went into Lewis's to warm up. A great blast of hot air hit you as you walked through the front doors, and then the smell of the perfume counters got the back of your nose. We tried the samplers.

'What about this one?'

'Mm. I quite like that. What is it?'

Coty L'Aimant. My sister Jo wore it a lot. She left a hefty trace of it in the house whenever she went out.

A thin snoopy-looking woman with corrugated hair

approached. 'Is it for yourself or is it a present?' she asked coldly.

'I'm thinking of getting some for my sister's birthday,' I said.

'Were you wanting a gift pack?'

'I'm not really sure; I'm just looking at the moment.' I sniffed my wrist. 'I'll have to have a think.'

We moved on, into the sweets and food and drink where the tasting samples were laid out everywhere on stalls. We tried fudge, ginger cake, cheese, tiny sausages, silverskin pickles on sticks. Some places we went back twice. No one seemed to mind.

'On the lam, are you?' said one of the women. 'Have a bit of this custard tart.'

We rode the escalator to the record department, flicked through shiny LPs. Three boys further up on the other side of the rack were looking at us. One had a long bony face, one looked like a koala bear, one wore a black leather Donovan cap. Ignoring them studiedly, we looked through the singles in their crisp paper coats, considering going into one of the listening booths but deciding against it as time was moving on. Had to be on our buses before school came out and the town got infected with loud green girls. Down two lots of escalators to the teen clothes department, where we riffled through racks of things we couldn't afford.

'I want one of these,' Pamela said, pulling out an electric blue dress, 'and one of these and—'

Pamela had a short thick neck. She was a big girl with

a wide confrontational face and footballer's legs but the clothes she liked to wear when she went out were soft and pale and fluffy. When we went to see *The Greatest Story Ever Told* she wore a big white fake fur hood that cradled her face like the face of a baby in its crib. It was hilarious; she cried her eyes out at that film all through the crucifixion, really sobbed and whimpered. Her face went beetroot red and her eye makeup was all smeared, and when we went outside and she caught sight of herself in a mirror she started to laugh. 'Look at me,' she said, 'face like a slapped arse.'

'The hood!' I said and we laughed ourselves silly.

'And I want one of these and one of these and one of these...', till she fell upon a coffee and cream op-art mini-dress that she just had to try on and dashed off into the changing room. I waited, looked at a black dress with a round neck and flower pattern, held it against me in front of a mirror. You couldn't tell, not against these horrible school shoes and green gabardine. The lighting in here was harsh. My face looked plain. I glanced at my watch. Better get a move on, what's she doing? I gave her another minute then lifted back the curtain. She was in one of the cubicles.

'Pamela,' I called, but there was no answer.

'Pamela, which one are you in?'

She swore under her breath and moaned, 'This one!'

'What's it like? Any good?'

'Get in here,' she whispered, loud enough for the other girls in the communal changing room to hear.

I slipped behind the curtain.

'It's stuck,' she said. 'Can you shift it?'

Her bra straps were grubby pink and cut too tightly into her back.

'How've you done this?' I said.

'God knows. I got it up all right, it just stuck when I pulled it down.'

The dress was too tight, the zip jammed just below her shoulder blades.

'Can't get it up, can't get it down,' she said and laughed.

'Stand still.'

I struggled with it for a bit but it was hopeless and we started to giggle.

'You'll have to buy it,' I said.

'They'll have to cut me out of it. I'll sue them.'

'What we gonna do?'

'Just pull,' she said, 'hard.'

I did. It didn't move but the material went into a bunch underneath where it was stuck.

'Oh my God, I've made it worse.'

We giggled some more. I had to sit down on the floor.

'My God, it's half past,' she said, 'if we don't go now we're bucked and fuggered. Pull it, pull it!' and she yanked and twisted till the dress inch by inch moved round back to front on her and the seam split in three or four places. She was going, 'Yo-o heave-ho, yo-o heave-ho, help me with it, come on...' till the zip was in reach. 'There, grab that.' We both pulled and the whole thing ripped down the back and I saw above her navy blue gym knickers a mass of bruising that stretched from just underneath her bra on one side down into her knickers on the other.

'God, Pamela, what's this?'

There was one bit somewhere in the middle that was redder than the rest, as if there was blood just beneath the surface.

'God, Pamela,' I said.

She smiled. 'Yeah, look at it,' she said, a bit embarrassed, 'mess.'

'How did that happen?'

'Mucking about.'

'Mucking about?'

'Mucking about on the tip,' she said, pulling her school blouse back over her head and kicking the ruined dress aside.

'What kind of mucking about's that?' I asked her.

'Mucking about kind of mucking about,' she said and laughed, getting dressed. 'I fell over.'

'Are you getting it seen to?'

'Course I am. Look at this, we'll have to sneak it back on the rail. Come on, we've got to go. You go out first.'

I went out. There was no one about. She came after with her school bag hanging from one shoulder, holding the dress primly so that no damage showed.

'OK, Pamela?' I said.

'Bit too small,' she said. 'Shame. Nice dress,' and slid it back in the middle of the rack. We walked quickly away.

Half way down the escalator she said, 'Don't look now but those boys are following us.'

I looked. It was the boys from the record department, above us on the escalator. The one in the black cap winked at me.

'Actually,' she whispered, 'the blond one, the one that looks like a ghost? He's not too bad.'

I wasn't sure. Oh God, you, my mum always said, nothing's ever good enough for you, is it? At the bottom of the escalator we walked on towards the front doors and the boys followed. 'The one in the black cap fancies you,' Pamela said. 'I'll have the blond one.' They caught up with us just as we were going through the door. The thin one leaned down close to Pamela's ear as they passed and she smiled, looking away.

'Oy, Big Leg,' he said, grinning with his lopsided mouth, 'I'd shag you if I was really hard up.'

Her face collapsed. Looking back, laughing stupidly, the three of them loped across the road towards the gardens.

'Stupid morons!' she yelled after them.

'Idiots,' I said.

Her eyes were spurting tears. 'I hate 'em,' she spat through gritted teeth, 'I really, really hate 'em.'

'They're just stupid,' I said, 'they don't know anything,' wanting to say more. But there was no time, we'd be caught, it was all rush rush rush, see you Monday, take no notice, and she went her way and I went mine and got on my bus with not a second to spare. It pulled away from its stop as I lurched along the top deck. As it rounded the bend I saw the first green girls appear from the corner of Chorlton Street, bending forwards into the wind, hair straining back from their foreheads. Further down the road we passed Pamela's stop and she was still waiting, standing at the end of the queue just outside the shelter, leaning her head against the metal pole. Her eyes were closed. She looked so tired it made me yawn. I thought about the bruises, how I'd seen the odd one before but never as bad as that, and about the look in her eyes when the boy said that nasty smug thing in such an off-hand way to her. I don't know how we came to be friends, good little me and big noisy her, it was before she got put up into my class from below. I think in the schoolyard, or maybe in the hall when it was too cold for outside, playing Jacks and Pick-up Sticks. She came in from seeing Miss Demery with her face fierce and bright red and tears in her eyes.

'Stupid bitch,' she said to no one in particular.

'What's up, Pamela?' someone said.

She had a way of being there, a big presence, yet nearly always on her own. She sat down pouting, legs splayed out in front of her. I was counting out playing cards, Happy Families with dogs. I'd brought them in but no one wanted to play. I really liked them. The dogs were beautifully drawn, lovely dog and puppy faces above their human clothes, the butcher, the postman, the policeman.

'What's them?' she scowled.

'Just cards. Happy Families. Dogs.'

'Gi's a look.' She grabbed them off me. 'That's like my Bobby,' she said.

She was always going on about her Bobby, a little shaggy white thing, very old with no teeth. I never saw him because she lived miles away and I never went to her house and she never came to mine, we only ever met up in town sometimes to go and see a film. We saw *The Sound of Music* and *The Greatest Story Ever Told*.

★

I got home at a time that I didn't think would look too suspicious. Our house was a semi at the end of a cul de sac off a main road. There were privet hedges all along the sides and the railway ran at the back. Our front garden was just long grass. Once or twice a year my dad decided to clip it with the hedge clippers but he never did a very good job and most of the time it just did its own thing. My brother Tony's motorbike leaned on the wall at the side of the house, looking cold in its grey plastic coat.

The hall smelt of aftershave and soap. Tony was watching *The Magic Roundabout* with his hair wet and a mug of tea on the arm of the settee. His Adam's apple was his main feature.

'Going out?' I said, poking my head round the door.

'Yeah.' He didn't look up.

Jo was in the kitchen making stinky cheese on toast, still in her work clothes, a boring grey skirt and cream-coloured blouse.

'Mum back yet?'

'No,' she said.

Good. All safe.

'You were seen,' said Jo, switching off the grill and turning away from the cooker with a hideous air of smugness. The white uniform of a dental nurse lay discarded on the floor next to the washing machine.

'What are you talking about?'

Jo's hair was dyed jet black and hung down just beyond her waist. She had plunging cheeks and bulging eyes and was considered striking. 'You. You were seen. In town. With that common girl you go about with. Pigging your faces at the cheese stall in Lewis's.'

'I wasn't in Lewis's,' I said.

'Mmmmmmm...' she said, very sarky, 'that's not what Mrs Shelley said.'

'Oh for God's sake! She's senile.'

'No she's not.'

She walked away, taking her cheese on toast upstairs. I followed. 'What did she say?'

'She was in town and she said she saw you with a big girl in Lewis's at the cheese stall.'

'I don't believe you. She never goes into town.'

'Well, she did today. Her daughter took her in.' Jo sat down in front of her kidney-shaped dressing table and adjusted the mirrors.

'Well, she didn't see *me*. I wasn't there.'

'You would say that, wouldn't you?'

The cheese on toast was on a plate next to her with a couple of bites missing. She pulled a square of tissue from a slit in a pink box, wrapped it over an index finger and picked in the corner of one eye. Mr and Mrs Shelley were about ninety and lived at the other end of our road. *She* was a nosy old badger, *he* was a miserable goblin, always moaning about everything and complaining when the kids from across the way chalked on the pavement.

'You always lie, don't you,' Jo said, examining a stale spot of old black eye makeup on the tissue.

'No I don't.'

'Yes you do. You're doing it now. You do it all the time.

Why don't you just admit it? I've never known anyone lie the way you do.'

'You don't know what you're talking about,' I said, picking things – hairpins, comb, pink nail polish – up off her dressing table and putting them down again in different places to annoy her. She slapped my hand.

'Pretty pathetic,' she said, 'the way you squiggle and wiggle to get out of it.' She picked up a hand mirror with a rose-patterned back and looked at herself. In the mirror her face had the same smug punchability of Sylvia Rose looking back at us in the cloakroom.

'It's got nothing to do with you anyway,' I said, 'nothing's got anything to do with you.'

'If you knew how stupid you sound.' She stroked her fringe, and her permanent look of wounded disapproval grew dreamy. 'Bugger off,' she said, 'standing over me like that.'

I went into my room and closed the door. It was true I lied. It was the only way to get through life. I'd deny everything. No one could prove a thing. For God's sake, who does it kill if we don't go and freeze out on the Games field? The brats were making a hell of a racket in the next room, Paul going *nurr nurr nurr*, Philip *nee-naw nee-naw*, then a series of crashing sounds as if they were bouncing off the walls. My room was such a mess that I walked across papers and flattened books and crumpled clothes to reach my unmade bed. My rug had a picture of tigers on it and was very worn out and I had a Rolling Stones poster on the back of the door. I emptied my bag. Homework, get it out of the way. Biology. Maths. Practise French Oral. In a whisper because if this lot heard, they'd take the piss. I upended my bag on the bed and flopped down, banged with the side of my fist on the wall. From downstairs came the theme tune of *The Magic Roundabout*. Next to my head was a picture I'd cut out of an old book the kids had ruined by spilling milk all over it. It was wavy at the sides and still a bit smelly and showed a white winged horse soaring up towards the golden clouds of heaven. Underneath it said: Pegasus Set Free. I liked to lie and look at it, the waving mane, the gorgeous freedom, and think, to be that, oh to be that.

I lay down to do my homework but my eyes kept closing and my mind wandered. I made myself sit up properly to concentrate on photosynthesis but was all shaken up and didn't know why. My eyes wandered along the mantelpiece over the disused fireplace where all my knick-knacks were lined up, my gold crown money box from the coronation that would only take sixpence, two glass dogs, pine cones, empty perfume pots and a cheap old crinoline lady with a silly face that the paint was cracking off. After a while I gave up, kneeled on the bed with my arms on the windowsill, looking out across the dark back garden (just more grass) to where the railway line ran at the back of our row of houses. I could watch the trains going by heading in and out of Piccadilly. There should be one along in about four minutes. It was still blowy as hell out there, the trees were fluttering along the railway embankment, and the sky was darkening. It would rain.

Christ, those kids were noisy. I marched out and pushed their door open. 'Shut your bloody faces,' I said, 'I'm trying to do my homework.'

'This is our house as much as yours,' said Philip righteously.

One on the bed, one on the floor, red-faced, glaring at me with pouty mouths. They'd been sweet when they were tots but now they were just irritating.

'Well, keep it down,' I said, 'I'm doing my homework.'

'Piggy!' Philip threw something at the closing door, so I turned back.

'If I tell Mum you wouldn't let me do my homework, she'll go mad,' I said.

They ignored me. 'Wait and see,' I said and went back to my own room.

I'm stuck between two lots of twins, neither of them identical. God knows, if I ever get pregnant, perish the thought, there'd probably be two of them. The only way to exist in this place is to be alone. It was the only, the desired state.

I heard Mum come home downstairs. She talked in the kitchen with Jo while they made tea and I thought she might be telling Mum about what old Mrs Shelley said. Hell with the lot of you, I thought, got under the top sheet and thought about Rob Callan. *He* didn't think I was a fool. He thought I was lovely. My books fell on the floor. I'd been going out with him for four months. He was a sweet boy, nice to be with. We could spend hours and hours doing nothing much at all, just feeling OK, as if we'd always been best friends from ages ago, hundreds of years. I never felt awkward with him. He was doing Maths and Physics and History and Geography for A Levels – four! – and he was gentle and slow and tall, with a big nose that turned up and had a cleft in the end, a crooked front tooth and a faint cast in one eye. At first I wasn't sure about his looks but when I saw how all the other girls acted around him I realised it was the flaws that made him attractive. Sometimes he put me in mind of a country boy in a fairy tale, the son of an honest woodcutter or something.

Here came the train, thundering past. Rattletyrack, rattletyrack. The sound of my nights. I liked it. When fear came in at the edges, always at the edges like shadows, dimming the parts of the room I couldn't see, I liked to hear my good old trains. If you looked out you could see faces in the train windows, indistinct behind the glass. Sometimes the train was slowing down as they passed and you could see the people getting their coats on and their bags down from the luggage racks. All their funny separate lives and each one thinking it was all about them. And me here. And no idea at all where I was going. I drew the curtains across; they only just met in the middle. They were green with silky leaves in stripes, and they smelt of dust. In one of them was a long jagged rip. I did that with my teeth one day when I was very, very angry, when it all came forcing itself up right through the middle of me like a geyser from the top of my head.

'But there's only two parts for girls.' It wasn't a popular choice, *Caesar and Cleopatra* by George Bernard Shaw. Miss Frith in Latin said it didn't matter and went on about how in Shakespeare's day all the roles were played by men, even Juliet, which we already knew of course. The performances were what mattered, she said. She was in charge with Miss Swett. We did a read-through with Miss Swett, and Frith showed us a film in 4 Alpha. It was awful. Everyone was posh. It had a kind of Eliza Doolittle/Henry Higgins feel about it, with Caesar as a big smug creep of about sixty and Cleopatra an idiot. I hated her. I had actually thought about playing her once. When they took us to see *Antony and Cleopatra* at the Octagon I think it was. Not that I ever could have done it. Too scared. It would just be, 'Good night, good doctor,' all over again. Oh but I knew how I'd play her, the big queen, the barge she sat in like a burnished throne and all that, the asp, the foolery – not that sap in the film. I'd actually tried in front of the mirror. I looked really stupid. The more I tried the more unnatural I looked and the weirder my mouth went. It was weird. I knew I could do it but I couldn't. Anyway, there was no point because it was always the same people who got all the good roles. Dotty always got in. Sylvia, of course: Raina in *Arms and the Man*, Lady Capulet, Constance in *She Stoops to Conquer*, couldn't act for toffee but could speak words without a stumble and make her voice carry. And of course if ever a bit of singing was required she was the one. But this Cleopatra – what a swizz. She was all screamy and cutesy and skittish and pranced like a four-year-old. And the voice! Froth: *Oh, ay'm so glaard you've cam, ay wors vewy lonely; did you heppen to see a hwite ket anywhere? I'm the bleck kitten of the sacred hwite ket* – all so very very farst and frightfully frightfully, as if she was at a tea party. Podgy parrot Caesar, wearing lipstick, teaches her how to behave like a proper queen and she squeals: *Oh, hwat will heppen to me if you never cam beck!*

'That's not Cleopatra!' I said. 'Look at her in *Antony and Cleopatra.*'

'Ah,' said Miss Frith with a knowing smile, 'very true. And what's the difference?'

'One's the majesty of the Nile, the other's syrup.'

'Not quite, Sally.'

'Syrup,' snorted Pamela.

'This is the *young* Cleopatra,' Miss Frith said, 'hardly more than a child, about the same age as you are now, girls.'

'God, I hope we're not *that* stupid.'

Miss Frith smirked. She was a tall scrawny-necked old woman with curly bronze hair and heavy powder. 'I will not comment,' she said.

'I don't believe she was ever like that,' I said. Sickmaking. But Frith said it was the ideal play for girls of our age.

Well, I thought, no way would I play that stupid thing. I just wanted to slap her.

The school play was quite a big deal, parents coming and everything, so they made a project of it with a trip to the Egyptian room at the museum to get us in the mood. Two by two, we crocodiled through town with Miss Frith and Miss Swett. Pamela was off sick so I walked with Sylvia. The Christmas decorations were going up and my mum had been moaning all week about it getting earlier and earlier each year. Sylvia strode out briskly at my side. We didn't speak much, just things like, 'Oh good, the light's changing,' and, 'glad I put my scarf on,' till by the Palace Theatre she said, 'Do you like going to the museum?'

'I love it. Great to get out of school.'

'Mm.'

'Not just that. I just like it.'

'Which is your favourite bit?' she asked a bit later, and I realised I should have asked if she liked going to the museum, so I said it now.

'Very much,' she replied solemnly.

'My favourite bit,' I said, 'is the Maori head.'

She nodded sagely, thoughtful about the mouth.

I could have looked at a mummy or a shrunken head all day but the Maori man's head was the best. It was on a stand behind glass. His face was tattooed all over in blue circular swirls and he had beautiful cheekbones. It seemed to me that something in his tight-skinned face, the parted lips showing teeth, the closed eyes, expressed remnants of wistfulness for his lost life, which I could not imagine. Walking like me, feeling like me, all the fears and fancies. And yet he looked serene.

We didn't speak again.

We knew the museum well, the stuffed animals and birds, the masks and mummies, the smell of old wood and polish and long brown cases with heavy lids that you pulled up to look at the faded insects pinned onto boards. Miss Frith and Miss Swett slid off somewhere probably for a cup of tea or something, leaving us in the study room where we sat at rows of desks just like school and the museum man stood in front talking dully at us. We always had the same man and he always looked miserable. I'd have loved to work at the museum but to look at him you'd have thought it was the most boring job in the world. Imagine being able to go and look at the mummies any time you liked? Imagine walking past the lovely stuffed furry things every day so that you got to know all their faces and they'd be like friends. I said this to Gail Turnbull who was sitting next to me. 'I dunno,' she said, 'probably depressed as hell seeing all those dead things all day long.' I hadn't thought of it that way. We watched a slide show about the Pharaohs, and when it was over the man told us to open our books and copy down the timeline from the board, then he left us alone to get on with it.

We only had about fifteen minutes left. It was that tired time of the afternoon and the room was overheated and windowless.

'If he comes back and tries it on with me again,' Gail said, 'I'm going to kick him in the balls.'

She said the museum man had once put his arm over her shoulder, pretending to turn the page of her exercise book, and he'd touched her tit.

'Ugh!' we all cried. The museum man was old and drab.

'I'd bash his face in if he did that to me.' Susan Grech slouched sideways with one arm hooked round her neck. 'He wouldn't do it twice.'

Sylvia kept gawping at me and it was getting on my nerves. She didn't lift her head, just her eyes, and if I met her gaze she didn't turn away or smile or pretend to have been looking over my head, she just gave me one of her looks, appraising, disapproving. I thought about the play, who would be Cleopatra. If you were good enough you should be able to show the steel under the silly child. After all, she was a terrible woman, she poisoned slaves and prisoners. Sylvia was looking over again; I saw her face turn towards me from the corner of my eye. I should say something. Want to take a picture? Something like that.

'Are you going in for the play?' I said instead.

'No, I don't think so.'

'Why not?'

'There isn't a part I'd like.' She said it as if she could play any of them if she wanted to but didn't feel like it. Then she put her head down and went back to writing conscientiously in her Rough Book. Her parting was greasy. I finished writing all the stuff down off the board and started drawing a mummy in my Rough Book.

Couple of Parents' Evenings ago, they put me and her on the refreshments table pouring out tea and coffee and orange juice at a table next to the stage. Trying to talk to her was like talking to a mute. Whenever she served one of the parents she'd smile adequately and say, 'Thank you *so* much', in a stuffy voice as she gave them their change. She wore ugly shoes and a horrible skirt, a kind of old lady's pleated tweedy thing that came down below her knees. Pamela came to get an orange juice. 'What are you wearing your mother's skirt for?' she said. This was before we'd started knocking about together. Sylvia didn't react at all. You shouldn't say things like that. But it *was* like her mother's skirt. I saw her leaving later with her parents. You could hardly tell her apart from her mother from the back and her father looked really old too.

'Can I see your picture?' Sylvia asked me.

'What, this?' I was pleased with my mummy drawing. Pity I didn't have any crayons, could've got that dull red-brown of the skin. It was a woman shrivelled on her side

CAROL BIRCH

in a box. Lying there surrounded by faces, fascinated by her hip bones and the wisps of coconut fibre still clinging to her skull. I shoved it over to Sylvia and she studied it with raised eyebrows and a frown line as if she was the art teacher.

'That's actually quite good,' she said after a while.

'Thank you,' I said.

'No, really. It is.'

Susan Grech and Sheila were talking about ouija boards. Sheila said she'd done séances with her cousins and once they got an ancient Briton called Celbold. He spelled his name out for them. She said it was sad talking to him, you felt sorry for him. He'd been killed in battle at Verulam.

'You ought to look him up,' I said, 'see if that's a proper old English name.'

'Was he fighting the Romans?' asked Susan.

'I don't know. We lost him after that.'

'Oh dear. Bad line.' Gail had peeled a caramel stick and was sucking noisily.

'I've got a book you might like,' Sylvia said.

Was she talking to me?

'A book?'

'It's about Egypt. Are you interested in Egypt?'

'Er—'

I suppose so.

'—yeah.'

'It's interesting,' she said.

'Oh, right.'

'It's old.'

'Can I have my picture back?' I said. 'I'll do a bit more before he comes back.'

She had finished her work and underlined it using a ruler. Even her Rough Book was neat. 'I don't quite know exactly how old it is,' she said, capping her pen and pushing my picture across the desk. 'There's no date on it.'

'Thanks,' I said. My pencil was getting blunt but it was good for shading. She seemed to expect me to speak, so I said, 'Where did you get it from? The old book?'

'From Egypt,' she said.

'Really? You've been to Egypt?'

'That's where I was born.'

Everyone perked up.

'You never told us that.'

'I never thought of it.'

'Sheesh!' said Sheila.

Sylvia was born in Egypt, the word went round the room. Somehow it changed her in our eyes.

'My father was posted there,' she said, 'in the army,' and it sounded like something out of a book.

'I don't really remember it. We came over here when I was three.'

'Can you do the sand dance?' Sheila got up and cavorted. Up jumped Gail and joined her. They collided, clumsy and laughing, bouncing off one another.

Susan Grech shushed them. 'He'll come in!'

I ran to the door and peeped out. 'All clear!'

They sat down, red-faced, laughing.

'Oh dear, dear,' crooned Sheila, 'well, well, well, I never did in all my life,' and after it had all calmed down and the clock had ticked us a few minutes further on and the yawning had begun, I said to Sylvia, 'So are you going to bring this book in then?'

'I can do,' she said, 'if you'd like to have a look at it.'

We paired up again in the crocodile going back. On the way out we looked at the Maori head.

'Seems wrong,' I said. 'Can you imagine if that was you and one day you're in a museum being looked at by people in the future? As if you're not even real.'

'Don't,' she said.

Back at school it was a free period before hometime and we were supposed to make a start on our homework. I was meeting Robin in the park after school. The girls at the window, who spent most of their time leaning on the radiators looking out like prisoners from their cells, announced it: *Sally, your Robin's here.* I didn't go and look, I knew he'd be there on the bench with his back to the school huddled up in the cold in his brown corduroy jacket.

I was proud of Rob. That'll show 'em, I thought, though I wasn't sure who it was I was showing, or what or why. All I knew was it felt good to go out into the park as if I didn't care, and for him to stand up with his big grin when he saw me coming. Casually, he would take my heavy bag from me and sling it over his high shoulder while they straggled by with their nosy sideways-glancing eyes, putting back their shoulders and walking nicely. Other boys showed up occasionally for other girls but none of them was as fanciable as him. But get this. Sylvia Rose fancied him like mad. It was so obvious, the way whenever he was there she hung about on the other side of the path faffing about with things in her bag. Something in the way she held her mouth, the furtive glances, the forlorn eyes. I don't suppose anyone else would have noticed it but me. I liked that, seeing her with the bright pink flush burning her cheeks as if she'd just run a mile, knowing that he didn't notice her at all. I'd actually said to him one day, 'Look at Sylvia, she can't take her eyes off you,' and he'd looked up, quite touchingly flattered, and said, 'Who? Looking at *me*?' 'Sylvia,' I'd said, but by then she was briskly walking away, 'she's in our class.'

At hometime, when we all poured out, he was freezing there, the tips of his ears going red. His hair was fair-brown, his eyes blue. It was me he stood up for and came towards with his smile, me he put his arm around. Pamela for some reason was shy of meeting him and had gone the back way and Sylvia was walking in front of us. And it was the suddenest thing, the way her ankle just went out from under her as if someone had kicked her. She went sprawling on the path so that we nearly fell over her, clumsy with her arse in the air and her legs splayed, and I hate to say it but I laughed, but then I've often laughed when I shouldn't. Sometimes you can laugh with horror even. And there's me trying to control the grin on my face and Rob being all sensible, taking control.

She was up immediately, trying to stand but unable to put her right foot down, holding it tippytoe in her brown shoe, testing it again and falling sideways while he lunged forwards and grabbed her arm. 'Oh gee,' he said like an American, 'what happened?'

'There's stones all over the path.' I kicked them aside.

37

'I'm all right,' her prissy voice said, 'I'm all right, I'm perfectly all right.'

'You're not,' he said, 'here, sit on this bench.'

Leaning on him, she hopped, head hanging so that her hair hid her face.

'There,' he said as she sat, while I scrabbled about picking up her things and putting them back in her bag, the red fountain pen, the clean rulers, the exercise books, blue, salmon pink, green, not dog-eared like mine but smooth and flawless as the day they were handed out. Her knees and hands were bloody.

'It's swelling right up,' he said.

A big fat steaming tear trickled down her cheek. 'I'm perfectly all right, I'm perfectly all right,' she said, jerking her head back and widening her eyes as if shocked by it. A cluster of girls had gathered. He was unlacing her sensible shoe, easing it gently from her foot like Prince Charming, and indeed yes, she was swelling up like one of those elephantiasis cases you see in *National Geographic*. I'd cry too if that was me. As he coaxed the shoe from her toes, one hand above her ankle holding her steady, I felt rather than saw a thin line of thrill running from his hand up her leg and all the way to the top of her skull.

'What's happened?' people said.

'Sylvia.'

'Sylvia?'

'Sylvia Rose.'

'Who's that?'

'Boy.'

'Who?'

He set her ugly shoe down next to her foot.

'It's all right, Sylvia,' Dotty's round hovering face said, 'Susan's gone to get someone.'

Robin stood up, realising the sudden girl influx and becoming a bit bashful. I put her bag down next to her on the bench. 'Does it hurt?' I asked, and she looked at me with dull eyes.

'A lot,' she said faintly.

'Sally's boyfriend,' someone said.

How dare she, I thought. Ever after I have wondered if she did it on purpose, to give fate a nudge. If so, she got more than she bargained for with that ankle. Maybe she didn't even know she was doing it. People don't always know. Miss Bredbury in her long grey tights and navy shorts, Miss Tucker with a billowing gown, scurrying from the back of the school and along the path with consciously worried faces. 'Sylvia? *Syl*via? What happened?'

'I don't know,' she said.

Rob faded into the background. Tucker and Bredbury got her on her feet and the last I saw of her was the back of her hopping into school between the two of them, holding her elephant leg up like a wounded dog. Rob was a short way off leaning against a tree, holding my school bag.

'Poor wee girl,' he said, as I came close.

'She's not *that* small.'

When we got half way along Canal Street and hardly anyone was about, we stood and kissed. He had big soft lips, and when he kissed me it was warm and sweet but not a thing ever moved inside me. Not like in the songs. You know, all that stuff, *It's in his kiss, And then he kissed me,* and, *Kisses sweeter than wine,* and so on. Nothing happened when he kissed me. Oh well. Arm in arm we walked along. 'That was Sylvia,' I said, 'you know, Sylvia who fancies you.'

He laughed.

'She does,' I said. 'She always hangs around and gets all flustered and pretends to be looking in her bag whenever she sees you.'

Our faces were close together and everyone walking past could see how close we were. He snorted. 'Looked like a nasty sprain,' he said. 'Hurts like fuck a sprain like that.' He had the faintest Irish burr imaginable and sometimes came out with these things. Och. Away and scratch. How about ye? It was so cold we made it to Piccadilly in no time and went into Lando's Snacks, our old favourite, round the corner between the joke shop and the dry cleaners. It sold chips and pies and bacon barm cakes and you could sit and drink coffee for as long as you liked. If you went at night it was full of interesting weirdos.

'Poor old Sylvia,' I said. Something got into me. It did sometimes, and it was a horrible thing, like watching a story or film unfold of myself being a nasty person who stirred things and put people down. I started telling him about Sylvia, the way she sang in that posh voice, the way she was never easy and always aloof, how she sat in corners looking judgemental.

'Poor girl,' he said.

I wanted her to seem ridiculous in his eyes.

'She's like a Puritan,' I said, 'no fun, no silliness, no daftness, no just being stupid.'

'Poor girl,' he said again. He went to the counter and bought two coffees and two Wagon Wheels.

'If she'd just relax a bit,' I said as he returned and set everything down on the Formica top and sat down opposite me, 'if she'd just fool around sometimes. She looks like her parents buy all her clothes for her. I mean, those shoes she wears. She needs to...'

He placed his hand over mine. It was big and covered mine completely. 'Why are you letting it get to you?' he said. 'You shouldn't do that. People are just people. You don't have to let it affect you.'

'I don't.'

He laughed. 'Well, you are. You're angry. What's to be angry about?'

'I'm not angry.'

'You seem it.'

'Sorry,' I said, stirring my milky coffee, 'I'll shut up.'

True, I thought. Not worth thinking about. 'It's just when someone's always looking down their nose at you...'

'Their loss.'

'Yeah.'

'So, this Saturday,' he said, 'can I come over yours? Our kid's got the chicken pox. Have you had chicken pox?'

'Yeah.'

'Well, you'd better not come over mine anyway, he's got it bad. Awful. Covered in big scabs. And I'm playing football Sunday, I think, so if I could come over to yours on Saturday...'

'OK.'

I smiled at his simplicity. I always felt older than him

even though he was a year older than me. He was stupid at times, all those pathetic double entendres he came out with. I drifted. I had a right to feel miffed. People had no right to look down like that, like the big twins sniggering and snurfing, *You know what Sally did? We were on this boat on the canal going through a lock and the gates were closed and there's these other boats coming along and she says, 'Shall we stop and wait for them?' Hilarious! When she got a boil on her bum and didn't want anyone to know, I go, 'You OK, Sally? Want to sit down, look, sit here,' and she's, 'I don't want to sit down...'*

'What are you talking about?' I said. 'Sorry, I zoned out.'

'You,' said Rob. 'You need to relax a bit. Take things as they come.'

'OK.' I wasn't arguing.

'No one's perfect,' he said, his clumsy big thumb stroking the back of my hand. The amazing thing about him was how much he liked me, so quickly, so thoroughly. Smelling of sick or in my school uniform, it didn't make any difference.

'Considering this is your actual life, your *actual* life,' I said, suddenly annoyed with him, 'I don't know how you can be so complacent.'

He was amused. 'Rebel without a cause,' he said. 'Great film.'

'Don't you ever think, though,' I said, 'that it can't be just this?'

'Well, doesn't everyone?'

'You don't seem to.'

'Ha ha, how do you know?'

'I don't.'

'There you go.'

'I rebel against beige,' I said.

Like Sylvia, I thought. Then just as I was thinking, no, she's not really beige, it's more like sepia with a rusty tinge, but beige is a better word, he laughed and gestured round the ordinary little café with its Formica tables and squeezy ketchup-dripped plastic tomatoes. 'All this?' he said. 'What's wrong with it? It's great! I mean *look*, really look.'

'Can't do it,' I said. 'That's no way to live.'

'What? The human condition?'

'It's true,' I said, 'I want more.'

'You,' he said, picking up his coffee, 'will never get what you want. Fancy another coffee?'

He went to the counter and stood talking to the small Italian boy. Somewhere at this actual moment, I thought, someone is riding a horse across a mountain, or living in a gypsy caravan or – or travelling in some wild place or – and we're here with school and buses and homework and going home and it's all the same every day. Outside the café window buses chugged and groaned through slow traffic. The man behind the counter talked in Italian over his shoulder to someone in the kitchen, where a radio played, *If you gotta make a fool of somebody, if you gotta make a fool of someo-o-one.*

Time was pushing on. We went outside, looked in the joke shop window at the vampire fangs and fake blood and horror masks, walked a little way and stood in Mangle Street and kissed. His lips were big and soft and warm. It was just beginning to get dark. Overhead starlings rose in great hordes from the tops of buildings, sweeping darkly across roads and squares only to settle again, rise again, settle and rise in compulsive rhythms. 'Oh Sally-Sal,' he said into my neck, 'you're a mystery to me.'

I smiled, looking over his shoulder at the place where vans unloaded and people put out bins. Yes, yes, I am, I thought, deep, mysterious, not like all the rest.

There was a row when I got home. Mum had been talking to Mrs Shelley and she'd said about seeing me in town, so there was all that moaning and juggling with words and denial and dirty looks, and after tea I went up to my room and got under my top cover and let it enclose me. One day, I thought, I'll get even with them. They'll know, they'll see that I'm not like them, I'm different, special, me.

I closed my eyes and thought about the day of the fair, first time I met Robin, the brats' birthday, one of those gloriously tatty little fairs that spring up suddenly on waste ground and as suddenly are gone. It was a couple of miles from home and Tony had driven us there in his mini-van, all squashed up in the back together, me and Jo and the brats, him in front with his girlfriend of the time. I loved fairs but this one went bad. Started off OK, everyone in a good mood, Jo being all big-sister-nice with the little twins, who were hysterical with fun and wanting everything they saw. Tony and his girlfriend went off on their own; I saw them at the rifle range. The girl was shooting at ducks and missing every time, no wonder with him standing behind her with his chin digging into the top of her head. I ate a hotdog buried under thick greasy white onions, drank something fizzy and took the kids on the Big Wheel. It was lovely; we stopped at the top and made it swing about, and the noise and the grating sounds, the lights, the screams, the music, the colours, green grass, yellow fairy lights, red everywhere on the painted sideshows and waltzer cars, all of that that got inside your head in a way you could feel, like a finger making a ridge in your brain. I ate candy floss and it stuck to my lips, made me lick the sticky sugar membrane from my mouth for ages. It was like biting your nails. Everything would have been OK if they hadn't wanted to go on the Octopus. Jo refused point blank, so *I* took them on – it was their birthday after all – and after about thirty seconds I knew I'd made a terrible mistake. We rose slowly into the sky on the end of a spike, the carriage swung and my stomach flipped. We hadn't even got going. Onions slithered in my stomach like worms. Too late.

'Yeah!' yelled Paul.

Philip yodelled.

I clutched the bar. It felt too far away, as if I might slide out from under it. Up we went, over the top with a great swinging lurch.

'We're off!' Paul cried.

'Yeay!'

Then faster and faster with no quarter, an unstoppable descent into pure horror. There was no more world, only a sick bright wheel pulling itself apart, whirling me in ever more demented circles. I closed my eyes. The darkness was bright, gyrating. Eyes closed, mouth closed, endure. It was the worst thing in my life. It went on forever, and impossibly on. The brats kept sliding to the end of the carriage, giggling maniacally, to make the thing whirl faster and I had no strength to protest.

I clenched my throat. Fingers ran up my chest inside. It took a lifetime.

'Again!' they screamed. 'Again!' as soon as it began to slow down, which it did in wide flaunting gyrations of every carriage. Somehow we were upright, almost still. The twins cried, 'Again, again,' as I stood and got myself out of that thing. I will make it, I will. I held the rail. 'No,' I said. 'Yeah!' they bawled.

Jo's face loomed.

'I feel a bit funny,' I said.

The twins pulled my hands. A machine wailed, deep, electric. Everything went jangly. 'Again! Again!' they cried.

I was going to die.

'Sally! Again! Come on!'

'I feel funny,' I said and walked away.

Jo stuck her pointy face in front of me. 'Are you going to be sick?'

Couldn't speak.

'Go behind something,' she said.

'I'm going home,' I managed to say.

'Don't be stupid, you don't know the way. Tony's going to have to drive you. You shouldn't have stuffed your fat face.'

'I know the way.'

If I went in the van I'd die. I started walking. It was all rushing up through me wanting to burst out and I had to get away from people.

'Sally!' her voice, annoyed.

'I'm OK, I'm OK,' I said, walking faster.

'Don't be stupid.' She was following half-heartedly. 'You can't get home on your own.'

'I can.'

I just kept walking and soon I was away from it all, behind a tent on the outskirts of the ground, leaning over and chucking up everything in the grass, a horrible steaming stream that formed a vile pink splodge in the grass. Pink frankfurter meat, shiny. You're a filthy pig, you stink, the splodge said. Tears ran out of my eyes. I walked a bit further, sat on a wall, closed my eyes, thought about how nasty Jo and Tony were, and a terrible thing came swimming back into my mind along with the resurging nausea: Grandma and Grandad's house, Boxing Day. I was about six. At the half-way landing there was a painting of a man in a small boat poling his way between rocks on a river. The sky in the painting was thick with billowing black cloud. I couldn't get past that picture. It was the way his eyes looked sideways. Mum said it was just some old thing from a jumble sale and not to be so silly. Tony said it was cursed and Jo nodded. 'Sometimes,' she said, 'the man comes out of the painting, and if you're there at the wrong time he can take you back up into the picture with him and you can never get back.'

All the uncles and aunties and cousins eating cake, turkey sandwiches, limeade, lemonade, Vimto, cream soda, crisps, mince pies. The men drank beer. The women had Babycham, Cherry B and Advocaat. Uncle Frank played the piano, Philip and Paul were still babies and made a terrible mess. Uncle Gary was there, the only one who looked young and quite handsome, drinking quietly, standing by himself on the edge of things with a weary smile and downturned eyes. Auntie Ellen, who always got drunk, grabbed my arms and tried to make me dance. 'Come on,' she said in her grating voice, 'this is how we do it,' pulling me up in front of everyone when I didn't want to. The smoke was all going up into her eyes and she was squinting but didn't seem to mind, and the powder on her nose had gone into the pores. 'Like this,' she said, but I couldn't do the dances she wanted me to do. 'Oh, look at her,' she said, 'talk about an old soul,' and everybody laughed, and I had it then, even then, that feeling as if I was with them but also somewhere else looking on, and it made me cold. Auntie Ellen had a weird way of popping her mouth like a fish when she danced. I smiled unnaturally, trying to dance, but she was too big and bouncy and just pulled me about for a bit while I smiled. Jo came up and said, 'She's shy!' as if it was the most stupid thing in the world to be. Auntie Ellen said, 'Oh lovey!' and rubbed my head and set me free. I sat down in a sedate armchair next to the window, green plush with a cream-coloured antimacassar with a crinoline lady in a flower garden embroidered on it. The stiff brown curtains were drawn across behind me against the dark early winter night. Jo and Tony giggled and messed about, and every couple of minutes one of them brought me a cup of fizzy mineral or a handful of crisps and I stuffed them in mechanically till I realised my bladder was full to bursting. I thought I'd wait till someone else went up and follow them and wait outside the bathroom door, but then after they'd gone down I'd still be up there alone and have to come back down, and the landing to the right would be full of open doors and I'd have to go downstairs past the picture. I was OK. I could wait it out, I'd just sit very still. Scared? You're not scared. What's there to be scared about? Don't be such a silly girl. Go on, off you go, it's the only way to get over this kind of thing! I grabbed Jo as she passed. 'Will you come upstairs with me?'

'Why?' she shouted.

'I want a wee.'

'You what?'

'Aw, come on, Jo...'

'Don't be so silly,' she said.

I waved at Tony. He came over but when I asked him to take me to the toilet he just laughed and walked away. The record player played 'Don't You Rock Me Daddy-O' by Lonnie Donegan. Auntie Ellen danced with my cousin Graham. Jo was dancing too, pretending to be a teenager. She wasn't though, she was only a silly little nine-year-old. Tony and Jo giggled together. She ran over and made as if to *tickle* me. 'DON'T,' I said, and then Tony started making a face like Auntie Ellen's fish mouth, and I put my foot underneath myself and rocked. My stomach swelled. Tony was the worst. He kept walking past my chair making these faces, and then my dad put his beer down on a pedal bin by the kitchen door and Grandma stood on the pedal and it flew in the air and the glass broke and beer went everywhere and we weren't supposed to laugh but holding it in was torture. Tony started walking like Grandad, pulling his face into a long streak of droopy mouth, and the pain bled out of me in a glorious gushing release, hot and wet into the green plush of Grandma and Grandad's armchair. About two pints of Vimto, cream soda, lemonade and lime.

There I sat feeling sick and hideous in the cooling wet, knowing it was impossible ever to get up from that chair. I even went on smiling sickly, wide-eyed to keep away tears. My cousin Steven, a stocky blond boy, sat down at the table end nearest me, studiously scooping up all the spare bits of anything anywhere on any plate in his path. There was something quite peacefully mechanical in it. Still, from time to time, Tony and Jo danced by, grinning and knowing and braying.

'What's up, Sally? Why don't you get up? Come and see this. In the kitchen! Come on and look. Oh, come on, Sally, get up, Sally!'

I don't know how long it went on, seemed like an hour, could've been much less. There was no way I was getting out of this alive so I just sat. My face burned. Cousins Graham and Steven and Barbara and Sue were deafening and big and everywhere, and one of the baby twins had started to squawl.

'Whatsammarrer, me lovey?' The face of Uncle Gary in front of mine, close enough that I could see the lines growing in the corners of his eyes and the tobacco discolouration of his front teeth.

'Nothing,' I said.

'Not well, love?' His breath smelt of cigarettes and beer. My eyes filled with tears.

'Moira,' he called back over his shoulder, but my mum was talking loudly to Uncle Bill and didn't hear. 'What, you feeling sick, are you?' He took my hand and looked at me with his kind drunken eyes. 'Got a flush on you,' he said. 'Moira!' he called. My mother looked round with a laugh fading out of her eyes, and Uncle Gary pulled me gently up from the chair.

There I stood in my nice shiny dark green party dress with the sash, the back stained, soaked all over.

'What's that?' shrieked Jo.

Tony released a long-held spluttering laugh, full of spray.

'What's what?' asked big Barbara.

'It's all wet!' cried Steven, the one at the table eating all the scraps.

'Sally,' said my mum's face, suddenly there, stern, 'what have you done? Why didn't you say if you wanted to go?'

'I didn't...' I said but my nose filled with snot and I couldn't speak.

'Ugh, what's she done?' said Tony.

'Look at the back of your dress.' My sister Jo, bending down to my face.

Cousin Graham's face appeared over Uncle Gary's head, laughing: *Haar! Haar! Haar!*

'She hasn't, has she?' Dad, cheesed off.

The chair cushion was saturated.

Grandad said, 'Oh dear, well, we'll have to soak it...'

Grandma's face looking at more work.

'It happens,' said Auntie Ellen.

My father, embarrassed, took my shoulders and turned me. I passed Uncle Gary, his nice face distancing itself. My dad marched me into the hall and down to the front door. 'We can't have you sitting in there like that,' he said. 'Here.' And he made me stand in the porch. There was a red bristly rug the colour of a fox. 'You just sit here and wait till we're ready,' he said, closed the door and walked away. He turned the light off in the hall but left the one in the porch on. The porch was a tiny square, open on three sides to the black night air. There were three shelves full of things like old used jars and tins, and a couple of pairs of boots. I sat on the bristle rug in my cold wet dress and hugged my knees and waited.

I will hate you always, I thought, and my eyes smarted. Because it must be hate, mustn't it, this feeling like a horse with iron hooves kicking me in the chest. Right there, just under the throat to choke me. Or what else is it?

Oh, you know, it was just kids being kids.

I'd get even one day.

When I opened my eyes I'd forgotten where I was. I was going to throw up again. I did, all down the side of the wall. I didn't look to see if anyone saw. My forehead was blazing wet. When I could I straightened and stood blinking. It was like one of those Westerns where someone walks out of a desert. Dogged, suffering, away from the fair and down a plain little street with houses on both sides. I was sick again on the pavement outside someone's garden. I walked on and came to a main road. The petrol fumes made me sick again, on a corner, turning in towards a brick wall in a desperate attempt to be discreet. Too many people. Go for the side streets. I looked back to see if someone was coming after me, checking to see I was OK. No one was coming.

Somewhere near a tree I was sick again but there was

hardly anything left inside by now so I just leaned against the tree and hoped for invisibility and wanted to die. I ended up at an empty bus stop in some strange street, sitting on the ground with my head on my arms, hanging onto every moment as one more infinitesimal creep towards normality. I must have been there for ages. The sky was fading and I was getting cold.

I became aware of feet and the pedals of a stationary bike.

'You OK?' said a voice.

That was Robin. I didn't look up to see his face.

'I've been sick,' I said.

'Where you going?'

'Home.'

He gave me a lift on his bike. I sat on the seat, he stood on the pedals. I was home in a few minutes. I had to get in quick in case I was sick again.

'Thanks,' I said. I didn't look back. I was horribly embarrassed, I hated myself. I went to bed and cried. Next day, my mum said, 'There's a boy at the door for you,' and I went down and they were so bloody nosy, Jo and Tony and my mum, all standing behind the door listening.

'Just came to see if you were all right,' he said. That was the first time I really looked at his face. It was nice but not how I'd pictured a boyfriend's face to be, something hayseed about it and his nose was big. In truth, it disappointed me.

Next day at lunchtime Miss Tucker said, 'Sally, can you go to the Office?'

'What's it for?'

'I have no idea,' she said, gathering up her books and files. 'Mrs Gordon said to tell you to pop in, that's all I know.'

Being called anywhere, the Office, Miss Demery's room, usually meant bother. Was I seen crossing the park? Can't be that or they'd have called Pamela too. I'd been telling her about all the drama of yesterday afternoon, the museum, Sylvia's fall and the way she'd been looking at Robin. She wasn't as interested as she should have been. Something was wrong with her. She hadn't been sick yesterday, though she'd brought in a note from her mum saying she had a terrible migraine. All she told me was that she'd had to stay home with her mum because her mum was upset about something. She waited at the bottom of the stairs while I went into the Office. It had a very high counter. Mrs Gordon, a skinny lady with a very long neck, always seemed to be looking down from a great height. 'Someone left this for you,' she said.

'What is it?'

'It's your friend Sylvia,' she said, 'I think she wants you to take her some books.'

'Me?'

'Yes. Here you are.' She waved an envelope. I looked at my name written on it in scrawly handwriting.

'Weird,' I said later as we walked up to the greenhouse, 'it's from Sylvia. That's insane.'

'Joking.'

'No, honest.' I ripped the envelope open.

Headed notepaper. At the top it said in fancy print:

M.B. Rose, followed by lots of initials, an address in Didsbury, a phone number, then neatly typed: *Dear Sally, My daughter Sylvia has asked that I hand this in for you at your school. As you are no doubt aware she is laid up for a few days and, as she was supposed to be bringing in a book which she was lending you, she wondered if you would like to call and pick it up at your convenience, and if at the same time you might bring one or two things from her desk that will enable her to keep up with her studies while she is away from school. See below. Yours Sincerely,* M.B. Rose, blue ink, straggling line at the end, then *M.B. ROSE,* typed in capitals, and below, a short list:

Elton and Bindoff.
Tennyson and Browning.
The blue science book.
My ruler.

'Bloody hell,' I said.

'Let's see.' Pamela grabbed the letter, read it and brayed with laughter. I flapped my hands to silence her because we'd reached the science labs and had to get past Tasker and Tufton. Tasker was sitting at his desk in the Chemistry lab in front of the periodic table pasted on the wall. We sneaked past and dashed up the little wooden stairs. It was pouring with glorious shiny rain which rippled thickly down the greenhouse windows. To sit under that deluge on those benches surrounded by half-hearted plants was wonderful. For a second I could see what Rob was on about when he said things were enough just as they were.

'This is bonkers,' Pamela said.

'She wants me to take her books. All the way out there, Didsbury. I'll have to get a bus.'

'Who are you then? Her servant?'

'It's cos I was talking to her about that Egyptian book.'

'What Egyptian book?'

'Yesterday at the museum. When she was telling us about being born in Egypt and all that. She was going on about this book and was going to bring it in.'

'Bit weird of her, isn't it? Getting friendly, all of a sudden.'

Weird was right. I didn't even like the girl. I didn't know her, I didn't want to. Why was she asking *me*? Why didn't she ask Sheila or Gail or someone who sat near her or knew her better? I'm not her friend, I don't want to be her friend, she's too stiff and peculiar, I'd never live it down. 'I don't want to go,' I said.

'You don't have to.' Pamela got out her sandwiches. 'It's up to you. What have you got for your sandwiches?'

'Tuna and pickle.'

'I've got corned beef. Shall we share?'

'OK.'

Then again, I was nosy and thought it might be interesting to see where she lived. Was it a big posh house with frilly bits over the windows? Her dad was old and looked important. Her mum was small and perky and wore frumpy clothes and scraped back her hair. They didn't look the kind of people who ever slobbed about. I couldn't imagine them at home.

'I don't know,' I said. 'Maybe I do want to go. To see what it's like.'

'How the other half lives.'

'Something like that.'

'Yeah, go,' she said. 'I wanna hear all about it.'

The clouds were black over Piccadilly. Smart tic-tac-toc on the windows.

'That's hail,' I said.

'Don't strike me with lightning, Mr Sky.' Pamela screwed up the bread wrapper her sandwiches were in and tossed it into her bag.

'Let's open the door.'

Rainy hail blew in and scattered down the small wooden steps onto the greenhouse floor. It felt as if the roof was coming in. Say what you like, we had such laughs, and she never made me feel stupid or awkward like other people did. If I go, I thought, I couldn't pretend I hadn't, because Sylvia might say something, then everyone would know I'd gone there and think we were friends. She might start acting as if we *were* friends and that would be awful because we weren't.

I went on Sunday in the end, in the afternoon when Rob was playing football. I telephoned first and spoke to her mother, who sounded curt and official as you might expect. Sylvia lived out near Southern Cemetery in a huge house set far back from the street behind a lawn. In the middle there was a weeping willow, a ghostly yellow giant taller than the house. The house's upper storey was half timbered, and there was a constant chattering of birds in a thick creeper covering most of one side. The gate screamed when I opened it and I felt looked at from the leaded windows as I walked in the rain up the long pathway to the door, which was deeply recessed so you could stand out of the rain while you rang the bell.

Sylvia's mother answered the door. 'Hello, dear,' she said, 'are you wet?' Silly question.

'Not too bad,' I said. 'I've got my umbrella.'

She was a small breathy woman, smiling furiously, tortoiseshell glasses, a pink twin set, stockings and clumpy brown shoes. 'Let me take that for you.' Her eyes had a bald look behind her glasses as if she was straining to see. I looked about. 'Dreadful rain,' she whispered. Through an open door I saw a large high room painted lemon and cream, with a piano that looked somehow like a racehorse, and stands with sheets of music ready to play. There were framed pictures of composers on the walls, the books were in glass-doored cabinets and all the wood was polished.

'Sylvia,' her mother called, 'your friend's here.'

That jarred.

It was like a hotel. Everything was spotless and fresh as if it had just that moment finished being cleaned, and the air was subtly perfumed from a vase of flowers just passing their best on the hall table. Her mother ushered me through to the back of the house, to the conservatory where Sylvia was sitting by a small round table eating an egg. One leg, heavily bandaged round foot and ankle, stretched in front of her on a red pouffe.

'I brought you those things.'

'Thank you.' Sylvia held a teaspoon, frowning. 'That's really helpful.'

I sat down on a wicker chair. It was weird to see Sylvia out of uniform. She wore an odd puff-sleeved orange dress with smocking that looked too young for her. Her mother's court shoes clicked away along the hall. It was a sparse conservatory, a glass rectangle with plants all round the windowsills, none of them very big, looking out across another impressive lawn, this one irregular in shape, with well-kept trees and bushes at the end and all round the sides. In among the plants were family photographs in frames. One was of a man in uniform who must have been her dad.

'How's your foot? Or is it your ankle?'

Her naked toes stuck up from the end of the bandage.

'My ankle,' she said.

'Does it hurt a lot?'

'It did, but it's not so bad now.'

She ate the boiled egg with precision. It was like watching someone conduct a demonstration of the correct way to eat a boiled egg. No mess, no runs, no picking bits of shell out of the yolk.

'Oh, that's good,' I said and couldn't think of anything else to say. I'd come all this way. I got up and looked out of the window. A squirrel stood still, out on the lawn, close enough for me to see its beady little eye swivel. It undulated across to the foot of a tree, turned its head, then, suddenly electrified, flew snakishly up the tree and disappeared, shaking the top leaves against the sky. In some obscure way the squirrel made me want to cry. Wouldn't it be lovely to be able to open your door any time you liked and step out and see flowers like that and smell the green and watch a squirrel run up a tree? It wasn't fair. To have a squirrel in your garden seemed to me impossibly remote, so far beyond anything I could dream of.

'A squirrel,' I said.

'Yes,' she said, 'we do see them.'

'How fantastic.'

'There's the book.' She put her plate aside, wiped her hands on a real white napkin then dabbed the corners of her mouth. 'On the ledge. Would you mind getting it yourself?'

'Of course not.' I jumped up. It was a thick heavy book, far smaller than I'd imagined, with a plain hessian cover and red Arabic writing on the spine. 'Oh,' I said, 'is it all in Arabic?'

'That's just the cover. It's English inside.'

I sat down and laid it open across my knee. I leafed through, thinking what a pity it wasn't in colour. The Pyramids, the Sphinx, the desert, camels, columns carved with hieroglyphics. Beautiful eyes.

'Quite an amazing place,' I said.

She didn't reply and my comment hung, embarrassed. I nearly followed it up with, 'It must have been very hot,' which would have been even more stupid, and a thought came up of the scene in the play where Cleopatra wakes up catlike between the paws of the Sphinx. Pity she had to open her mouth. *Old gentleman! Old gentleman!* The pages of the book were cold and smooth and smelt like old rooms. Between the pictures, columns of faded text sat three abreast, page after page, and the writing was so small that I couldn't bear the idea of reading it.

'Perhaps that's why I don't mind hot weather,' she said thoughtfully as if to herself but also as if she'd heard my thought, 'having been born in a hot place, I mean.'

'D'you think so?'

Her face was expressionless. 'Possibly.'

We sat in silence for a minute or two, me leafing, her just sitting.

'What was it like?' I asked. 'Egypt.'

She looked sideways as if concentrating. 'We lived in a flat in a block. I can't really remember it.'

'Anything?'

'The heat. The big fan on the ceiling. And the beach we went to, and the carriages with big round wheels and the horses.'

'It's funny, isn't it,' I said, 'thinking about yourself before you could remember? When you think about it, it's like being dead.'

She didn't look at all interested. 'Sorry, don't know what you mean.'

'Well – I mean you see a picture of yourself when you were a baby and you think, gosh that's me, but it's not you, is it? And it doesn't exist any more anyway, that baby, it's gone. Feels like it's got nothing to do with you any more than if it was in another life and you've been reincarnated. So in a way you already have been reincarnated even though you haven't died.'

She looked at me as if I was talking gobbledygook.

'See?'

Her mother crossed the hall with a cigarette in her hand. *Pom-di-pom-di-pom*, she was humming. The idea of clacking round the house in shoes and stockings like that.

'I don't think I feel like that,' Sylvia said.

'Don't you?'

'No. I don't think I do really. I feel like I've always been here.'

Her mother came in and said to Sylvia, 'Daddy will be back very soon,' in a significant way. Sylvia nodded like a commander receiving news from an underling and Mrs Rose picked up the plate with its still spotless egg cup and neatly disposed fragments of white egg shell. I thought she might be hinting for me to go, but then she said, 'Would you girls like some orange juice?'

I was dead thirsty. 'Oh, yes please,' I said.

Sylvia ignored her.

'I'll bring some biscuits too.' Her mother backed out of the door, raising her scrappy eyebrows and smiling unnaturally.

I wished then I'd said no because I really didn't want to stay here too much longer. Let's hope she's quick. There was something unsettling about this peculiar social trial. Why was I here? Sylvia had lapsed into silence now, and her face was back in school mode, stiff, bordering on surly, the awkward set of her mouth.

'That your dad in the picture?' I said after an awkward while. 'In the uniform?'

She nodded. 'He's retired now. He's been reading the lesson at church this morning.'

'Oh.'

Nobody I knew went to church. Well, I suppose some of the girls at school went but I didn't count them. None of my friends went. None of my family. God maybe, I don't know, I wouldn't absolutely rule it out, but he's not in those churches. It's not like that. I'd make my deals with it as I went along, take it as it came.

'Do you go to church?' I asked.

'Yes.' She said it as if she meant, *Of course!*

Her mother came bustling and humming down the hall with a tray. 'Now!' she said, beaming and setting it down on the table. It was fancy, a dinky little teapot with violets on, two proper teacups in matching saucers, a milk jug that also matched, and a plate of chocolate biscuits. But she said we were getting orange juice, I thought, dismayed. I wanted orange juice. I didn't say anything of course. Only, 'Thank you.'

She left and Sylvia poured the tea. I could no longer stand the look on her face and cursed that I had to stay here long enough to get down a hot cup of tea. Still, I'd make the most of the biscuits. I took two to start with. Bourbons, lovely. Sylvia took one, nibbled it delicately with her two front teeth as if she was a rabbit. 'Do *you* go to church?' she asked.

My mouth was full. 'No, never,' I said. 'Only with the school.'

She sipped her tea, looking at me over the rim of her dinky cup. *This* was why I didn't like her: the look, concerned, more sorrow than anger, pitying. 'Don't you *like* religion?' she said.

What a stupid question. I couldn't be bothered to answer. 'I don't even know what you mean,' I said. Then we drank our tea, and I ate three more biscuits and could have eaten the lot. She had one, sensibly. I went to the loo before going for the bus because I wanted to see upstairs, but the doors were all closed. The only open one was the bathroom's. I counted six doors, and only three of them living here. The bathroom had fluffy white towels and a new bar of pink soap in the holder, and the bath mat wasn't squishy.

'I'll be off now,' I said, coming back to find her looking through the stuff I'd brought her. She looked vaguely in my direction as I got my things together.

'Hope you get better soon,' I said.

She indicated the Egypt book. 'Would you like to borrow it?'

'Not really,' I said.

Going home, on the bus, looking out of the window at streets I didn't know, streets with big houses set back behind big gardens, I imagined telling Pamela, my God, you should have seen it, they've got a music room, an actual room just for music, with a huge fireplace and music stands and pictures of composers on the walls. And the way she eats an egg. And squirrels in the back garden, and flowers in the hall. And how she said, 'Don't you like religion?' in that prissy voice. Who did she think she was? As if you had to go to church to be religious. All those people in sanctimonious rows thinking they're better than you, and how Pamela cried her eyes out when Jesus got crucified. *She* didn't go to church.

From that I got to thinking about how people didn't like Pamela. When she came and sat next to me at the start of the new year, Sheila Simpson and Dotty Spawl hissed behind my head, 'Oh no, Pamela's coming, quick, quick, tell her that's someone's place, Sally, don't let her in. Sally! Put your bag on the desk, quick! Get Linda, don't let her...' then going quiet and sulky because it was too late, there was Pamela plonking her big self relentlessly down, flinging up the lid of her desk, emptying out the chaos of her school bag into it, getting out her greasy package of cold toast. Great! It would be fun sitting with Pamela. It's true she had a nasty streak with people she didn't like. Some people were scared of her. She'd been known to slam a desk so hard with the flat of her hand that it flew across the room and crashed over. She was up for anything. Dare Pamela and she'd do it. The time she rang the fire brigade and told them there was a cat stuck on top of the Free Trade Hall. The time Mrs Stannard the Deputy Head took us for Biology when Mrs Kitney was away and made us look at the splayed-out insides of a small white rat pinned flat on a board like a rug about to be laid down before a fire. A white worm, bloated at one end and thin at the other, lay dead in the innards. 'Fuck that,' Pamela said to Mrs Stannard, 'I'm not going near that. It's cruel.' If you knew Mrs Stannard, you'd know that was a very brave thing to do. She got sent to see Miss Demery. Nobody swore like Pamela where I came from, the way you heard boys talk in the streets sometimes and on buses. My mum said 'sod' and 'bloody' and 'bugger', and that was it, but I never heard anyone else swear in our house, even my brother unless he was with one of his mates and thought no one could hear.

Monday morning before Assembly, me and Pamela laughed about Sylvia's silly mother and the dinky tea cups and the way her mother called her father, 'Daddy', as if she was an infant. I did a great imitation of Sylvia eating an egg. 'Like this,' I said, my fingers held like tiny pincers. By the time French came we were already in a ridiculous mood. Last week we'd had to learn a poem about a toad and test each other on it: 'Le Crapaud'. Of course everyone giggled about the title. Miss Oliver had said we all had to recite it in front of the class next week; we were getting marked out of thirty, ten for content, ten for pronunciation and ten for delivery. I could do the content but my accent was rubbish, whereas Pamela could do the accent but for the life of her couldn't remember anything beyond the first line.

'They'll have to give me twenty points anyway,' she said, 'that's enough for a pass. I'll go' – thrusting her big raw hands out as if she was in Shakespeare – '"*Le Crapaud!*"' And it was perfect, the way she did that thing in the throat on the *r*, the way she formed her lips round the *aud*, the soulfulness of the delivery. Just the title. 'See,' she said, 'that's all I need, ten for accent, ten for delivery. Bugger the content.' She did it too, but they didn't give her twenty marks. Everyone laughed and Sheila behind me said, 'Oh Pamela!' indulgently, and Miss Oliver rolled her eyes and said, 'Go and sit down.' Honestly, the whole thing was a laugh a minute, not just Pamela and her Oscar-winning cameo but everyone else too with their dreadful French accents. The whole room was in stitches. Again and again –

le crapaux, le cr-r-r-apeau-u-u, le crappo –

Even Miss Oliver was laughing. Mine was as bad as all the rest. In the middle of it all Sheila passed a note over my shoulder: 'Séance. Biology lab.'

I don't know why but I've always felt a certain guilt, as if everything would have been different if I'd never gone to that particular silly séance. And it was silly, very, with Sheila saying, 'Heavens to bloody Murgatroyd', and the sound of 3B who were on late lunch pounding around like baby elephants in the gym downstairs.

'Is anybody there?'

Loud silence. Pamela crunching loudly, sitting on the radiator with a packet of crisps, not joining in. She never joined in. Our six fingers on the glass: me, Susan, Sheila, Gail, Linda and Dotty. Mr Tasker and Mr Tufton down the corridor having a muffled conversation. Susan was Master of Ceremonies. 'Is anybody there?' she asked again. The cloudy glass someone had nicked from the dining hall sat unresponsive in the middle.

'Said the traveller,' whispered Gail.

'Ssh.'

Crunch, crunch. Far down below, outside, lads larking about. Traffic. The Biology lab was dark, heavily laden with boredom, high windows showing the sky through a filter of dust. A tap dripped audibly. We sat at a Formica-topped table next to the tanks with their stale smell and residual greenness. The glass moved, just set off, our fingers with it. It didn't go anywhere in particular, just roamed briskly without settling on any of the small squares of paper, the letters of the alphabet and YES and NO, that we'd put in a big circle reaching to the edges of the table. It stood still.

'It's a bit near the D,' said Linda hopefully.

'Ssh!'

Crunch.

'Ssh!'

'What's your name?' asked Susan.

Off it went. Sheila was writing it down. G – O – S – S – E, it said and sailed back to the middle.

'Oh stop it, that's dead creepy,' said Gail.

'Ssh.'

'Hello.' Susan.

It didn't answer.

'Gosse,' she said, 'is that your name? Gosse?'

Nothing.

'Are you dead?' I asked it.

Nothing.

'Do you live here,' asked Susan, 'in this building?'

It moved again, smooth, to NO.

'Can you see us?' asked Sheila.

YES.

Back to the middle, then nothing. Behind us Pamela screwed up her empty crisp packet with no respect whatsoever for proceedings. We kept catching each other's eyes and smiling, acknowledging how daft it all was, yet feeling the air around us thicken. The deep bellow of Miss Bredbury boomed in the gym below; elephants made thunder. A door down the corridor closed. We stared at the glass, waiting. Nothing.

Susan sighed deeply.

'Gosse,' said Gail, 'do you have a message for anyone in this room?'

Off it went: H – I – R – A – M

Centre.

'Hiram?'

Nothing.

'I don't think we've got a Hiram here,' whispered Dotty, and me and Linda smothered a laugh.

'Ssh,' said Susan but it was going off again, faster than before –

P – M – L – A –

'PMLA,' said Susan.

Rushing us now, our hands hauled about like a giant pink spider: P – A – M – L – M – A – P – E – L – A – P – L –

There was an indrawing of breath.

'It's trying to spell Pamela!' said Sheila.

It wandered aimlessly now.

'Don't bring me into it.' Pamela jumped down from the radiator.

'Do you think?' I whispered.

Susan looked up as if someone was on the ceiling. 'Have you got a message for Pamela?' she asked, dramatically hushed.

Nothing for ages.

'What about Hiram?' said Gail. 'Who's Hiram?'

'When he's at home.' Sheila laughed.

'Ssh!'

'I'm sure I've heard that somewhere,' I said.

Susan kicked me under the table. It moved again, this time at a stately pace. It said: L – E – A – V – E

'Fuck off,' said Pamela.

Again: L – E – A – V – E

'Leave,' we all repeated.

'Do you mean Pamela?' asked Susan. 'Are you asking Pamela to leave the room?'

'You're pushing it,' Pamela said, disgusted, walking round the table with one of her big flushed scowls.

'We're not,' we said.

'Honest,' I said, 'we're not pushing it, Pamela. It doesn't mean you, it probably means Hiram.'

'Oh don't be stupid!'

'Well, *I'm* not pushing it anyway,' I said.

'Me neither,' said everyone else.

'Anyway,' said Susan, peeved, 'it's stopped now. What do you expect the way you're all carrying on.'

'Don't fucking tell me to leave.' Pamela squared up to the table. 'I'm going anyway, this is *stupid*.'

'It did move,' said Gail.

'Yeah.' Nods. 'It did. I felt it go.' Linda appealed to Sheila, who nodded seriously. 'It was weird, you had to kind of go with it. Really. Honestly, Pamela, we wouldn't mess around.'

Pamela walked out and slammed the door so that the whole corridor vibrated and Mr Tufton came out of the Physics lab down the corridor and shouted something.

'Gosse, what kind of a name is that?'

'P'raps it meant Goose,' said Sheila. 'It's not a good speller.'

'Perhaps we've got the ghost of a goose,' said Linda. We all laughed.

'Ssh,' said Susan, 'let's just give it one more go now Pamela's gone. It may not have liked her sitting there watching and not believing. She might have put it off.' So we all got quiet again and sat there with our fingers on the glass in the middle and sat in concentration for a minute or two and nothing happened. A truck in the street blew smoke loudly through its nostrils.

'It's gone,' said Susan.

Nothing ever came through.

The door opened and Mrs Kitney, a tiny, pleasant-faced woman, walked in. 'What are you girls doing here?' She sounded surprised. 'You shouldn't be in here at this time.'

'Sorry, Miss,' said a murmur of voices. Susan swept the bits of paper into a pile and started scooping them into her bag.

'Oh, *I* see.' Mrs Kitney took in the upside-down glass in the middle of the table, a thin awkward smile on her face. 'You shouldn't be doing this,' she said. 'I'm serious. It's not a game.'

'We were only...'

'I know what you were doing.' She leaned on the table with her knuckles, looking at each one of us in turn. 'Whose idea was this?'

An awkward silence. She seemed embarrassed. 'It's not a game,' she repeated, still grinning, but it was an odd stiff grin. We called her Mrs Kidney. Not to her face. 'It's up to you what you get up to out of school but you can't be doing this here. You may think it's just a game but people have had some nasty experiences playing around with this kind of thing.'

This was terrific. She was OK, Mrs Kidney. She never wore a gown and piled her glossy chestnut hair high up on her head.

'Have you done this before?'

'Two or three times,' Sheila said. 'We didn't think...'

'I don't think it's a game,' said Susan Grech seriously.

'Then you should know better than to mess with it,' Mrs Kidney snapped.

'What kind of nasty experiences?' asked Dotty.

Mrs Kidney said nothing.

'Aw, go on!' we all cried. 'Tell us!'

She raised her eyes as if wishing she'd never started it. 'That's all I'm saying. And I'm telling you you shouldn't be doing it.'

We packed up, the bell was about to go.

'What can happen?' Susan Grech said. 'I'm really interested in these things.'

'Are you, Susan? I'm not sure that's such a good thing.'

'But it's *fas*cinating!'

'Oh really?' She folded her arms. 'Well, I do hope you don't get more than you bargained for, Susan. My brother once did this at a friend's house. There were six of them. They made contact with something but all suddenly felt a sense of dread, and at the same time a drinks trolley flew across the room and smashed against the wall, and the curtains, long heavy floor-to-ceiling ones, came down as if they'd just been *ripped* from the rail so hard that the rail came down and all the curtain hooks flew off.'

We gasped. 'Wo-o-ow,' said Sheila.

'Oh God!' said Gail.

'I'm not saying what it is.' She moved to her desk and started lining up her books. 'It may be some kind of group thing, mass hysteria, there are all kinds of explanations. But I saw those people just after, because they all got out of the house and drove straight to our house and I can tell you that two of them were crying, it had shaken them so much, and I'm not just talking about the girls.'

We were dumbstruck.

'OK,' she said, becoming brisk, 'off with you all now. I won't say anything more about this for now, but if I find any of you up here one more time at lunchtime, and if I find anyone doing anything *remotely* like this in school again, there *will* be trouble.'

She wasn't naturally strict and you could see that she found this difficult. I would have liked, I think we all would, to have stayed and talked to her about everything she knew about ouijas and séances and things like that, because clearly she knew far more than she was letting on. But she wasn't having any of it. We slid away into the corridor. Oh God no, now it was Chemistry. Mr Tasker was standing outside the lab waiting for us, looking away over our heads as we approached. He never acknowledged any of us outside the Chemistry room. Not even in it either if he could help it. He was a short bulky man, dark-haired and black-suited, and his breath when he leaned over your shoulder to correct something you'd written was heavy and ripe. My mother thought he was attractive, 'in a funny sort of way', when she saw him at Parents' Evening. Oh vomit! We were all talking about Gosse and Hiram as we found our places along the benches and got out our Chemistry books, making up stories about what it all might mean.

Pamela was in a mood. 'I hate that,' she said. 'What they wanna go bringing my name into it for? Someone was pushing it.'

'It didn't feel like it,' I said, because it was true, then thought I ought to play it down. She was so rattled. 'Well, someone *might* have been pushing it, I suppose.'

Susan and Sheila were at the front telling Mr Tasker about the séance. He said nothing, just looked down with a rare and suitably sarcastic smile, then stood up and clapped his hands once, a deep hollow echoing sound that made everyone jump. I snoozed through Chemistry. There was some sort of fuss going on in 4 Alpha when we went down to our classroom at hometime. I got the details later from Gail. It was her little sister in the first form, Christine: she went into 4 Alpha for something she'd forgotten, came out screaming, charged downstairs and collapsed at the bottom. Said she saw two silhouettes in the back row. Crying and hysterical, Gail said, had to go down to the sick room.

'Silhouettes?'

'Yeah, but she's a moron,' Gail said. 'Kid's demented. And look, I'll show you' – scrabbling in her bag – 'she did these drawings—'

'*Which* room?' asked Pamela.

'4 Alpha.'

Our old classroom from a few years back. It was at the end just before the stairs and we still had Geography in there. There was a map of the world, a timeline of British kings and queens, a list of words most commonly misspelled: necessary, mischievous, independence. These whatever-they-were were sitting next to one another in the back row underneath those posters. Gail pulled out a sheet of paper and spread it over the desk. We all laughed. The things looked ridiculous, like dancing dollies cut out of paper, with round heads and pointed shoulders.

'She said she couldn't describe them but she'd draw them,' Gail said.

Shadows.

'Honestly,' Gail said, 'she's a moron.'

'It's the séance,' said Susan. 'What if we called something up?'

'Nah,' said Sheila.

That night I asked my dad, 'Have you ever heard of the name Hiram?'

My dad was an avid reader and knew a lot of things. In Mum and Dad's bedroom there was a huge collection of old *Reader's Digests* in three piles against the wall. Our bookshelves groaned with encyclopaedias and dictionaries and ancient school textbooks from the thirties. Though horribly jumbled, these were often useful for homework.

'Hiram,' he repeated thoughtfully. He had his bare foot up against the coffee table, cutting his horny toenails.

'Isn't it from the Bible?' my mum asked, still in her nurse's uniform. 'Sounds like it might be.'

'Why?' said Dad.

'I just heard it somewhere.'

'I think it might be American. You know, one of those old Western names, a cowboy name. Look it up.'

But the books were in such a mess I couldn't be bothered. Instead I went upstairs and kicked *Caesar and Cleopatra* off the bed, lay down and listened to a train rattling south away from Piccadilly.

Christmas came and went. I got *Rubber Soul* by the Beatles from Jo, talc from Tony, soap from the kids and a jumper and a Mickey Mouse watch from my mum and dad. Same old thing, turkey, Christmas pud, etc. All my friends were with their families, Rob too, so nothing much was happening. Christmas dinner was irritating because the little twins had a tendency to giggle in relays at mealtimes in a stupid forced kind of way. And they ate with their mouths open. New Year's Eve, though, that was the thing, a party at Shanna Glassman's in Blackley near Boggart Hole Clough. Loads of people from school were going and I was taking Rob. Last year I hadn't gone anywhere and Jo had lorded it over me because she was going to a party with a boy who'd bought her a lovely choker for Christmas and called her the meaning of his life. This year she was only going to a firework display with a friend. I was in my room getting ready; Rob was calling for me at half past seven and I had nothing to wear. My clothes were all horrible. I dragged them out and laid them on the bed and not one thing was reasonable. A grey pinstripe skirt with a fake brown silk top with long sleeves – that got me by lots of times but it wouldn't do for a party. My green leaf-pattern dress, worn too many times and starting to hang a bit baggy at the back. That yellow thing she was throwing out, oh I hate that thing – I pulled it off its hanger, threw it on the floor and walked over it in my heels. I loved my legs in heels, I liked to watch them walk by in mirrors and glass windows. I didn't look like a kid any more. Useless, though, without decent clothes, and getting money out of Mum and Dad was a joke, they just didn't understand how important clothes were. I ran downstairs. The telly was on. My dad was asleep, stretched out in his chair, his legs taking up all the space in the room. Mum was knitting a baby blanket for Mr and Mrs Shelley's expected grandchild, shades of peach and cream because she didn't know what sex it would be. Her hair was awful. She used to have it curled under at the ends and a bit fluffed up on top but now it was a kind of dyed blonde, lank and straight as if it had just been poured over her head, and where the roots were coming through you could see the grey. Awful to let yourself go like that. God, look at them. Moira and Stan. Hope I die before I get old. Tony's shy girlfriend was waiting for him on our settee with a nervous smile; the brats were together in one armchair looking actually quite sweet with their knuckle-kneed legs sticking straight out, sucking on lollies from the freezer and sharing a big football picture book they'd got for Christmas.

'Hey Jo,' I said, 'do you mind if I borrow your purple dress?'

Of course she had to make a drama out of it. 'That's one of my best.' She coiled her hair round her fingers and made a great production out of a sigh.

'I know,' I said, 'it's a lovely dress. You won't be wearing it for the fireworks, though, will you?'

Another heave of the breast. 'I don't know,' she said, 'how do I know you won't go getting silly and come back with drink spilled all over it?'

'There's not going to be drink at this party, is there?' my mum piped up.

'Course there isn't!'

'Huh,' said Jo.

'What do you mean, huh?' I said.

'Just huh.'

Tony came in with foam on the back of one ear. 'Ready, Stell?' he said.

'Yeah,' she whispered.

'Have a good time,' my mum said mechanically, and Stella got up awkwardly. She was worse than me. That was nice. I liked people who were worse than me, more dumb and stupid, more likely to say the wrong thing. Trust me to say it, cringing as I said it. God, life was tough. The way to look, the way to be. Rob, now, I never thought he worried about that sort of thing; I used to think it was because he was shallower than me but I don't think that now. Now I think maybe life really is simpler after all. Then I thought it was a tangled knot. I used to get a feeling in every scene that I was realer than all the rest and it was so scary that I turned myself off, floated myself up and off somewhere, some place a little above my head, slightly to the right, like an oncoming migraine. It was great up there, Godlike, like I was a huge eye in the sky of the room and I could move them all around like in a story, make them do things.

'Right, Joey-jo?' Tony said.

'Right.' Jo yawned, putting her hands over her face. Her nails glittered. They had this thing, those two, a twin thing, I suppose.

'I promise,' I said, 'I won't spill anything on it. And if I do I'll pay for it to be cleaned.'

'You haven't got any money,' she said.

'I've got my pocket money.'

'Oh let her borrow it, Jo.' Mum frowned at her knitting. 'You don't wear it these days.'

She looked miffed. 'Go on then,' she said, staring at the telly.

'Great! Thanks, Jo.' I ran up and grabbed the dress and took it to my room quickly before she could change her mind. It was purple with a black trim, not as mini on me as on her but never mind, it was better than anything I had. Looked good on me too; I knew because I'd tried it on a million times when she was out. She hated me trying her clothes on.

'Oh, you do look nice!' my mum said when I went down.

My dad had started to snore.

We got the bus to Blackley and walked past the creepy old gates of Boggart Hole Clough just as a few flakes of fine snow came swirling down out of the darkness. My dad had arranged for a taxi to come and pick us up at a quarter past midnight so we'd have time to bring in the New Year, though all that usually meant was getting snogged by boys you didn't want to snog in honour of conviviality. This year, though, I had Robin so it wouldn't happen. He was quite the thing to walk into a party with, walking along warm next to me with his wide shoulders and collar turned up, chattering his big teeth and shivering as the snow landed in his hair.

'You know,' he said, 'I'd love to walk across Boggart Hole Clough in the middle of the night.'

'Oooh! So would I!'

'Let's go out tonight before the taxi,' he said. 'Yeah! Let's go out just before midnight, let's climb over and wait for midnight then go back in time for the taxi.'

'Oh yes!'

My hand was warm in his pocket.

Shanna's house was all lit up. It stood at the top of a small slope, and the short grey path curled up to a front-porched door which stood open. Music poured out: the Yardbirds, 'For Your Love'.

A quick look round showed me he was the best with his big memorable face, not handsome or neat in any way but quite lovely with the thick curving lips and soft eyes. I swanked it. You wouldn't have known, I didn't show it. But look at them, just look at them, other people's boyfriends. There's Dotty, always on about her Mike, Mike this Mike that. Well, *I* wouldn't go with him. That mouth. Robin, though – look at him move his head. The way his neck is there, the side of it in the half light, that's just Michelangelo, that is. Here in the everyday, Michelangelo.

I stand back and watch at parties, but only in my mind. Outside I'm opening bottles and giggling and going from room to room, and taking another sweet cider to embolden me and *being there*. There was Coca-Cola and soppy stuff, and there were some stern dark bottles of Newcastle Brown that many of the boys and one or two girls were knocking back, and some monster bottles of cider and a few six-packs of something. We drank New Year's Eve in. There was Dotty and Linda and Susan and Sheila and me and Shanna and Gail and others, and there were boyfriends and older brothers and sisters and other sundries. Pamela, of course, had not been invited; she was my friend, not theirs.

Those bright rooms just shone. In those times we had no sense of lighting. We were not sophisticated, we were young things under harsh lights. Shanna's mum and dad were gone somewhere till two-ish. There was all of the bright downstairs and the kitchen with its bottled Manhattan and the dog in a basket under the sink. A stocky black-haired boy with a piratical air had brought exploding cigarettes; he kept handing these things out to people and offering a light, then standing back and roaring with laughter when it exploded and they jumped back and screamed. Even when it wasn't funny any more he went on, crocodile white laugh and mad, merry eyes like a big kid. I don't know how but Robin got wet in the bathroom; we were fooling about and we came out, downstairs, his arm round my neck, me in the purple dress with the black trim I'd have preferred an inch or two shorter, he bare from the waist up. How did we end up that way? I saw the way they looked. I had him.

And there, suddenly, was Sylvia, who must have been there for a while and I hadn't noticed. What's she doing here? She's milking it with that stick, I thought. She'd come back to school after about a week with that and a faint limp, which she said would pass away with time. She told me this very stiffly her first day back when I asked how she was. Neither of us said anything about the peculiar visit to her house and I didn't want anyone to know about it or think we were friends. We pretty much ignored each other after that and she always looked sulky. Who invited her? Well, Shanna, obviously. But none of her friends, if you could call them that, the people she sat with for lunch, the people at her side of the classroom, none of them had come. I suppose it was quite brave of her to come alone. But look at her, it's painful and I should know, *I* used to be shy. She's in her head, all stuck. Her mouth's stiff. Oh, I know! Poor Sylvia, stiff, stuck-up, in the corner, no one talking to her, everyone's forgotten—

But could she care? That face looking down on us all, stern, sniffy, strung up.

Well, I was feeling kind. Don't laugh, I mean it. She was a pain, a kick-in-the-face pain, but I'd felt that dread of the room full of others.

'Have you got a drink, Sylvia?' I asked.

'Err...' she started and appeared flustered as if I'd just asked a complicated question.

'I'm getting one,' I said. 'Shall I get you one?'

'Thank you,' she snapped.

'What would you like?'

'Oh.' A long thought. 'Is there a Tia Maria?'

Tia Maria. What?

'I'll see,' I said.

Shanna's parents' cupboard – yes! Tia Maria. I took the top off and sniffed. Nice. Coffee. I had a little swig. The glasses in that cupboard were much too tiny and precious-looking to use. I poured some in the bottom of a mug then foraged ice and handed it to her where she sat like the

Sphinx at the entrance to the kitchen. She'd done something to her hair and it hadn't worked.

Poor girl.

Poor girl, I thought, basking in the knowledge that my hair hung long and shiny, even if it wasn't as long as Jo's. Sylvia's stuck flat on top of her head. The dress she wore was off-white, very plain with a Peter Pan collar. 'Thank you,' she said, frowning as she sipped.

'Oh, it's you,' said Rob, suddenly there with a drink in his hand, his shirt back on if unbuttoned. 'The girl who fell over.'

She coughed.

'So how's it going?' he said. 'How long you got to have the stick?'

'Not much longer,' she said, a hand in front of her mouth.

'Why don't you have a comfy chair?'

And because he was talking to her, suddenly we, the table, the depleted bowls of crisps and nuts, were surrounded.

'Ey,' he said, turning round. 'You shove over. Don't you give a seat to a girl with a bad foot? Christ, what are you? Bet you never get up on the bus for old ladies, do you?'

He was like that. That's what he liked in me at the start, I think. He could sniff it out even if it lay deeply buried, the stiff and awkward, the shy and dumb, he'd include you in the conversation with his nice eyes and big smile.

'There you go,' he said, 'sit here. Sorry, what's your name?'

'Sylvia.'

She stood, tall and thin and spiky in the off-white dress that hung straight down to the middle of her knees. Settling uncomfortably at one end of the settee next to two girls she didn't know, she sipped her drink. 'Here's your stick, Sylvia.' Someone handed it to her. Because of Rob's attention, the girls from school crowded round.

'All right, Sylvia?'

'Is your leg all better now then?'

'Won't be able to walk far, will you?' said Sheila. 'How are you getting home?'

'My father's picking me up,' she said.

'*We're* walking,' said Dotty, as if it was something special, swinging the arm of her froggy boyfriend.

'I wouldn't walk with a bad leg,' Susan said, 'not in the snow. Don't want to slip again.'

'Must be a drag,' said Rob, 'limping about.'

'It is rather.' Sylvia looked down at the ice melting in her Tia Maria.

I looked at the new Mickey Mouse watch I got for Christmas. Twenty-five to twelve. 'It's nearly time,' I said.

'We should sing "Auld Lang Syne",' said Dotty's froggy boyfriend.

'Not yet!' She shook his arm.

'Sylvia sings,' I told Robin. I don't know why I said it.

'You sing?' he said. He was sweaty. He had a beautiful chest, brown and smooth and strong.

'Yes,' she said in her stuffy way, 'I do.'

'Go on then,' he said, 'give us a song.'

'She's the best singer in the school,' said Sheila.

Look at her. She looks as if someone's stuck a pole up her back. Or a string, you know like they say, imagine there's a string coming out of the top of your head for deportment.

Deportment. At the end of our Reports. I always got: Acceptable. Pamela always got: Poor. Occasionally, Very Poor. God knows what Sylvia got.

'Not now,' she said.

'Aw, go on,' said Rob.

'Yeah, go on, Sylvia.'

'She's got a lovely voice.'

'She really has,' Linda said, 'she wins the singing prize at the Arts Festival every year.'

'Not here!' Sylvia reddened.

'Go on, Sylvia.' I encouraged her. I wanted him to hear the stupid way she sang with the stupid mouth and the stupid ends of the words and the whole ridiculousness of it.

'Oh well,' said Robin. 'If you don't want to.'

But she did really, of course. 'Well, all right then.' She cleared her throat and began at once: *Plaisir d'amour ne dure qu'un...* no hesitation, no jitters for the one thing that came naturally to her. Someone turned down the jingle-jangle record player music and her voice filled the room. It was gorgeous. She sang the whole thing, French and English, four verses, simply, without exaggeration. I never heard her sing like that before. Why now? Why suddenly?

When it was over there was applause and a small cheer.

Encore! Encore!

'No no no,' she said.

'Go on.' A final, definite shake of the head, a furtive smile on her face.

'You've got a lovely voice,' Robin said.

'Thank you.'

'It's nearly time! It's nearly time!' someone shouted and a

cold draught blew in as someone threw open the back door at the end of the kitchen. 'It's snowing again!' There was a rush to the back door and some people ran out and danced about in the snow. Linda, fresh-faced and glowing, looked back from the doorway. 'It's getting slushy out there,' she said. In the kitchen some poor girl had her head in the sink. A kind curly-haired boy with Bambi eyelashes was holding her hair back in clumsy sixteen-year-old hands.

'We should go,' I said, making for the front of the house, thinking too late of the darkness in the park and me and Rob bringing in the New Year in Boggart Hole Clough with the snow falling around us. The house was a tumbling jumbling chaos of bodies and voices and it started: Ten! Nine! Eight... too late, so I turned back into the heaving mass of the hall and couldn't get through – Five! Four! Three...

I pushed.

... Two! One!

Explosion of whistles, shrieks, cheers, whoops, someone even rang a bell somewhere. Everyone kissed everyone else and I stood in the doorway and watched as Rob kissed Sylvia on the settee, smiling as he did so as if it was great fun. Her neck stretched back, long. Their eyes were closed. A round-shouldered boy with a face like a friendly rodent blocked the view, opened his mouth, closed in for the kill. Clamping his mouth onto mine, he thrust his three front teeth between my lips. I pulled back but he hung on desperately, beginning to gnaw. His milky eyelids flickered next to my wide open eyes. Fireworks screamed through the sky, crackled, hissed.

Happy New Year!
Happy New Year!
Happy New Year!
'Happy New Year!' I cried, shoving hard, wiped my mouth, lurched into the room. Robin rushed to meet me, sparkly-eyed and grinning, flung his arms round me and lifted me off my feet, holding me close against him and kissing me hard. We opened our mouths. People pushed past us. 'Happy New Year,' he said, putting me down but keeping his arms round me.

'Happy New Year.'

Sylvia sat alone on the settee.

'We were supposed to go to Boggart Hole Clough,' I said.

'Oh fuck' – he kissed me again – 'forgot.'

We stood out in the snow, watching for our taxi. It was lovely. People drifted along the pavement. A firework exploded somewhere on the far side of the park, a mighty red spray blossomed above.

'We should have had this at Christmas,' he said, looking up at the floating flakes against the dark sky. 'What's the time, wee love?'

I looked up. Sweet. He was.

'Nearly quarter past,' I said.

His mouth could have been ugly but wasn't, was somehow just about right. We kissed and kissed. I liked the warmth and the softness but I still never got the thrill. Kissing has been a huge disappointment. Yes yes yes but really? This? I was always standing outside myself watching. But when he kissed Sylvia— She got far more out of it than I ever did—

He kissed her, Sylvia. And I'd kissed a poor boy with a

ratty mouth at the midnight hour when everyone started cheering.

'Here it is,' I said. We got in the back and gave the man the address, drove through town, our heads fuzzy with unaccustomed drink. Lights on snow, fireworks, glittering colours in the sky. There were things in my head, dramas half-heard through closed doors. There I was in the centre of each one. And this lovely boy to cuddle in the back of a taxi. You couldn't better him. Look, the sweetness in his eyes, the depth, the fun, and below all that, the place where he could be hurt. It was a long ride. He said he loved me as the taxi crossed Ardwick Green. I'd been expecting it. He whispered it so the taxi driver wouldn't hear.

Love, the big thing. I didn't feel it. 'Love,' I smiled, 'what is that?'

How profound I was.

'I just do,' he said. 'Make of it what you will.'

'You don't know me.' Thinking of the terrible things I'd done, the fool times, the stupid times, the shitty times.

'I will, though,' he said.

'But why?'

'Fuck knows.' We went limp, leaning against each other and smiling dreamily with the lights strobing across our eyes.

'Love is such a thing,' I said, not knowing or caring what was coming out of my mouth, 'love is so – *massive* – a thing—'

'Yes,' he said into my hair.

'Listen,' I said, 'don't fall asleep. We'll be at my house soon.'

He smiled, eyes closed, on my shoulder. 'Doesn't matter,' he said, 'doesn't matter.'

We dozed.

'Nearly there,' I said.

'I love you,' he said again and I kissed him tenderly in gratitude but couldn't say it back. It would have been easy to, but it wouldn't have been true. He just wasn't the One. The One? Ha, ha.

'Do you want the Stockport Road end or the other?' the taxi driver asked.

'The Stockport Road end,' Robin said.

'Love,' I murmured, feeling wiser than him, 'that word's too big, don't you see, don't you realise? That word, I don't know what you mean when you say that, it's not what *I* mean, it's like people just throw it about meaning anything, and *I* don't, *I* don't, I mean something more, something beyond, something that when you have it makes everything that ever was OK, anything, it doesn't matter, because it's just bigger than everything else.' All the profundity of fifteen, that moment, the drink in my head. 'I suppose,' I said as the taxi turned into my street, 'I'm talking about God.'

'God!' he said, as if I'd said something outrageous.

Rob was an atheist. He liked talking to that bloke who walked up and down Market Street with a placard held above everyone's heads saying *Atheism Is The Truth*.

'I'm not like that,' he said. 'Sorry. I'm simple. I just don't understand that language.'

The taxi pulled up near my door.

There was one long serious moment on the pavement,

his hand over mine. 'I'll always look out for you anyway,' he said.

Mum and Dad and the brats had already gone to bed, and Jo didn't appear to be back. Tony was snogging with his girlfriend in the front room, lights low, some kind of music playing so quietly you couldn't even tell what it was. I peeped round the door and saw his foot in its brown sock hanging over the arm of the settee. There was a sound from the girlfriend, poor awkward whatsername, something in her timid little throat in response to what he was doing to her. The gas fire was turned right down and the settee cushions were on the floor. Mum had a thing about the settee. She'd spend half an hour getting it all nice with the cushions all swept and plumped up, arranged just so, the knitted-square thing tidily arranged over the back with all its lines straight, and then some horrible person would come along and sit down and watch TV and wriggle about and do things and then go out, and she'd come in and survey the wreckage and despair. 'I don't know why she doesn't just put a sign up,' Tony said once. '*When sitting on the settee, kindly refrain from moving as this disturbs the cushions.*' I went into the kitchen and looked in the fridge. Only interesting things were a lump of cheese and a leftover bit of sherry trifle, actually quite a good chunk beginning to dry out which needed rescuing, so I grabbed it and a big glass of Coke and floated up to bed. The lamp was already on in my room and my mum had made the bed and tidied up a bit. Like a gift, in the dark uncurtained window, lovely snowflakes drifted down like passing nymphs. Our back garden was lit from the window light and I could make out the slope of the railway embankment. There were no trains, New Year's Eve. It made me think of Sylvia's back garden with the trees and bushes, and the squirrel. I listened to the silent house as I took off the purple dress. There were a couple of tiny stains on one of the sleeves but she'd never notice them. I stuck it on a hanger and hung it on the hook on my door, put on my nightie, turned back the blankets and made everything ready to receive me. My head spun just a bit and I drank the Coke, which got me hiccupping, then suddenly, I wanted to cry. I wanted a train to break the stillness. I was all fuzzy that night, everything running round and round in my head, the party, the fireworks, Robin kissing Sylvia, me and him in the snow, the taxi with the lights passing over our closed eyes. I didn't care about him kissing her. It was a kindness kiss. That was OK. Not like when he kissed me. They all saw that.

I finished the Coke and still was thirsty so I went to the bathroom and ran the tap till it was really cold, and drank and drank and refilled the glass. Someone came in downstairs, Jo. Voices. Kitchen light clicking on. I left the curtains wide open, got into bed and watched the ghostly grey flakes sifting through the light from the railway, drifting, inevitably, down into sleep. I hoped it would go on snowing and snowing like on a Christmas card forever, and it did in fact snow the next day and the next and I spent it all watching the little black shapes of birds on the railway embankment, hopping, calling, piping their winter songs, living their lives around the spiky black winter bushes.

★

I didn't want to go back to school.

It came round too soon. The dreaded morning arrived and I couldn't get out of bed. I hate school, I thought. This can't be life. Why am I going to this place? Mum was on an early shift, Dad had gone for his bus twenty minutes ago. College hadn't started yet and Tony was still in bed, and it looked so cold out there I couldn't bear the thought of trudging to the bus stop along the slippery pavement, the slush that freezes through your strong hated school shoes, looking down at your raw cold red knees. I let myself fall back to sleep.

Jo shouted up the stairs, taking the brats to school on her way to work, 'Sally! Sally! You're going to be late!'

It was awful, I just couldn't, couldn't get up. Kill me, I thought, I don't care, I can't face it. History first thing then Gym. Curtains, stay closed. I turned over and shut my eyes and lay in bed for some long queasy time knowing I was putting off the inevitable, whining in my soul: what's wrong with me? Why can't I spring forth? I lay for so long it seemed impossible that I should ever get up again, but then I thought of the explanations I would have to make, and about having to get a note from my mother and all the rest of it, and it was all just horribly too much – and I'd still have to go in tomorrow when everyone else would already have settled in. So I found myself meagrely washed and half-awake getting off the bus in the middle of town in some strange indeterminate morning time when I shouldn't be about. It hadn't snowed for two days but there was still slush piled up in the gutters, and though it was cold it was blindingly sunny. I couldn't look straight ahead as I forged through the glare, and the grand municipal buildings rose up on either side all the way from the bus stop. There was nothing for it but to go back, because there was nowhere else to go. Still, it would be nice to see Pamela again. Me and Pamela, we knew so well what we didn't want, but we had no idea what we really wanted. Or did she? Maybe it was just me. I thought she wanted a lovely boyfriend and getting married and all that stuff, but I wasn't sure what I wanted. I wasn't sure of anything much, just that I wanted out of school and all the stupid rules, having your hems measured to make sure you weren't showing too much leg, your hair measured if it came down too far below the lobe of your ear. And though we talked all the time about how we'd be out of it as soon as we could, I knew that really she'd get out long before I did. Because she'd muck up the exams and be out, and I'd do OK because I always did, and I'd go on to A-levels and college or university just as everyone expected me to.

I got there near the end of the second period, just before break. I had my excuses ready, I'd practised on the bus, a wild story: the little boy next door taken ill, had to help his mother – and to my amazement, Mrs Stannard, encountered ferociously outside the Office, frowned earnestly and stood still to wave me through: 'Oh yes well, hurry along then.'

How clever I must have been.

Our classroom was empty. Pamela's desk lid was up, careless. Her Rough Book lay spine-squashed, flattened on the floor under her chair. I dumped my bag. A stick of shoe whitener had rolled underneath the chairs. I'd missed History. Mr Justin's neat chalk-writing was still on the board.

I'd have to report to the Office. I should put Pamela's desk lid down. There was her toast in its greaseproof wrapper, her Wrigley's Spearmint Gum. There were her pictures, cut out of magazines and taped to the underside of the lid, the Stones, The Beatles. She once declared seriously, 'I am in love with each and every one of the Rolling Stones and each and every one of The Beatles.' I closed her desk, picked up her Rough Book and put it on her desk. Second period, Gym, that's where they'd be. I went along to the dark end of the corridor where the Gym door stood open but no one was there, only their clothes lying over the benches and their gym bags open-necked, shoved under. Miss Bredbury's hollow booming voice sounded like a bittern in the reeds from the yard below. She's got them out in this weather, she's mad. Thank God, thank God I'm not there. I climbed onto the warm radiator and looked through the high window, grey ropes hanging down at the side: there they all were in their yellow gym blouses and those silly little flapping grey skirts, all dashing and jumping around with their legs red from cold. Their long shadows ran with them. Pamela was tearing along with the ball. She threw it to Sheila. She'd had her hair cut and it stuck flat with sweat to her forehead. The heat from the radiator was burning my knees. I was very tired still. My God, was I tired. I yawned. Maybe I'd caught something. The yard, the netball posts, the bins, the back gate, the warehouse opposite, the running girls with bare pale legs, the voice of Miss Bredbury, the feel of the high polished Gym yawning dreamily behind me. The peremptory staccato peep of Miss Bredbury's whistle. I felt I'd fallen asleep for just a second with my head against the glass. The girls were drifting to the back door. A tic of fear. Now where did that come from? Everything was exactly the same as the moment before but I wasn't, I felt as if something far in the corner of one eye had offended me, but when I turned my head that way, this way, nothing was amiss. The sharp electronic grinding of the bell jolted me. Half way across the yard Pamela stood still, looking down sideways to where her gym blouse was half out of her skirt. She pulled it and it came out and hung loose.

Her long shadow did the same, stretching out in front of her. It had no head. I swear. No head. I ran back to our classroom.

Part Two

Umbra

'WHAT DO YOU WANT TO DO with your life?' I asked Pamela as we waited at the bus stop.

'I haven't got a fucking clue,' she said. 'Why? What do *you* want to do with your life, oh wise one?'

I wanted to be Cleopatra. The barge she sat in like a burnished throne, the way she hopped on one foot while still majestic and never in a million years even if she hadn't been Queen of Egypt would she have been beige. Let me not be beige.

'I don't know either,' I said.

Her bus came and she got on it and I had to wait another five or six minutes for mine.

Caesar and Cleopatra was in March. We could have got into the crowd scenes. We thought about it but really there didn't seem much point just standing about going rhubarb, rhubarb. Dotty was Caesar. Cleopatra had gone to a girl from 5 Alpha called Hilary Brogan. It was a big do in the evening with parents coming and prefects posted at the doors to welcome people and hand out programmes and show people where to go. Rows and rows of chairs were set out right to the back of the hall and all of them were full. My parents didn't go, neither did Pamela's. My parents never went to anything like that, it just never occurred to any of us that they would. But we'd heard so much about the damn thing we wanted to go, so we met in town, me in my new black coat which I wasn't sure if I liked, it had an odd kind of popperish finish a bit like seaweed that you could pop your nails against, and Pamela in her brown suede skirt and short denim jacket, a witchy green glittering over her eyes. First we had a shandy in a big red pub; no one asked our ages. I drank carefully, aware of my pink lipstick and already feeling embarrassed about it. By the time we reached school we were in a silly mood. It was funny seeing other people's parents. I saw Sylvia's, but her mother who'd given us Bourbons and tea didn't recognise me.

We sat near the back. The Sphinx looked like McDonald Hobley and we couldn't stop laughing. Sheila and Shanna and Sylvia were in the crowd scenes, wearing togas. But Cleopatra. You know I could have done it much, much better than her if I just could let myself, because by now I know *exactly* how she would be. Dotty made a reasonable job of Caesar, but Hilary Brogan was terrible, wooden and flaky as an old plank. A wooden Cleopatra just doesn't work. She didn't think she was wooden because she'd practised a lot and put in all the right inflections at all the right moments, but honestly? You could have fallen asleep listening to her. It's not really what you want from the Queen of the Nile, is it? She wore a ridiculous wig and Shanna said she was going round backstage saying, 'Do I look like Sandie Shaw in this?'

Next thing, the Arts Festival was coming up and you were supposed to put your name down on the lists on the notice board if you wanted to take part. The weather was nice by now, so we changed into our summer uniforms of stripy cotton dresses and straw boaters. The stripes were awful. Rows and rows of vertical lines hurt the eyes. Me and Pamela weren't going in for anything but in our class Sheila was reciting 'The Solitary Reaper' by Wordsworth, Gayle and Linda were with the recorder group, Susan Grech was playing the piano, and Sylvia, of course, was going to win the singing again. She was doing 'The Trout'. We walked past the music room door one late afternoon and it was a little bit open, and there was big posh stork-like Miss Frith standing at the front and young Mr Phelps, hollow-eyed, sitting at the piano. 'Well, look who it ain't,' whispered Pamela, pulling my arm so we moved past far enough to see Sylvia standing at the music stand in front of them. She had her fancy hankie out and was fussing it round her nose, turning aside to have a good old blow. She always did this before she went on stage, a good old nose blow and a throat clearing, all very discreet of course.

'When you're ready, Mr Phelps,' said Miss Frith, and Mr Phelps played. The piano did its ripply thing for water. Miss Frith raised her arms to conduct, drew in her rouged cheeks and stretched up her long ropy neck as if she was about to heave a fish down her throat. Sylvia stuck her hankie back up her sleeve and began.

I stood beside a streamlett thatt sparkled o-on i-its way

'Bloody Nora,' whispered Pamela.

She was doing it again, that awful thing with the ends of the words.

And saw beneath the ripples a tiny troutt at play.

Triddly trill trill, triddly trill trill. The piano sounded smug. Miss Frith's black gown flapped like the wings of a great black bird. I felt sorry for Mr Phelps. Sylvia's performance was something out of Greek tragedy. Her eyes, the taut shoulders, the look of disapproval as the fisherman comes and boldly stands upon the shore, the beginnings of melancholy in her glorious contralto as she hopelessly sang as we giggled. She'd seen us.

She clenched her fist. 'She's going for the Oscar,' I said. We moved further from the door out of the sightline of Miss Frith. Sylvia's voice dropped an octave. From there to the end was horrible, the whole thing full of exclamation marks—

and HID... her eyebrows shot up... *the fish from VIEW...* her eyebrows collapsed into her eyes.

We couldn't help it. Talk about stitches, it was awful. I sniggered into my sleeve, squashing my nose in desperation to stay silent. By the time she sang of her heart being full of sorrow for the catching of the poor trout we were nearly weeping with laughter. Her eyes switched towards us once or twice, full of utter disdain.

My troutt is free forever, my troutt will nott be caughtt.

The bell rang and soon everyone was crowding down and it was all babble and rush. We ran down to the cloakroom. Sheila and Dotty hooted loudly on the other side of the coat rack.

'If she says Heavens to Murgatroyd one more time,' I said, 'I'll kill her.'

'Small brain,' said Pamela, 'poor love can't help it.'

Then Sylvia appeared, struggling with the straps of her bag, passing the end of our aisle.

'Don't you ever get sick, singing like that?' asked Pamela.

There must have been noise going on all around us but it didn't feel like that, it felt like *High Noon*.

'I beg your pardon?' said Sylvia. No one said I beg your pardon. It was snotty.

'I said,' Pamela fiddled with her shoe, 'don't you ever get sick of singing like that?'

Sylvia turned her body in a peculiar stilted way till she was staring at us full-on, then went completely still. 'Like what?' she said.

'Like that,' said Pamela, 'all stupid – like – *stood beside a streamlett-t-t* – like that.' Pamela was a good mimic.

'Because that's the right way to do it,' said Sylvia. 'It's a classical style of singing. It has a right way and a wrong way and that's the right way.' You wouldn't understand, she didn't say, but it was there.

'No one sings like that any more!' said Pamela.

Sylvia was rooted. 'You don't have to like it,' she said.

I'd been thinking of saying something like, 'Well, you sang really lovely at the party,' but then I didn't because it was too awkward. Pamela hadn't been invited to that party. Not that she cared. Anyway, with Sylvia there looking down on us with those sombre eyes as if it would kill her to just lighten up a bit, shrug, tell us to shove it up our arses or something but no, always so bloody po-faced, I just didn't feel like being nice.

'It *is* exaggerated,' I said.

'I don't have to like it,' said Pamela, cramming her bag shut and yanking on a strap. 'Have to listen to it, though, don't I?'

'Oh well' – Sylvia turned to go – 'I'm sorry if it's so painful for you,' and started walking off.

'It's not painful,' said Pamela, 'it's just stupid.'

She turned back. Her face flushed scarlet as she hauled up her school bag.

'Why d'you wanna be such a boring old crow, Sylvia?' said Pamela, opening up a fresh packet of gum.

'I beg your pardon?' she said again, freezing.

'That's what I mean!' cried Pamela, and I couldn't help but laugh, try as I might not to. 'I beg your pardon! I beg your pardon! Why d'you *talk* like that?'

It was a horrible moment. The air turned thick and nasty and a few heads turned to look. Sylvia clenched her teeth and clamped her mouth shut. She put her bag on as nicely as always and marched out, stony-faced.

Pamela shook her head. 'She won't have a laugh with you, will she?' she said. 'She's not just got a poker up her, she's got the shovel and tongs an' all.'

'She shouldn't get special extra practising time,' I said. 'That's not fair.'

'Yeah. What about everybody else?'

I never should have said that. It was another stick on the fire.

★

I don't know which one of us saw the door to below first, whether it was that afternoon as we were going home or a couple of days later. We were in our coats. I was waiting outside the toilets and suddenly saw this anonymous brown door that I must have walked by hundreds of times, tucked in under the stairs at the side of the cloakroom. 'I wonder where that goes,' I said when Pamela came out.

'Cupboard,' she said.

'Is it?'

'Let's have a look.' She walked over and turned the handle and it opened onto a dark brown passageway with a couple of doors on one side, then the top of a flight of stairs that went down.

'That must be under the ground,' she said.

'Well, *this* is under the ground.'

'But that's *under* under the ground.'

We knew we weren't supposed to go down there even though nobody had ever expressly forbidden it. Of course they hadn't, there'd been no need to. It was just a thing that was there. We tried the doors. We had no need to, we were just nosy. Both of them were locked. There was a switch so we turned on the light and closed the door behind us then went down the stairs, which twisted round once and opened onto another passage deeper still beneath the building, and at the end of it was a door that stood open, and a dim light beyond.

'Ha,' said Pamela, 'curiouser and curiouser.'

Behind the door was a cosy little space where three people were sitting on benches round a big boiler drinking coffee or tea out of flasks and eating sandwiches. They paused with hands half way to mouths and looked at us uncertainly.

'Y'all right?' said Pamela.

There was a small plump woman with short brown hair and two men in overalls, one shaped like a Zeppelin, the other small and thin and narrow-jawed like a hobo on the range, both very dusty.

'I don't think you're meant to be down here, are you?' said the woman. 'Got lost, have you?'

'No, no,' said Pamela, 'just exploring, I suppose.'

The three of them smiled, looking us up and down.

'Do you work down here?' I asked.

They nodded.

'Is it nice working down here?'

To me it seemed very nice, much nicer than up there. There were no windows. Beyond the dimness, all the strange and unknown underground things that kept the old building going hummed and murmured. Huge pipes ran along the ceiling in all directions. I looked into the murk on all sides, saw the openings to passageways and thought of a vast underground world stretching away on all sides, spreading out underneath the entire city, going down deeper still, who knows how deep?

'It's not too bad,' the woman said.

'You know, said Pamela, 'I'm gasping for a puff, do you mind?'

'Well, we don't,' the woman said, 'but you don't want to go getting yourselves in trouble.'

We sat on the end of one of the benches and Pamela got half a cigarette out of a pocket in her skirt.

The woman raised her eyebrows. 'I've not seen you,' she said.

I never saw Pamela as much at home as she was in that place. It was calm. We went down there a lot over the next three weeks. No one could find us there. They let us sit with them and share their tea and biscuits, and they let Pamela smoke. They asked us what the school dinners were like and what we were studying, did we like it, all that. I never said much, but Pamela would sit back with her head at a proud angle, crossing her legs and smoking with a casually professional air, arms crossed under her breasts, wrist cocked out, bent back. The boilermen, or whatever they were, were shy and hardly ever spoke. I never got their names. The woman was called Mrs Rouse and she had a motherly Mrs Tiggywinkle feel about her and talked about her cat called Millie who brought in mice, and how horrible it was when they were half alive. Pamela talked about her old dog Bobby. Sometimes Mrs Rouse knitted. Once she told us how a school hamster got loose and lived down there with them for six weeks completely wild. It was finally captured by the Zeppelin, who'd nearly fainted afterwards because he was terrified of small hamstery things. I remembered that hamster. It had got out of its cage in the Biology lab, got down six flights to the underworld and come home all grey and dusty and wide-eyed. Couldn't tell us anything more than what was in its startled black eyes about its odyssey with all its wonders.

It sometimes seemed to me that the place was not quite

real, so cut off it was from the rest of the school. Pamela and Mrs Rouse and the hobo smoked. The Zeppelin and I didn't. Nothing could have been more different from the greenhouse with its open skies, but the feeling was the same. Those places kept us sane. It didn't last long. One day when I was too hot sitting next to the boiler, too full of coffee and smoke fug, I went upstairs for a pee and a drink of water. Sylvia was standing between the stairs and the entrance to our cloakroom, against the light so that I couldn't see her face but I could recognise her anyway, the shape of her hair, the way it tweaked up above her ears. She was very still, between me and the cloakroom, looking as if she'd been lying in wait.

'Hello, Sylvia.' I walked past her.

Her face came into the light. There was an awful blank hardness in her eyes. Just for a second I was scared. 'What's up with you?' I said brashly to break the feeling. Her eyes went over my shoulder.

'You've left the door ajar,' she said.

Scared of what?

'Why are you getting all weird?' I said and turned my back to walk towards the stairs, but she followed close behind, very fast. It irritated me beyond measure. I swivelled round and she was about a foot away. Behind her the door to below opened wider and Pamela appeared. Sylvia didn't see her.

'Why do you think you're better than everyone else?' she said, quietly furious.

'I don't.'

'You do.'

'I don't know what you're on about. You're mad.'

Pamela turned off the light and closed the door behind her.

'The rules don't apply to you,' Sylvia said, 'that's what *you* think. What makes you so special that you get different rules from everyone else?'

'You know, I really think you're going off your head, Sylvia,' I said. 'I have no idea what you're talking about.' Her eyes were dead and penetrating. Pamela came up and Sylvia walked away, down the corridor and into the toilets.

'*Who is Sylvia?*' sang Pamela inharmoniously, '*What is she?*'

'Did you hear that?'

'What?'

'Her. Being really weird. Going on like, you think your better than everyone else.'

'Who, me?'

'No, me. Being really horrible.'

'Bonkers,' said Pamela. 'Doolally.'

'Doolally.'

'She's the one thinks she's better than everyone else. That face of hers.'

'Looking down her nose all the time.'

'Literally.'

'Can't stand her.'

'*I* think she's got a screw loose.' Pamela smelt of cigarettes. The bloody bell went.

And it *had* to be connected to what happened later. Over the next couple of days I kept catching those looks of hers. A seethingness came off her, and once or twice my flesh crept faintly on eye contact. Everything was suddenly serious.

We were down by the boiler and Pamela had just taken a light from Mrs Rouse and was leaning back and proudly exhaling her first cloud of smoke. The door scraped open, light poured down, the awful clack-clack-clack of terrible brisk heels descended. Oh horror, it was Miss Demery herself, wide like Henry the Eighth in her robes, the head on top of her like the Queen of Hearts. Mrs Stannard, her deputy, right behind her. Grave, remorseless, calm: 'You will go to my office. You will wait in the ante-room. Mrs Stannard will go with you.'

Oh, this was trouble now one way or the other, oh yes, we were truly bucked and fuggered. The smoke from Pamela's pinched-out cigarette heaved slowly, blue-grey. We stood up.

'Go,' she said. The tone was more disgust than anger, but her eyes were merciless.

We went without a word, up the stairs and then the long walk along the corridor to that foul little ante-room, Mrs Stannard stalking our heels. There was nowhere to sit. It was just a brown space where you stood looking at Miss Demery's door awaiting your fate. Mrs Stannard smiled, half nice, half nasty. 'What were you thinking?' she said, then closed the door on us and went away. We looked at each other.

'Well, that's it,' Pamela said.

'Bucked and fuggered,' I said, and she said, 'Yeah, bucked and fucking fuggered.'

Her face was tight. She looked as if she might be going

to cry. You never could tell with Pamela, she might cry or knock over a desk. We heard the click-click-clack of Miss Demery's shoes passing the ante-room door and going into her office. After a fraught moment she called, 'Come in!'

I went first. The desk she sat behind was wide and intensely polished. Her hands were folded on the blotter. We stood side by side in front of her grandeur, the wide disdain of her powdery face, the red of her hair and eyebrows, her eyes like bores. She'd done stage acting and she'd been good at it. 'Well, you have made perfect fools of yourselves, haven't you?' Miss Demery said.

I felt about twelve and silly.

'Well, what have you got to say for yourselves?'

'Sorry,' I said, 'we were just having our sandwiches. We didn't realise...'

'Of course you realised, you're not a fool.'

She stared and stared at us. Pamela didn't say a word. Mostly, Miss Demery seemed to look at me, but then her eyes would switch to Pamela and there'd be a subtle change. Pamela looked ahead and slightly down with an expression both blank and surly. I felt itchy, my upper lip, my nose, my neck, but I was scared to scratch.

'And you, Pamela? Nothing to say?'

'No,' said Pamela.

'No what?'

'No, Miss Demery.' The way she said it didn't sound respectful.

Miss Demery looked sideways, a strong performance, disappointed, saddened by our idiocy. She lectured us for twenty minutes. She stood up. She talked about the Blitz.

She gazed pensively out of the window over the park across which we'd so often sneaked on a Friday afternoon. She wondered what our parents would think. In a community such as this each one of us bears a responsibility not just to herself but to each and every other member of this community. We have rules for a reason and as with law no one is above them. She spoke about our future, our womanhoods, how supremely lucky we were to be enjoying the blessing of an excellent education and if we had any sense we'd be making the most of it instead of indulging every childish whim that crossed our minds.

We should grow up.

For our punishment, she was sending letters to our parents, and we got a week's detention each but not together, and she said if we put one more foot wrong, either one of us, they'd split us up.

When we got out we collapsed in giggles. We nearly cried, taking her off: '*When we were young we didn't have time to waste in…*'

'*Where do you think we would have been in those days if everyone had behaved like you?*'

Sob, sob, sob.

'Bet it was Sylvia,' I said as we were running up the stairs.

'The sly cow!'

'She saw us and she was acting all funny.'

'She's a right creepy sod,' said Pamela, 'she's always snooping and snoozling around, she gets on my wick, she really does. Who does she think she is?' Her cheeks were blood-red and hot, and her eyes were moist. 'I'm going to tell her, I'm going to…'

'We don't know it was her,' I said.

'I bet though.'

'Maybe someone else saw.'

'I'll get battered,' Pamela said. 'I'd like to bash her head in.' Get battered. I hadn't heard that since primary school.

'They won't really batter you, will they?' She shook her head and snorted but I thought of the bruises on her back.

'We'll have to keep it from my dad,' she said.

We were late for English. Everyone looked at us as we walked in. Word got round. Miss Swett was off so Mr Phelps was taking us and he just told us to get on with some revision. Gail was groaning in the back row.

'What is it, Gail?'

'Terrible cramps.'

Talk of periods was a surefire way to get out of anything with Mr Phelps. 'Do you need to go to the sick room?' he said, going pink and looking down into the book he was marking. He looks like Keats, I thought.

'Can I?' she whimpered.

'Of course, if you need to.'

Gail stood up, her face one big wince. 'It's a bad one,' she said, 'ooh!'

'You'd better go.'

'Shall I take her, Mr Phelps?' Shanna Glassman jumped up.

'Sit down, Shanna, she can get as far as the basement.'

We pretended to revise but I was all shaken. This was a horrible thing, parents involved, fuss, the lot. Made you want to run away. But it was all just stupid, stupid, stupid. Why go through all this? What have we done? Really? So bad? I looked at the back of Sylvia's head. Of course it was her. Poor Mr Phelps had a headache again, I think. He put his long white fingers on his forehead and they trembled slightly. I was worried about Pamela. My mum and dad wouldn't care too much, but what went on at her house was unfathomable. The sleepy lesson ticked onwards till History, tick, tick, tick, hometime.

'What happened?'

'Oh nothing. Stannard and Demery came down into the basement and caught us. Not the basement, the boiler room thing. Underneath.'

'You went right down?'

'Yeah, it's great down there.'

'You should have realised though,' Sheila said.

'Realised what?'

'That you shouldn't go down. No one else goes down there, do they? It's kind of obvious.'

'It's not. What does it matter to anyone?' Pamela got mad. You could feel the rage like heatwaves coming off her.

'What you getting so het up about?'

Sylvia had already gone.

'Because it's stupid!'

It kept feeling as if something was going to happen, as if electricity was coming off things. Part of me was always watching to see what would happen, if you did this, said that, pulled this string, cut that cord. It was like when I got outside myself. I'd never seen Pamela so upset.

'Silly cow,' she said as we walked up to Piccadilly, 'what's it to her? What does *she* care where we go? No skin off any bugger's nose, is it? What's wrong with people?'

'Who else knew?' I said. 'Who else?'

We know, we know.

Who else knew we went down there?

Snitch.

Miss Demery said she was sending a letter to our parents explaining why we'd got a week's detention. It would get there the day after tomorrow, which gave us time to prepare them for it, somehow explain and make it sound better than it was. I never got to see the letter but I knew my parents wouldn't be too bothered about it, they didn't really care about that sort of thing. The big twins were worse. Jo was in that night when I got home. She'd just got back from work and was letting her hair down as she always did the minute she got in. She wore it twisted on top of her head for work. Tony and the twins were there too, milling about. I didn't say anything. I waited till they were all back, then I told Dad first, who told Mum, and then it was all over.

'She's in trouble again,' Jo said.

'What?' Tony, hardly listening.

'Some daft thing she's done.'

'What's it to you?' I said.

'Her and the Pamela girl nosing around where they shouldn't be.'

'Curiosity killed the cat,' said Tony impressively, Aristotle pronouncing a truth, looking at himself in the hall mirror.

'You're not at all impressive, Sally.' Jo stood in the kitchen doorway. 'You're just silly.'

'Ah, shut up,' I said, half way up the stairs.

'You always have to be different, don't you? Think you're different but you're not. You're just ordinary.'

Never.

'True that,' said Tony.

I still don't think it was that bad to make such a fuss over. It was much worse for Pamela. She told me later, her mum and dad went mad. I don't know what happened but I could tell she was upset by how awful she looked when she came in that first morning after. In her family a letter home was big trouble.

At Assembly, Miss Demery was grave. She said certain parts of the school were out of bounds as we all knew but certain girls had taken it upon themselves to flout these reasonable boundaries. She wanted to make it absolutely clear: any girl found in breach of these rules would be suitably punished and she hoped that the girls involved in the present misdemeanour, Pamela Dunne and Sally Hare of Form 5B, felt suitably ashamed of their disgraceful behaviour... and blah, blah, blah...

'Worse things at sea,' my dad said when he finally read the letter, and my mum just frowned and tutted and said, 'You don't just want to do whatever that Pamela tells you, you know.'

Things changed after that. The door to the underschool was kept locked, and we never went down again. I wondered if anything had happened to Mrs Rouse and the Zeppelin and the hobo, if they'd got into trouble about letting us go down there, but there was no way of ever finding out because you never saw them above the ground. I thought of them sometimes down there in the shadowy underground tending the big boiler, drinking coffee and tea out of flasks as they sat round in its warm glow.

The confrontation came in the toilets. We were washing our hands at the sinks and Sylvia came out of one of the cubicles.

'It was you, wasn't it?' Pamela said, shaking the water off her hands.

'Are you talking to me?'

'I'm looking at you, aren't I?'

'I don't know what you're talking about.' She turned on the tap.

'Oh, you do.'

'I don't. I never know what you're talking about. I don't think *you* do.' Her face, bowed over the sink, was flushed and heavy.

'You know, Sylvia,' said Pamela, 'you're really not a nice person. You really are not. You are...' She stopped, as if it was too awful for words.

Sylvia ignored us.

'You told on us.'

'Of course I didn't,' she said stiffly, washing her hands.

'Someone did.'

She was the only one who knew we were down there. I'd said it, time after time. It had become a mantra.

'How do you know?' Sylvia turned and said, 'I dare say loads of people have noticed you going down there. People do see things, you know.' She looked at me and I turned my head away. 'I do not lie,' she said. 'If I am asked a thing, I do not lie,' and she walked over to the roller towel.

'So you told.'

'No.' So noble. So pure.

'What's that supposed to mean?' said Pamela.

'Exactly what it sounds like.' Sylvia walked out.

'Oh, very nice!'

'Ignore her,' I said.

'Wish I could. She sets my teeth on edge.'

Pamela had gone strange because of something she wouldn't talk about, something at home. She'd gone all red, her face and the veins showing in the whites of her eyes. And she was always angry.

Same day I ran straight into Miss Demery striding out of her room. 'Ah, *Sally*,' she said, 'I've been meaning to talk to you and this is as good a time as any. Do come in.'

Oh God.

I had to go in through the ante-room and wait till she called me. She was sitting behind the desk as before with her hands clasped on the pink blotter.

'Take a seat,' she said.

I sat.

She looked at me and gave a loud sigh. 'Now you know as well as I do why you're here, don't you?'

'No,' I said.

She leaned back like Churchill. 'You are here,' she said, 'because of the dramatic deterioration in both your behaviour and academic performance over the past year. Do you have anything to say about that?'

I didn't know what to say so just looked at her.

'I know you're not a stupid girl,' she said, 'and it's a great shame you've been taken in by this teenage rebellion nonsense, which may be all the rage with a rather pathetic but bumptious minority, but I had thought you might have the intelligence to see through all that. It demeans you. I am dreadfully disappointed in you.'

Not again, why now, just me?

'Now you tell me, why do you think this has happened?'

'I don't know,' I said.

'I think you do.'

'I'm sorry, I don't.'

She just stared at me then with a pitying smile, and I stared back. After about a minute I realised I should drop my eyes or it would be interpreted as insolence. I would have done so once but not now. Why was it insolence when I did it but not when she did?

'Surely you've noticed,' she said, leaning forwards onto her hands and widening the smile, 'that the change began when you became friends with Pamela Dunne.'

'I don't think so,' I said.

'It's very clear.'

I looked down.

Miss Demery leaned back, drawing in a very deep breath through her open mouth and pulling a file towards herself. 'This could have gone the other way,' she said, her face suddenly dismissive. 'You could have had a good influence on that girl. You could have set her a good example. But you chose not to. You chose to let her influence you in the most puerile way imaginable. I have considered separating you two, but I won't.' She opened the file and uncapped her pen. 'I think we'll see this as a test for you.' She began writing. 'Keep out of trouble from now on. Keep *her* out of trouble if you possibly can. However' – and here she looked back at me with Gorgon eyes – 'if I don't perceive a change in both your behaviour and your attitude I'll have no hesitation whatsoever in having you separated. You may go.'

Robin was waiting in Lando's Snacks and I had a good rant. He'd bought chocolate éclairs and we sat in the window watching people rushing along, starlings massing on high buildings. 'It's ridiculous, I'm not going to stop being friends with Pamela just because someone says so. I'm not. What have we actually done? Really? What have we *actually* done?'

'I agree,' he said, 'it's a pain.'

'So now we've got to watch it. The least little thing and they'll be down on us like a ton of bricks, and it's Sylvia's fault. It is. She's a bloody nightmare.'

He watched me rant and his eyes were laughing.

'It's not funny,' I said.

'Sorry, sorry.' He smiled and put his hand on mine. 'I'm not laughing. It's just that you look really nice.'

'What?' I could have thumped him. 'This is serious.'

'Won't it all just blow over?'

All this love stuff bothered me. Not that I didn't like it, but it was a huge responsibility and I didn't know what to do. One night last week we'd been kissing in the empty bus shelter, and, 'Oh God, look at you, I love you,' he'd said. I couldn't say it back, it wouldn't come. And at the weekend, embarrassed, looking down into the canal as we wandered along, he'd said, 'Don't use my love against me.'

'What's that?' I'd said. 'A line from a song? Blow over? If

anything it's getting worse.' I took my hand out from under his. 'She watches us all the time, I swear she lies in wait. Such a sneak. Hanging about with that snobby look on her face. Snitch snitch. She's horrible. I'd hate to be like her.'

'Well, you're not, so no prob.'

Sometimes I wanted to make him angry just to see if it was possible.

She – she –

She was the Puritan elders, the Spanish Inquisition, she was *them*.

'Forget her,' he said, leaning across the table and putting his face close to mine. I drew back.

'It's serious,' I said, 'she's getting us in trouble. That horrible moral uppitiness. I can't stand it.'

'Her problem,' he said. 'She sounds dead miserable. People like that do more harm to themselves than anyone else.'

'I don't know about that.' The coffee was awful. '*She* didn't get in trouble, did she? It was us. *She* didn't get a note sent home.'

'I agree,' he said, smiling, 'it's rubbish. She sounds bloody awful. But there's always people like that and you just have to say fuck 'em.'

I pulled a face at the coffee. 'Agh! Why do we come here?'

'It's cheap,' he said. 'Are you going to eat that?' He eyed my half éclair. 'Because I'll have it if you don't want it.'

'I'll have the top half,' I said, 'you can have the rest.'

I watched him eating it. Big kid. He'd come straight from school and was in his school blazer. Sometimes his sense of humour was about on a level with the brats'. Let a medieval damsel cry, 'Oh, I am undone!' and he'd reply, 'Never mind, love, let me do your zip up for you.' Big babies, him and his mates all swearing and smoking like outlaws. And he's such a sop when he's with me.

It was trying to rain and the starlings were sweeping across the square from one rooftop to another, a massed applause of wings. The sky was chattering. The masks in the joke shop hung like severed heads above little glass shelves full of fake dog muck, big noses with round glasses, itching powder and exploding cigarettes like the ones that silly boy had at Shanna's party. My bus stop was right across the square. He had to turn off half way across to get to his. We kissed goodbye on the corner, and after I'd crossed at the lights I looked back and saw him walking away through the beginning drizzle. I liked it in town when it rained, the way the lights looked on the wet pavements. It made me feel happy, but something about his retreating back made me equally sad. Going off like that with his school blazer on.

When I got home my mum was sitting at the table doing a jigsaw, and the brats were upstairs. 'There's some stew on the stove,' she said without looking up, 'just wants heating up.'

'I think I ought to finish with Robin,' I said, standing in the doorway with my bag pulling my blazer off my shoulder.

'Oh you,' she said, 'you're never satisfied.'

I went in and sprawled. 'It doesn't seem right in a way. I mean, I know I'm not going to stay with him forever so how's either one of us ever going to meet someone else if we stay together?'

'You've only been going out with him for what – six months?'

'Going on a year, I think.'

'Well, that's not long,' she said.

'Yeah but – is it fair on him?'

'He's such a nice boy,' she said, 'I don't know what you're expecting.'

'I know he's nice.'

'Well then.'

'You don't just settle down with someone because they're there,' I said. 'What if I meet someone else?'

'Who's talking about settling down?' she said. 'You're only fifteen.'

'Sixteen soon.'

'Sixteen! It's all the same.'

What could you say to such stupidity?

'Where's the others?' I asked.

'Jo's at Margaret's, and Tony's – I don't know what Tony's doing. Kids are upstairs. Your dad's popped down to the Lion. Did you say you were going to be late?'

'Yeah.'

I might have done. What did it matter? This little room, its hissing white-barred fire, its telly, the sound on so low you couldn't tell what was going on, a small box in which we lived. I wasn't hungry. 'He'll want his tea when he gets in,' she said, lining up a few jigsaw pieces on the table. 'Put the stew on, Sally.'

'I don't know what you want out of life,' she said as I went out the door.

I yawned as I lit the gas, looking down into the brown

sticky depths of the stew. I could hear my mum in the other room talking to her jigsaw pieces. That's what she did. 'What do you think you're doing over there?' she'd say. 'Ah now, I've been looking for you. Get over here, you're in the wrong place, you stupid thing.'

I looked for the wooden spoon. The hall door opened and my dad came in, a bit boozy, straight into the kitchen, rubbing his hands together. 'Something smells nice,' he said. 'Getting a bit nippy out there now.'

It was in the dirty water in the washing up bowl and I had to fish it out and rinse it under the tap.

'Can you put the kettle on, Sally?' my mum called.

'OK!' I stirred the stew, pushed my dad out of the way into the hall where he took off his coat and hung it on a peg. It fell off immediately. Some kind of shrillness was going on upstairs. Strange how high boys' voices could be. I suppose I'm expected to make the tea and all. So I did, and gave my dad a plate of stew on the arm of his chair and poured out a big mugful and went upstairs to avoid the news, which was full of starving babies. I couldn't be bothered to tell the brats to keep the noise down, it would only be back up anyway in the next minute. It was dark but I didn't close my curtains; I stood with my mug of tea looking out at the darkness, and the lights along the railway embankment, thinking tearfully and dramatically, oh me oh my, what is my life, oh what, what, what shall I do? Poor babies with baby suffering eyes. I heard Jo in my head say, 'You think you're better than the rest of us,' because I felt different, and Tony picking his chin and sniggering, 'Don't be such a pretentious twat, Sally,' always making me the fool, and I thought about Robin kissing Sylvia

Rose on New Year's Eve, her throat stretching back, her posh house, the humming mother shuffling along with her silver tray, the polished smell of the music room on the way out.

They were getting the hall ready for the Arts Festival. That didn't mean much, just a banner across the top of the stage and bringing in the chairs. Everyone had to do the donkey work, apart from those who were actually competing. They were all off rehearsing. Me and Pamela were hauling chairs. That morning I'd caught a look from old Sylvia, a really dark nasty look, and it made me mad. Who did she think she was? She's not our teacher. Not even a prefect. She's got nothing over us. Looking down her nose like that, then pulling her stupid handkerchief out of her sleeve, shaking it out so the initials show, fussing it round her nose as if performing some delicate operation. Wouldn't catch her hauling chairs. I rambled along in this manner to Pamela as she lifted four or five chairs with half the effort it took me.

'I wish I was in a book,' I said, 'so I could run away with the circus or the gypsies or whatever.'

'I don't know,' Pamela said, 'I don't know what I could do in the circus. I don't think I'd be much good on the trapeze.'

'You know,' I said to Pamela, 'you know,' and this idea popped up, something I'd never dream of actually doing, 'I'd love to bring her down a peg or two, just stick a pin in that smug mug, you know something mad like put a frog in her pocket as she's going on the stage, or that stuff that makes your voice go funny, what is that stuff? I don't know, just something.'

Pamela snorted. 'Can you see her face? Aargh! A frog!'

'Too cruel for the frog,' I said. 'Anyway, where would we get one?'

'A frog? Easy.'

'Easy?'

'Honest, I could get a frog, bet you I could get a frog.'

'Have you got a pond?'

'No!' She laughed at the thought.

'But really, though,' I said, 'it'd be an awful thing to do.'

'Funny, though. Aargh! A frog!'

'Have you seen that joke shop with all the horrible masks?' I said.

'Ha ha! Put a mask on and wait for her coming out of one of the toilets.'

'Itching powder. Itching powder just as she's going on stage.'

'Yeah! Trying to stay still. Put it in her shoes.'

'It'd have to be in her socks.'

We had History next with nice vague old Mr Justin who tolerated us with dry long-suffering. We were in a really stupid mood, the whole class, because of the Arts Festival beginning tomorrow, when all routines stopped for a while. Pamela put her head down and walked her fingers across the top of her desk, going, 'Blobbablobbablobbablobba...' in a silly deep voice, God knows why, I can't remember, and Mr Justin said wearily, 'Oh, put a sock in it, Pamela,' and the whole class laughed. Except for Sylvia, who turned her head and scowled towards us in the most obvious way.

She had no right to do that.

We didn't talk or plan anything, but after school we

wandered about for a bit and ended up looking in the joke shop window. The itching powder came in small white packages with a cartoon of a man trying to scratch himself all over at the same time. Looking at that cartoon I realised how absolutely horrible it would be. You couldn't do that to someone. 'Can't possibly work,' I said. 'Think about it. You'd have to get it in her shoe for a start. How would you do that? How could you time it?'

'Well, there's always a way, me dear,' Pamela said.

'Nah.'

I felt bad for Pamela. These days her face in repose wore a hurt squint and she was always angry. 'I hate this place,' she said about fifty times a day.

'Do you want to go and see a film?' I asked her. We hadn't been out for ages.

'Can't,' she said. 'I've got to look after Bobby.'

'All the time?'

'Yeah. He's a wreck. Have to mash his food. Put him on the paper all the time cos he pees. Can't leave him on his own or he screams the house down. Howls.'

'Surely you can get out for an hour or two.'

'Not really.' She wouldn't say any more.

In the end we didn't even go in the shop. I went to my bus stop and she went to hers. There she was again leaning on the glass pane of the bus stop as I sailed past looking down from the top deck, but she didn't see me because she was watching out for her bus. She was all right before we had all that trouble. It wasn't fair.

And next day, nothing that followed was my fault because I didn't do anything.

In the morning we had events. Recitation, Sheila over-acting 'The Solitary Reaper' by Wordsworth, someone else performing 'The Journey of the Magi' as a jolly travelogue. After that the recorder group with Linda and Gail plodded through Handel's 'Largo' and Susan Grech played the piano. There was something dreamlike about that day. You know those times when fate just keeps pushing one way.

In fact I tried to stop her. 'You're not,' I said, 'you're not.'

'Am.'

But first we found Sylvia's hankie lying on the floor under one of the sinks in the toilets. 'Oh look,' I said, holding it up and showing Pamela the swirly letters embroidered in one corner. 'S.F.R.'

Pamela smiled. 'Sylvia Fucking Rose,' she said.

'Indeed.'

We'd had lunch, everyone was heading up to the hall for the singing.

'She'll be missing this,' I said. 'Lost without it.'

'She doesn't need to keep blowing her nose like that,' Pamela said. 'It's a nervous thing.'

'Probably.'

Miss Tucker stuck her head round the door. 'Come on, stragglers,' she said, 'don't want to miss the beginning.'

'We're coming,' I said.

'Must have fallen out of her sleeve.'

'Maybe it'll put her off her stride,' I said, 'like losing your lucky rabbit's foot.'

Pamela balled it in her hand. 'I've got it,' she said as if to herself.

'Got what?'

She raised her eyes, looked straight ahead, thinking.

'Well, come on then,' I said, 'are we going or what?'

'Idea,' she said.

'What?'

She dashed out and I followed. She was going up the wrong staircase. 'Where you going?' I called.

'Won't be a min,' she called back.

I waited for her outside the hall. She came out of the dining room at the far end and ran towards me, grinning frantically and shaking out Sylvia's hankie. 'Bloody good job,' she said, as we slipped inside. It hadn't started yet. Some of the teachers were still taking their seats on the stage where they would sit behind the performers. The girls competing sat in a special row of chairs just for them, along the wall near the front of the stage. Sylvia was third along. Pamela went straight up to her and said, 'Is this yours?'

'Oh!' she said – she hadn't realised it was gone – 'thank you,' and shoved it up her sleeve. Disgusting habit, hankie up your sleeve, I thought. It made an unsightly lump under her jumper. Funny, someone like her, so proper. 'Where did you find it?' she asked.

'In the dining room.'

She screwed up her nose.

The judges, Mr Phelps, Miss Frith and Miss Swett, with pens and paper to make notes, took their seats behind a table at the side of the stage. Old Miss Oliver was at the piano. Pamela came and sat with me on the end of our class row.

'What was all that about?' I asked.

'Pepper,' she whispered.

'What!'

'Pepper in her hankie.'

Miss Demery swept from her room and up onto the stage with her majestic stride, black gown billowing behind her. Silence fell.

I hardly heard a word of Miss Demery's usual spiel, talk, talk, talk as smooth and polished as always, the wrinkles in her forehead rising in unison and perfect symmetry as she spoke.

'She'll see it,' I said.

'So then it won't work, will it?' She wasn't bothered.

I watched Sylvia. Why wasn't she getting her hankie out? She always got her hankie out. You'd have thought someone told her when she was little she'd die if she didn't clear her nose before she opened her mouth. I bet she gargled too.

I gave Pamela a nudge. 'How much was on it?' I whispered.

'Lots. It didn't show.'

'It must have done.'

'Well, it did but I gave it a good shake so it wouldn't be obvious.'

'Oh, she's bound to see it.'

Mrs Kidney hissed at us from the end of our row so we shut up. Miss Demery retired to her seat of honour. Miss Tucker took her place to announce the first contender, Mavis Linsky, a tall thin girl with a lopsided skirt and dark hair that stuck out in a clump at the side of her face. Mavis sang 'My Love's an Arbutus', warbling away quite competently with a bit of screechiness on some of the high notes. I couldn't see Sylvia any more because the girl in front of Pamela had shifted in her chair.

'Is she getting it out?'

'No.'

After the song and the polite applause, a solid block of a girl from 5 Alpha sang – how we sniggered – 'Who Is Sylvia?'

'I don't know why they bother,' someone said behind me, 'everyone knows who'll win.'

Nothing was going to happen. It was a relief in a way but then again –

Who-o-o-o is Sylvia? Wha-a-at is she?

Sylvia's face was red. She looked straight ahead, glassy-eyed, preparing mentally. She had won now so many times that it had grown boring and she must have known that everyone secretly hoped she'd come second this time at least, just for a change. I don't know why she put herself through it again and again, she always looked miserable in the run-up. Only when she actually sang did she become sure, oblivious of everything but the song pouring with absolute conviction from her throat. Oh, but if only her face hadn't performed so, if her whole demeanour could have been toned down a notch or two. As the applause rose at the end of 'Who Is Sylvia?', Pamela said, 'She's doing it!'

I still couldn't see and felt like punching the girl in front of Pamela in the back of the head.

'She's got it out!' Pamela leaned forwards, a look of delight on her face.

'What's she doing?'

'Nothing.'

The judges wrote on their bits of paper. Miss Frith said something to Mr Phelps and he smiled and nodded. Miss Tucker stood up and came forwards as the applause died down.

'She's doing it!'

'Is she blowing her nose?'

'Yes! Oh, very ladylike.'

'Sylvia Rose of 5A will sing Schubert's "The Trout",' Miss Tucker crisply announced, and there was Sylvia going up the steps at the side of the stage, walking to the centre, perfectly fine, the hankie shoved back up her sleeve.

'Aw,' said Pamela, disappointed, sitting back and leaning left to get a good view. Sylvia stood in preparatory pose, dead centre. It had failed. The back of Miss Oliver's head was pathetic and strangely moving in its incomparable dowdiness. Nothing was going to happen. But why were Sylvia's eyes so shiny bright? The piano rippled, diddly diddle dum dum, diddly diddle dum dum...

Sylvia's nostrils flared, her whole face glistened.

We were nasty girls. We gave them something to remember.

Pamela grinned, bright-eyed, and I went hot and cold with fear out of all proportion to what was happening. It was like suddenly realising you're in a nightmare. The moment fell into its designated slot in the dream, neat as can be. Sylvia's throat lurched as if a tiny animal was running up it, frantic to escape. She opened her mouth to sing and sneezed instead, but it wasn't a normal sneeze, it was an eruption. From both nose and mouth came a visible spray. Too late, she slammed both hands violently into her face, eyes streaming, a look of startled horror in them as if a bout of vomit had just got out of control. Miss Oliver stopped rippling and turned on the piano stool with a look of alarm. Sylvia pulled her hankie out of her sleeve and wiped her face, nose, lips, brow, eyes too.

Miss Frith jumped up from behind the judges' table and tried to make all well. 'Take a little time, dear,' she said kindly. 'Would you like a drink of water?'

Miss Demery calmly gave orders. A prefect ran for water.

Instead of laughter there was, after the first few giggles and murmurs and false exclamations, a terrible quietness. The sodden hankie fell to the boards and Sylvia swabbed her face with both sleeves. Between each desperate swipe her face was visible, wet and distorted, shining with snot, and still the sneezes came and came and came, like convulsions. There was nothing I could do about it, no way to place the feeling, a mixture of gleeful hysteria and the sickness of knowing how it felt to be standing in front of everyone with your wet dress sticking to your legs. I *knew*, I knew how she was feeling, the horror and humiliation. I looked at Pamela. The grin was eager. Me too, I was grinning, covering my mouth. I felt sick, and I was glad. Shouldn't have lorded it like she did, should she?

A prefect came running on with water in a dining room glass. It was no use. Miss Tucker, holding her by both arms, guided Sylvia, everything streaming, from the stage into the bit behind the curtain that we called the wings. Pamela was stifling herself behind her hands. A hushed babble arose. Miss Demery came forwards with arms outstretched as if smoothing the waters. 'This is very unfortunate,' she said.

'Sylvia is going to the sick room,' and as she was saying this Sylvia came stumbling down the steps between Miss Tucker and the prefect who'd brought the water, her eyes clenched and her face giving off heat.

Miss Demery raised her voice. 'Kindly do not gawk. It is in no way helpful. We shall carry on with the competition. Miss Frith, will you please announce the next competitor?'

Miss Frith had just sat down but she got up again and said, 'Of course,' then beaming around as if everything was normal, 'the fourth competitor is Helen Toves of 4B. She's going to sing for us the traditional song, "I Have a Bonnet Trimmed with Blue".'

Pamela fell against me, almost sobbing with laughter. I thought I'd burst. Hysterical. The double doors closed on Sylvia and her helpers. Helen Toves, who looked more like a first-former than a fourth, stubbed her toe on the way up the steps to the stage and tried to pretend it hadn't happened, probably unnerved by suddenly being thrust on in the wrong order. Miss Oliver frantically rearranged the music on the stand in front of her but some papers fell on the floor and Miss Frith helped her to pick them up. By this time me and Pamela and a few others who just liked a good ruckus of any sort were in torments of rising hysteria. It was like trying to plug a volcano.

'Silence!' Miss Demery blasted us.

Helen Toves stood next to Sylvia's forlorn abandoned handkerchief and started quacking on about her bonnet trimmed with blue, and the piano attempted jovial fun under the worn old fingers of Miss Oliver. It was too much. Pamela actually got onto the floor, pretending she'd dropped something, and I had to look down into my lap and just shake and shake. We did it. *She* did it. *I* did it. It was all my idea. All of it, apart from the details and the doing of it.

Sheila and Dotty talking behind me.

'Someone put pepper in her handkerchief.'

'Well, what a horrible thing to do.'

'I bet you anything it was Pamela. Tell us, Sally. Was it Pamela? Did you know about it?'

'I don't know anything,' I said. 'She never said a word to me. Why would it be her?'

'It was obviously her,' Dotty said. 'She gave her the handkerchief. Lots of people saw her.'

'So what? She found it on the floor in the dining room. What was she supposed to do?'

'What was she doing in the dining room? She never has her lunch in there.'

'Don't you interrogate me,' I said, angry. 'What are you trying to make out?'

'Whoever did it,' said Linda from across the aisle, 'it was a damn mean thing to do.'

God, listen to them all. It's not as if any of them really liked her.

'Poor Sylvia!'

'It's a crying shame.'

She hadn't come back to sing. She'd been too upset and gone home. Someone won with 'Is My Team Ploughing?', no one I knew. It was like football fixing or sabotaging a boxing match.

'She's in with Miss Demery,' said Shanna, coming in. 'I saw her go in.'

'Sylvia?'

'Not Sylvia. Pamela.'

'Serve her right,' said Sheila.

That's when Miss Swett called me out to say Miss Demery wanted to see me.

Pamela was in the ante-room with tears running down her face and Mrs Stannard hustled me straight through. Miss Demery was the worst I'd ever seen her, glaring me down, not even raising her voice, using words like abominable, despicable and heinous. 'Tell me everything you know about this,' she said.

'I can't tell you anything. I don't know anything.' I stuck to the story. 'Pamela found the hankie in the dining room. I wasn't there. She gave it back to Sylvia in the hall.' That was all there was.

'And the pepper?'

'I don't know anything about it. Honestly. I have no idea.'

She went on at me for a good twenty minutes trying to break me down but I didn't crack. All the time Pamela was in the ante-room and Mrs Stannard was trying to calm her down. I found out later she'd sworn blind she was innocent, she just picked up the hankie, it was all scrunched up already, she didn't open it up, why would she? Who wants to look at someone else's snot? Then she'd burst into tears, crying, 'Everyone always blames me for everything, it's not fair, I wish I'd never picked it up, I should have left it there, well, that's the last time I do anything nice for anyone, it doesn't make any difference, I still always get the blame.'

In the end they sent us back to class. They couldn't prove anything. Pamela was threatening to explode – two breakdowns in one day, they couldn't have that. It was awful going back and facing everyone. Miss Swett was trying to talk about 'My Last Duchess' but no one even pretended to listen. Everything stopped. 'It wasn't me!' Pamela made her declaration. 'I told her. I said, I said why would I have given her the hankie in front of everyone if it was me? I'm not a fool, am I? Of course, it's always me! It's always the same. But I told her, I did, I told her and she had to back down.'

'All right, Pamela,' Miss Swett said kindly, 'the day's nearly over. Dry your eyes now.'

'I think it was just an accident,' I said. 'What if someone spilt the pepper and saw the hankie and used it to clear up the mess and then just left it there, not thinking?'

'So why haven't they come forward?' Sheila said, as if it was some huge police investigation with appeals for information.

Next day Miss Demery made a speech from the stage, saying she hoped the girl (*girl*, take note, not *girls*) responsible felt thoroughly ashamed of such a despicable attack, and that as long as she lived she would always bear the weight of what she'd done. She may think it funny now, but when she finally matures, we can only hope she will see, and understand, just how truly disgraceful such an action was. Pamela brazened it. I looked blank. A few people looked at us slyly but no one dared actually turn round and stare.

'Attack?' I whispered to Pamela as we filed out. 'That's a bit strong, isn't it?'

She shrugged.

It could have been a lot worse.

Still, after that people sent these looks our way – suspicious, deploring – well, not really my way, it was Pamela who'd done it, everyone was sure, I'd only been called in as a witness. Everyone knew that.

It had been Sylvia's nightmare, that stupid thing of a moment, that prank. She'd never let it go. Well, we all had to live with it, didn't we? Human embarrassment. Mortification. Why should she be any different? And yet looking at her made me scared. I couldn't place why. Had it been so terrible? As bad as standing there wet in front of everyone? And *I* had to not care. Anything else would not do. It was a horrible thing we'd done, *she'd* done, I wasn't sure any more how much to blame I was. Sometimes it seemed it wasn't anything to do with me, I hadn't done anything. Not actually. Everyone was being nice to Sylvia. Sheila was always going over to talk to her about something or other. People kept asking her to sing but she wouldn't.

'You're not stopping singing!' said Linda.

'No,' she said, 'I just don't feel like it at the moment.'

She was still stuck up. She sniffed in my direction sometimes.

'You know, I had nothing to do with it,' I said once, finding myself in the cloakroom the same time as her one day when no one was around.

'I know,' she said.

Pamela she never spoke to at all. She would just turn in her chair sometimes, only slightly, and look at her, back under her lids at a funny angle so that it wasn't easy to see that she was looking. Pamela showed no sign of noticing but I watched Sylvia watch Pamela many times, and there was such intensity in it that it made me go cold. It wasn't me she looked at, only Pamela, and I'm glad it wasn't me because that look could have made you believe in the evil eye. There was nothing good in it. There wasn't even anything as definite as malicious intent, it was just a still, concentrated coldness. And everything carried on as normal, all of us going about the routines as the school droned on, while underneath it was as if a seam under the ground was opening up and sending up noxious fumes.

Suddenly the O-levels were close. I counted the days and it was horrific, only thirteen. I'd known but not known and now it was real. I didn't do too bad in exams usually but this year I couldn't get down to it. There were bits like French and English I was good at, but things like Geography and Physics were a blank and History wasn't much better. I'd have to kill myself cramming, start from scratch, stay up all night. We had an official revision period one day and Miss Swett left us to get on with it. A gentle hum of reading and quiet talking made me sleepy. Behind me, Dotty was testing Sheila on the Napoleonic Wars and every time she got a question wrong she made a stupid quacking noise and said, 'Heavens to Murgatroyd.' If she does that one more time, I thought, I'll kill her. How could anyone concentrate? Pamela was dozing on her desk with her head on her arms. I wanted to do that too but panic was mounting in me and every time I looked down into my Physics book my brain shut down. I was going to fail. So? So? Why bother? But you had to do well, didn't you? There was such fuss if you didn't. You'd have to get a job. What job? My brain shut down again.

This was getting me nowhere. I took my Physics book and my Rough Book and a pencil and pen and slipped out quietly. No one took any notice. I went up to the greenhouse. It was empty and I had half an hour before History with Mr Justin. I'll mark down the essential bits I really must have. I'll just do a big memory thing, pack it in, recite, repeat, repeat, repeat. I thought if I write it down like doing lines it'll stay in. Long enough anyway. I read it twice and couldn't understand. I tried looking at the words one at a time, thinking yes, I know what that one means, and that one, and that one, so why can't I make sense of the whole thing? Every so often I looked up questioningly at the big grey turret with its iron crown. The sky behind it was pure blue, cloudless and dazzling. I could hear distant singing, a song we used to sing in the second form, a round called 'I Have Twelve Oxen'. I always used to get the words wrong. Now it got in the way of concentration. It began, one half of the class in full voice: *I have twelve oxen, they be fair and brown…* lanky Mr Phelps conducting, bringing the second group in – *and they go a-grazing down by the town.* I used to think it was *they go a-crazy down by the town.* The song, round and round, was like sleep in my head. I may even have nodded off.

When I looked up I saw Sylvia sitting on the brick ledge below the turret, six feet from the ground. My first thought was Joan-the-Wad.

You used to see Joan-the-Wad all the time in the newspapers, small box ads with a line drawing of her: send your money, P.O. or cheque, and they'd send you a metal charm to hang on a bracelet for good luck, Joan-the-Wad, Queen of the Cornish Pixies. I sent off for one in secret once but they found out and made fun of me. I carried it round for a bit but it got lost. I didn't take care of it. Joan-the-Wad was naked with one leg pointing down to the earth, the other knee raised. Sylvia wasn't naked of course but she was sitting like that with one leg down and one up, in her stripy summer dress. Joan-the-Wad has the face of a gargoyle. She smiles from ear to ear. Sylvia never smiles – well, no more than a tight twitch in a still-worried face now and then – she can't do anything naturally. Yet there she was with her face thrust forwards, a Joan-the-Wad grin plastered across it, staring in at me.

It was so unnatural that I ran, the sight still taking form in my head. Half way down the wooden steps, hurtling, heart hammering. Her eyes were both brighter and more full-of-fun than I'd ever seen them and the grin had already been there long before I looked up. I reached the science floor. All the lab doors were open so it must be lunchtime, that meant I'd missed History. Surely not? Mr Tufton came out of the Physics lab. 'You just run a marathon?' he said sarcastically and I realised I was panting.

I went downstairs. I'd left my books up there, no time now to go back for them. I wasn't going back up there anyhow. Girls were strolling back to classrooms, it was the *end* of lunchtime. Impossible.

How did she get up there? She hadn't gone through the greenhouse. Was she mad? Trying to scare me? I went into the classroom and there she was, Sylvia at her desk the same as ever. I'd run down all the stairs from the roof and she was here before me. All her pens and things were arranged in rows and her hands were folded calmly and neatly in front of her.

'Where've you been?' Pamela said. 'Justin didn't even notice. Everyone else did though.'

'I was revising in the greenhouse.'

'Are you all right?'

'Yeah.'

She couldn't have got down past me. Sitting there with the same old face, writing something up in her Rough Book as if she'd been there forever.

It was as if my heart never really calmed down again after that, and I went about the school all afternoon in a different state, saying nothing to anyone. Everything seemed turned upside down.

'Are you all right?' Pamela asked again.

'No.'

'What is it?'

'I feel sick.'

I did too but not as if I actually might throw up. It was more like a hand inside my stomach opening and closing. Miss Frith said I could go, so I went down to the sick room where you went if you threw up or had a bad period. It was a dark little room with a couple of bunks and a small office attached, and there was a matron woman who was quite nice and wasn't a teacher. I told her I felt sick and she took my temperature and told me to lie down on one of the narrow bunks. The grey blanket scratched my chin. How did she get onto that ledge? I fell asleep.

'Why don't you ever want to go up to the greenhouse any more?' said Pamela. 'Look at it, the weather's really nice. We could go out on the roof.' We were playing Jacks in the hall. I said I liked it better up there when it rained, and she made an annoyed sound, tossing the ball and swiping up nine.

'I don't know,' I said, 'I've just been feeling creepy about the greenhouse.'

'It's always been creepy,' she said.

It was stupid. I couldn't give any good reason. All I'd seen was Sylvia on the roof.

'The whole *point* of it is that it's creepy.'

'I know but—'

'We could go out on the roof,' she said again.

'We've only got – what? – five days? Four till the exams?' I tried to change the subject, but, 'Yeah great,' she said, 'we could revise on the roof in the sunshine.'

'I just don't feel like going up there.' I tossed the Jacks.

'Suit yourself.'

All week it had been niggling and gnawing at the back of my mind that I'd seen Sylvia in the wrong place and there was no possible way she could have got from the rim of the turret to her desk in the time it had taken me to get downstairs. Every time I looked up I saw her a couple of desks down across the aisle, same as ever, and wondered: did she know? I couldn't make a place for it in any kind of sense I knew.

'I saw something,' I said.

'What?'

'When I was up there revising. Sylvia was on the roof.'

'*Sylvia?*'

'On the turret.'

Pamela laughed.

'I saw her.'

'On the turret? What was she doing on the turret?'

'Not right on top. You know that wall that holds it up? She was on that.'

She thought it was funny. 'Why?'

'God knows. I just looked out and she was looking in and she had a horrible smile.'

Pamela shook her head. 'She scared you?'

'You don't expect anyone to be out there. It gave me a fright. It felt – not right.'

'What the fuck was she doing up there?'

'I have no idea but it was weird.'

'Didn't you ask her?'

'No, because I...'

'You didn't say anything to her at all?'

'No, because...'

Pamela laughed again. 'You're bonkers,' she said, 'you should have gone out and asked her what she thought she was playing at.'

'Well, I didn't. Listen...'

'I wish I'd been there,' she said, '*I'd* have had something to say.'

'It wasn't normal.'

'Damn right.'

'No, I mean, it wasn't...'

'She was spying,' Pamela said.

'No, but listen.' It was time to tell. 'When I got downstairs she was already in the classroom. Sitting at her desk. And she couldn't possibly have got there in time.'

Pamela sat back and folded her arms. Here we go, I thought, she'll go all sensible and blah-blah, I shouldn't have opened my mouth.

'Why not?'

'I ran downstairs. Soon as I saw her. I ran all the way. She couldn't have got past me.'

The bell went. Pamela gathered up the Jacks into their pouch. 'There's another way down,' she said.

'What other way?'

'I don't know but there must be.'

'There isn't.'

'We don't *know* that.'

'Yes, we do.

Walking back to class Pamela started working herself up. 'She's trying to mess us about. She's pissed off about the pepper thing. It's me she's getting at.'

'No, it isn't. Not just you.'

'I'm not having it.' She stuck out her chin and her boobs. 'Wait till I see her.'

'She's allowed to go up on the roof,' I said, thinking, oh God, more trouble. 'We can't stop her. Not if *we're* up there. If we tell on her she tells on us.'

'I don't care. She's following us around. It's intimidation.' She started striding.

Done it now, I thought.

Sylvia was seated at her desk lining up her pen and pencils and mapping pens for Geography, all nice. Pamela went right up and plonked her bag down heavily on Sylvia's desk, knocking her pencil sharpener askew. 'What were you doing on the roof?' She said it as if throwing down a gauntlet.

Sylvia closed her face, a subtle effect as if a ghostly hand had just passed in front of her and drawn a shutter. She was ramrod straight. 'I have no idea what you're talking about,' she said with her mouth practically closed.

It was all my fault. I sneaked into my seat and started unpacking my bag.

'You've been up on the roof.' Pamela jerked a thumb at me. '*She* said.'

Sylvia looked away. 'I have never been up on that roof in my life,' she said, sounding suddenly very tired with it all. 'Why on earth would I?'

'You tell me,' said Pamela.

Sylvia shook her head. There was something in it of the way Miss Demery looked when she despaired of us and stared out of the window in righteous sorrow, immeasurably wise and far above us. 'You're being ridiculous,' she said. 'I have absolutely no reason to go up on the roof. It's out of bounds.' She straightened her pencil sharpener. 'I don't break rules like some people.'

Pamela leaned over Sylvia's desk. 'What's that supposed to mean?'

'Nothing.'

'I'm telling you,' Pamela said, 'don't go up there looking in on people.'

Sylvia looked at the space between Pamela's eyes. 'I haven't got a clue what you're talking about,' she said.

'I'm talking about spying, Sylvia. Spying is what I'm talking about. Spying.'

'Can't you two give it a break?' Sheila called over.

Pamela didn't look round. I just kept out of it. Miss Tucker came and Pamela had to let it go for now. She was sitting down when Sylvia said clearly, 'You're unstable.' It fell into the lull of silence just before Miss Tucker turned from the board and the lesson began. Everyone heard. Pamela heard but didn't react, and later as we were getting our things together at hometime she leaned close and said in my ear, 'She's gone too far.'

I thought she meant the spying.

'Not that!' she said. 'Calling me unstable! If anyone's unstable it's her.'

'We should let it go now,' I said. I was scared.

'Hah!' We walked to Piccadilly in silence. She chewed the skin inside her mouth and her face was pained. I should have kept my mouth shut. Such a relief, though, to get it off my chest. It sounded so stupid when you tried to put it into words. Even Pamela thought it was stupid and I couldn't imagine telling anyone else. People just laugh. Anyway, I didn't want to think about it any more. You have to start considering meanings and implications and it's just too hard. I wanted it out of my head, gone.

'See you later,' she said, turning off to get her bus.

'See you later.' I walked on.

How had everything turned so serious? How could I revise with my head full like this? I was going to fail. Where had the light gone? We had fun once. Not this thickness in the air. I imagined telling Robin – I wasn't seeing him till after the exams, oh, what a hideous week this was coming up. Two exams a day, morning and afternoon. Cram, cram, cram all the times in between, all the time allowed. Why should we do this? Run away. Oh God, Monday morning horror. Too much to do. I lay my head against the vibrating bus window and closed my eyes and the sun and shade strobed my eyelids.

Next day was another revision day, with P.E. in the afternoon. Sylvia and Pamela ignored one another. Miss Swett sat at the front marking, and the room hummed with a low buzz of soporific study. It was a glorious day. I fell asleep for real for about ten minutes I think. I'd been revising till three the night before. Anyway, I woke up or seemed to, when everyone was getting out their dinner tickets and going to queue for lunch.

'I don't know about you,' Pamela said, 'but I'm going up to the greenhouse.'

She marched ahead.

'Oh, I don't know...'

'Don't be ridiculous.' She turned, grabbed my arm and pulled me along. 'We've got to. It's like getting back on the horse when you fall off. You don't keep off the roof because of *her*.'

'But it's not *her*,' I said. It was impossible to explain the growing conviction that what I'd seen sitting on the turret was not Sylvia.

'Oh, come on,' she said, 'don't give me all that. We've got to get back to normal.'

'Normal.' I laughed. 'How did we become not normal?' I said.

'We didn't. It's everybody else. We're going up to the greenhouse like we always did, and no one's stopping us.'

We dodged Mr Tasker who was noisily locking the Chemistry lab, breathing heavily down his nostrils like a horse. The door to the Biology lab was open. Little things with skins were pinned out on boards. We sneaked past the door and ran up the old wooden stairs. The greenhouse was stifling, rank soil and hyacinths growing ripe. 'The heat!' Thank God the door wasn't locked. I threw it wide and let the air in, but the air itself was hot. How could you get any work done? How could you sleep? Tomorrow was the last day before the last weekend and I was going to fail in History and Geography and Physics. Probably Chemistry too. We sat out on the roof eating our sandwiches. She had cheese and Branston Pickle, I had ham. I had a Wagon Wheel. She had the usual soggy dregs of old toast in a smashed-about brown paper bag. We sat on the roof with our backs to the greenhouse and our legs stretched out in front, facing the grand old turret. The sky was brilliant and gorgeous, eye-watering. An hour passed, near enough. She tested me on my Latin, it was OK-ish. I tested her on her French, it was patchy but she got the accent right because she didn't care how she sounded. My French was self-conscious. She could say, *Quand je serai grande j'aurais des moustaches,* perfectly. The city mumbled below. Like old times. Pamela lit a cigarette. We didn't stand up or go near the edge to get a better view of the municipal gothic skyline, the fire station, the Magistrates' Court.

'We should go back down,' I said.

'True.' She stubbed out the cigarette on the roof, rubbed it in more with the toe of her shoe when we stood up. 'Inwards and downwards,' she said, but when we got inside, the light in the greenhouse, though darkened, stabbed my eyes and made me woozy. I sat down quickly on one of the benches.

'Are you all right?' she said.

'Yeah. Bit dizzy.'

'Altitude,' she said, closing the door to the roof. P.E. Miss Bredbury. I hadn't whitened my pumps. She sat down with her back to the windows, the turret looming behind her. The sun made the slates shine.

'Adjusting my eyes,' I said, looking up and blinking. Sylvia was outside, close up to the glass, looking right at me over Pamela's shoulder. I screamed. She wasn't smiling any more, just looking. There was absolutely no need to scream. It was just seeing her there so sudden.

Pamela jumped, turned, saw her.

'Fuck off out of it,' she roared, 'you fucking spy!'

She dropped the bag she'd been packing up. Next second she's on the steps, at the door, which stuck of course so that she had to push and bash at it. Sylvia showed all her teeth at that, turning away and sauntering off. She disappeared round the base of the high grey tower.

'I'll kill her!' The door flew open. The bell went. Pamela scrambled up and out. 'I'm gonna knock her fucking block off!'

'Pamela, the bell's gone!' I yelled. 'There's no time.'
But she'd gone.

'Pamela!'

They were off in the maze of ridges, towers and turrets.

I ran downstairs. The classroom was empty. Lately I'd been getting scared sometimes for no reason, going down to the toilets, the row of cubicles with doors open or closed and not knowing what was in each one. Stopping on the stairs and standing still to listen. For what? I didn't stay in the empty classroom. I grabbed my things for P.E. and ran to the Gym. The buck was set up. I hate the buck; I can't get over, always end up hanging off sideways with a crick in my knee, feeling stupid.

Sylvia was in the line in her gym clothes. The laces of her immaculately whitened pumps tied in double knots. That made me cold. I sat on a bench to change into my pumps. Miss Bredbury walked up to me, bent down and put her face very close to mine so that I could see all the details of her brown wrinkles and yellowish-red veins in her old eyes, and she said in a very low voice as if telling me I had bad breath, 'Don't ever come into this gym with your plimsolls in that filthy state ever again.'

'Sorry,' I said.

My arms were all goosebumps. What could I do? I'd been a scaredy-cat long before this, way back when, in Grandma and Grandad's house, the picture of the thin man poling along in his boat at the turn of the landing. And before that too. How come this feeling had followed me to school? Was it innate?

Miss Bredbury walked away barking and clapping her

hands. I changed quickly and joined the line-up for the buck, looking back at the door, waiting for Pamela to come through it, but she didn't. Ahead of me, Shanna, Linda, Dotty, then the straight back of Sylvia with her short brown hair tucked neatly behind her ears. Does she know? Should I go up to her and say, 'You're on the roof, what are you doing here as well?' I got a sick feeling low down in my stomach. Things changed in that unbearably insistent yet subtle way, as they do when you find yourself suddenly standing too close to a high cliff edge. This was worse, much worse than before, because this was a confirmation, the end of the possibility of misperception or false memory. Sylvia couldn't be here but there she was, sharpening herself up for the run at the buck just the way she sharpened herself up before she sang; you could see it in the back of her neck and the stance of her shoulders. I might be going to faint. I had fainted twice before, once from heatstroke on a beach, once when Tony jumped out at me on the stairs wearing a demon mask. It had felt a bit like this.

There was no one behind me. Thunk thunk thunk went the girls, one at a time leapfrogging over, grunting, panting. Soon be me. My mouth was bone-dry. There went Sylvia, sailing over, legs bowed, arms trembling, shoulders humped. We shuffled forwards. Dotty's gone, heavy legs pumping. She gets over, just, thighs rubbing along the scuffed top of the buck. There goes stick-thin Linda. Pamela's not come.

I walked out of the line.

'I'm going to be sick,' I said to Miss Bredbury.

'Well, off you go then,' she snapped, 'be quick.'

I ran down to the toilets. The outside corridor was dark

and high and there was no one in the toilet block. I made it to the first sink in the long double row, hung over it gripping the taps with my fists and tried to be sick but I couldn't. I stuck my finger down my throat: nothing. Pushed it further down, just about shoved my whole hand in my mouth – nothing but a dreadful retching that made me wish I was dead. I got scared of the toilets in their long row, the doors all closed or half closed so that there might be anyone behind any of them. Another Sylvia, lots of Sylvias, a Sylvia behind every closed door.

Get a grip. Voice inside. Get a grip. Drink water, walk upstairs. Pamela would be there by now. She went down another way, she'd say. Crafty. And it would be any other ordinary day. I couldn't stop shivering. Always cold down here. I went out into the corridor and looked down to the junior cloakroom and the sick room at the far end. All the lights were off down there. The basement was a huge area, wide, plain, brown-tiled, the ceiling so high it was out of vision. It echoed with a layer of silence slightly less than audible. It was like hearing the water in the pipes and electricity running its secret ways through the walls. I could go to the sick room, tell them I've been sick and need to lie down. The nice lady will give me a drink, maybe tea too sweet and weak, and I'll lie there and listen to the walls under her protection. Send me home till tomorrow, a new day, back to normal. I was in my P.E. things, I'd have to go back, get changed.

I had stood there a long time when I became aware of a stir going on somewhere. At first it was difficult to separate from the tumult in my head, but no, this had the brashness of reality. Something was going on. I raised my eyes to the hubbub above. At this time of day? I went up by the dining room staircase. Girls were running down from above and being shepherded back up by Mrs Stannard, smartly clapping her hands. In every face there was a look of serious concern veneered with an almost gleeful excitement.

I saw Shanna.

'What's going on?' I asked.

'There's a girl on the roof.'

We sneaked past Mrs Stannard and out the back doors into the yard. Crowds of girls were staring up with their necks bent back. A third-form game of rounders had been going on in the yard by the look of things. Several teachers walked about anxiously and Mr Justin, batty as ever, was saying in a panicked tone to a tight-mouthed Mrs Stannard, 'We should put coats down on the ground.' Pamela was standing right on the edge looking down. At first all I could see was the shape of her head against the brilliant sky. It was hard to look up and my eyes watered, but when I blinked and put my hand over my eyes I could make out her round face and the dark hair around it.

'She'll go on the railings,' someone said.

'Here' – Mr Justin moved an arm in a spreading motion across a part of the playground that he thought might fit her descent – 'get lots of coats from the cloakrooms and...'

'The man's mad,' someone said.

Five storeys if you included the basement, because that's where you'd land, down in the sunken area that bordered it, if you didn't hit the spiked iron railings. You could look down through them into the area, but no one ever went down there. It was mysterious, like the underground realm of Mrs Rouse and the men in overalls.

'Oh no no no, I can't look.' That sounded like Dotty. Smaller girls stood at the back, seriously staring, ignoring the prefects who were trying to get them to go back indoors. Some of our class were there, still in their gym clothes. Sylvia was there too.

'What's she *doing*?' Another voice.

Oh God, Pamela, go back. Please, Pamela, go back. I couldn't see her face well. The windows were crowded with faces. Every now and then they'd clear when a teacher or prefect called them back, but soon they'd reappear.

'It's OK,' said a voice, 'she's just messing about.'

Another step in the awful unfolding.

Oh God, she'll be in trouble now.

A siren approached.

'Coats on the ground!' someone said. 'The man's an idiot.'

Another girl giggled. 'She wouldn't land *there* anyway. She'd fall down into the area or get impaled.'

'Shut up, Marion!'

She couldn't jump that wide.

Sirens whooped in the street and stopped abruptly. Miss Demery billowed from the back doors. 'This is disgraceful.' Though she didn't shout, her voice carried everywhere – 'Prefects excepted, every single girl will return to her form room immediately' – so that a general movement, made slow and clumsy by the fact that everyone was still craning their necks up, began towards the bottleneck of the back doors. Me and Shanna hung back.

'I don't believe this,' Shanna said.

'Neither do I.'

Susan and Linda came over. There was a jam at the door and the prefect was looking worried. Pamela looked over her left shoulder. I couldn't honestly say I saw her lips move but I felt she was talking to someone out of sight behind her on the roof.

'Hurry it along,' Mrs Stannard said tonelessly.

'Someone's gone up,' I heard.

All under control. The police are here. Look at that, they've sent a car, we'll be on the news, a siren, and an ambulance just in case. I stood with Susan and Linda and Shanna, imagining how I'd tell this tonight when I got home. That's when she stepped off the roof. Didn't jump, just stepped. There were screams, muted and foreshortened, hands clapping to mouths, hoarse gasps.

She plummeted, unstoppable, feet first, arms flailing feebly like old rope. It was a slow moment. Hundreds of times I relived it, feeling it in my stomach every time as if I was falling in a lift. How many seconds did she have on the way down? Sometimes I think it was three. Other times, I think it was forever and still happening. Just before the railings she tilted forwards a little, and for one hideous moment it looked as if she would hit the spikes; but she went straight down into the area instead, and there was no look on her face, no look at all, not that I could see. But then it all happened so quickly.

Here's the strange thing. I got the urge to laugh hysterically. I even think a smile spread across my face. There wasn't a thing I could do to stop it so I covered it up with my hands. We were hustled inside. I looked around: the teachers deadly serious, the girls, blank, red-faced, shocked, some with a kind of wildness almost of enjoyment in the eyes, some actually starting to cry. I saw police uniforms at the end of the corridor. Back in the classroom I sat next to Pamela's empty desk. Everyone was quiet and a prefect we didn't know was standing at the front, plump and brown-haired with glasses, trying hard to be an adult. 'Away from the windows, please,' she begged, 'sit down, everyone.'

'There's an ambulance in the yard!' said Linda.

Sylvia was looking down into her lap, head bent as if praying.

'Sit down now, please,' the prefect said. 'There's no good to be had from looking out there.' She seemed so relieved when Miss Swett came in and said she could go.

'Calm now,' Miss Swett said, and then she looked at me and smiled tiredly. 'Sally,' she said, 'are you all right there? Would you like to sit somewhere else?'

On Pamela's desk her Rough Book lay open with her fountain pen on top, the nib leaking ink onto a scruffy paragraph of her large round handwriting.

'OK.' I nodded.

'You can sit wherever you like.' I sat with Shanna and Linda. Miss Swett said we had to leave the room because the police wanted to look in Pamela's desk. 'Why?' we asked, and she said she imagined it was to see if there was any indication of why she'd done what she did. 'Those of you who have someone at home may leave now,' she said, swallowing as if there was something bitter in her throat. 'No more school today. The rest of you can stay till hometime but we'll have to go into 4 Alpha. How many of you want to leave now?'

About half of the hands went up. Mine was one.

'Straight home,' she said. 'Use the front doors.'

Going home on the bus, I had a terrible fear, deep down through every bit of me. My bus huffed along as if this was just any other day and passed the bus stop where Pamela used to wait, where I'd looked out and seen her leaning wearily against the post, eyes closed. Who to go round town with now? Such fun we had going round town. Couldn't stop the thoughts. What's it like? When you hit the ground? Tomorrow was Friday. Surely they didn't expect us to take the exams after this? Why was I sitting here on the creaking bus when everything had changed? Why was everything the same as ever when nothing was the same any more, and how had the day come to this? I felt as if there was something I should be doing or feeling, but my mind was so struck it didn't know what to do, and the old world rolled past the windows same as ever and in no time I'd be home. I saw Sylvia, clumsy, trouble in her face, jumping frog-fashion over the buck. The line in front of me, light from the high windows slanting into the gym, my filthy plimsolls down there on the polished boards when I dropped my eyes. Pamela dead meant nothing. We passed the pretty green and yellow tiling of Peveril of the Peak. Should I have told someone? Miss Swett the most approachable? Anyone? But what could I say? Pamela's not come down from the roof. She went silently, like a stone – why do we say that? A stone, a brick, a raindrop, it's all the same. Is there blood on the ground where she landed? Will they have cleared it up? Has she gone now? Where've they taken her?

There *was* someone else up there on the roof with her. She looked back over her shoulder.

No, no, she was just looking back. There was no one there.

When I got home the brats were watching TV in the front room and Tony was in the kitchen spreading Marmite on toast.

'My friend died,' I said.

He frowned. 'Kidding,' he said.

'My friend Pamela.' I leaned against the door frame. I couldn't name the feeling I had. It didn't quite hurt but it scared me anyway and made me light-headed.

'What happened?'

'She jumped off the roof.' I could hear myself, how unemotional I sounded.

'Christ!' he said, throwing the smeary knife into the sink. 'You mean on purpose? Killed herself?'

'Yeah. It's just…'

'My God.'

'I know, it's just…'

We looked at each other with the awkwardness of strangers.

'At school,' I said, 'you know my school. Five storeys. We were in the yard, I saw her jump. She just sort of… stepped off. And went down. It was…'

'Jee-sus!' Tony took a bite of his toast and chewed. He looked puzzled.

'I'm going to lie down,' I said, 'I feel a bit funny.' I did, my head was dizzy.

'You *saw* it?' he said.

'Yeah.'

'Christ, how did she? Was she depressed? How did she...'

I shrugged.

He swallowed and the point in his throat lurched up and then down. 'Did you actually... see her land?'

'Oh,' I said, pushing myself away from the door frame, 'no. She fell down into the area.'

'The area?'

'Round the basement. We just saw her fall past.'

I left him with his shocked eyes, so much more feeling in them than anything that showed in my face, I'm sure, and went upstairs past the open door of the living room. The hearty voices of jolly presenters sing-songed out. Upstairs I closed my door and lay down on my bed. Did you see her land? he asked. Wanted blood and splatter, I suppose. Well, there would have been, wouldn't there? I didn't want to see it but there was an image in my mind of Pamela in the area, face-down with one hand up beside her head, a splash of red coming out from underneath her.

I had to tell the story three more times, Jo, Mum, Dad, and then again at teatime to all of them, even the little twins, who actually shut up to listen. I didn't say anything about Sylvia being on the roof. Jo said depression was a weird thing, it didn't always show on the outside.

'There's usually some sign,' said my dad.

'I'm not so sure.'

Mum smiled at me. 'Oh Sally,' she said, 'you must try not to dwell on it too much. It's horrible, I know.'

'Terrible, terrible.' Dad shook his head. 'Poor kid.'

'A young girl like that.' Mum shook her head too.

I thought about ringing Robin but couldn't face having to go through it all again. 'I can't really eat.'

'I'm not surprised.' Mum gave me a wan smile.

'And I've got loads of revision to do.'

'Oh, leave it,' said Jo.

'Well, I don't know.' My dad shook the sauce bottle over his chop. 'Might be good to take your mind off things.'

'They ought to stop the exams,' said Tony. 'Everyone'll be upset.'

'They can't!' Jo was scornful. 'They're not allowed.'

'They could.'

'They couldn't.'

'Maybe that's why she did it,' said Tony, turning to me. 'Was she worried about the exams?'

'Pamela couldn't give a toss about the exams,' I said.

'Well, that's what she *said*.'

'No,' I said, 'she really didn't. That sort of thing didn't bother her at all.'

I had an early night and didn't do any revision. I thought this was sort of like being ill, no one expected you to work when you were ill, did they? I couldn't get my mind to settle down, it kept thinking about what had happened, everything playing and replaying neurotically. I kept getting all these images of Pamela. I saw her leaning over her Rough

Book, writing in her slow laborious way, with her head low to the page because she was a bit short-sighted but wouldn't wear glasses. I saw her grinning widely on the school photograph, standing with her skirt blowing out in front of her so that she looked fat. Raising her head from where she'd been dozing on her arms on the desk. Her thick, bitten-nailed, inky fingers. Dead. Impossible. I said the words 'Oh Pamela', in my head in a conscious way, hoping it would make me cry. I should, like being sick. I could feel it lying heavy inside. I imagined talking to her about all this. 'Oh Pamela, you didn't,' I said, and she kind of laughed. One step. Oh! Too late. One second. I tried again. 'Oh Pamela,' I said, then, 'This is terrible, terrible,' and my eyes did burn after that but no tears came. It worried me.

I went down to the hall and rang Rob.

'My friend Pamela died,' I said.

'Oh, Sally!'

'She went off the roof at school.'

'What!'

I couldn't face going through it all again.

'I just wanted to let you know,' I said. 'I can't really talk about it.'

'Oh fuck, Sally!'

'I'm OK,' I said, 'I am.'

'Oh love!' he said. 'Shall I come over?'

'I don't think so. I'm really tired. I think I'll just go to bed.'

'She went off the roof? You mean, she fell?'

'I don't know.' I felt a rising panic, suddenly, out of nowhere. 'I can't talk about it, Rob.'

'OK.'

'Anyway. I just feel – really weird.'

Lame.

'I don't know what to say. I wish I was with you.'

'I'm OK.'

'No really.'

'No really, I'm OK.'

'I'll come over if you like, if you want to…'

'No, no, no.'

Long pause.

'Everyone thinks she did it on purpose,' I said.

'Jesus.'

'I'm not so sure.'

Sylvia was with her on the roof, I know, just as I know she was also downstairs in the yard looking up. Pamela looked back. It would terrify you, wouldn't it, seeing that? A shudder went through me. I couldn't tell him. Not that he'd laugh or make me feel a fool, he wouldn't ever do that because he was too nice. He'd sit there and not for one moment believe a word I said. He'd say things like, 'I believe you believe absolutely that that's what you saw,' choosing his words finely, as if crossing stepping stones, careful not to put me down.

'Shall I see you tomorrow?'

'It'll have to be quite quick,' I said. 'I'm a million miles behind with my revision.'

'Aw, Sal, Sal!'

'OK,' I said, 'come about seven.'

'Right.'

'OK?'

'Yeah.'

When I put the phone down there was a ringing in my ears that scared me. Why shouldn't there be? I was changed, irreversibly, unfathomably. I went upstairs and lay down in my clothes under the covers. I must have fallen asleep because I woke suddenly on the dot of three, still with my light on, still in my clothes, looked at the clock face beside the bed, thinking no, no, not three a.m., the creepy time of night. Does that thing walk about? That Sylvia-thing on the roof. Doppelgänger. I tried to push myself back down into oblivion but I was up and down all night, and only when I woke up properly, half seven or so, did I think – my God, that's a whole night's revision gone, what will I do? The exams were as unstoppable as an approaching avalanche.

Mum and Dad and the brats were already out of the house when I got down and the big twins were still in bed. I knew no one would mind if I stayed off today but I had to go in and see what was happening. On the bus I kept thinking, I won't go, what does it matter? They won't make me. What if I see it again? What is it? *What* is it? Does she know, does Sylvia know? Is it something she's doing? Did it push her? Did it kill Pamela? I turned my mind off, listened to the slow groaning progress of the bus through rush hour traffic, watched the streets of every day alternately roll and jerk by, people squashed under bus shelters surging forwards to flood the platform, on and off, at every stop. Shopfronts opening, traffic lights, prams, couples, lorry rolling casks down a ramp into the cellar of a pub. It was a lovely day, the sun bright, the sky blue. From Piccadilly Gardens I walked with the sun in my eyes. I was not wearing my boater, I'd left it at home on purpose. Let them tell me to put my hat on, tie back my hair, roll my sleeves down, I just won't. They can't do anything. It doesn't matter at all, it's the most stupid thing in the world to think about getting a detention for not wearing a hat when people jump off roofs and smash on the ground and die. I'll laugh at them if they do.

I was a bit late. Not much, but everyone was at their desks, and Miss Swett was already coming down the corridor. She smiled at me. 'Sally,' she said gently, 'will you pop in and see Miss Demery after Assembly?'

'OK.'

'Good. How are you? Bearing up?'

'Just about.'

'I know. It's a hard time.'

The class was solemn. Tension hung in the air like a vibration from a tuning fork. Pamela's desk had gone, the whole thing, chair and all. Her desk lid with the pictures of The Beatles and the Rolling Stones, her cold toast. Someone had moved the furniture around and I now sat in a threesome with Shanna and Linda, looking forwards to where I'd sat with Pamela. Miss Swett took the register, everyone was quiet. We marched downstairs and took our places in Assembly just like any other day, but it was a special Assembly that went right over my head. Rather than listening, I watched the faces around me, all wondering what was going on and how were they supposed to look. Nothing like this had ever happened before so we didn't know. Funny how some of them cried, people who'd never liked her. Sylvia had surely hated Pamela, blamed her entirely for the pepper thing. Her face was blank. And when the whole school at morning Assembly sang 'Lord of All Hopefulness', Sylvia sang perfectly as always, head held high.

'First of all I want to convey my sincere condolences,' Miss Demery said when I sat in front of her, 'I know you were very good friends.'

'Thank you,' I said.

'She had a troubled home life. It's assumed that she committed suicide.'

'Yes.'

She waited as if expecting me to speak. When I didn't she continued, 'I have spoken harshly to you about Pamela, a girl who refused absolutely to confide the least thing in me.' She looked towards the window. 'Those eyes, the way she would look at you – such sullen yet rather pathetic defiance. And you know,' turning back to me, 'many a time she's stood there in front of me on that rug and simply stared me down as I was trying to actually make a genuine connection. She was a deeply troubled girl. I regret *very* much that I never succeeded in winning her trust.' She smiled painfully. 'Neither you nor I,' she said, 'must blame ourselves in any way for not seeing quite how deep that trouble was. I'm sure your friendship was extremely valuable to her and all credit to you for that.'

'But it wasn't hard being friends with Pamela. It was really easy...'

'And you'll treasure that. Tell me, Sally, had she said anything to you? Had she been acting strangely? Anything at all? Was something worrying her?'

I looked as if I was genuinely trying to think. 'Only the

usual stuff,' I said, 'the exams. She was upset because she thought everyone blamed her about what happened at the Arts Festival.'

That made her wince.

'This is hard for you, isn't it?' she said, sitting back in her throne. 'I think perhaps it's been harder on you than anyone here. Would you like to take the rest of the day if there's someone at home?'

'My mum's on nights,' I said. 'She'll be in bed. But I can get in, I've got a key. It'll be OK.'

'Good.' She looked at the window again and sighed. 'We have a few hard weeks ahead. It's unfortunate that the examinations are so imminent but there's nothing that can be done about that. The Board will of course be made fully aware of the situation, and the fact that the entire form and indeed the whole school has been affected by what's happened will be taken into account. You mustn't worry on that score.'

She stood up, smiling without humour and accompanying me to the door, leaning in front of me to open it. 'And perhaps the best thing for all of us at a time like this would be some sheer hard work and concentration. You must try not to brood, Sally. This is crass advice, I know, but I'm afraid it's the best there is.'

'Thank you,' I said.

When I got home I went straight to bed. It felt funny going to bed in the morning but I was so tired. 'You should have seen them,' I said to Pamela, as if she could hear me, 'you should have seen – Dotty was crying. So was Shanna, I think. And everyone's really upset.' Then I slept.

★

The exams came and went as things do. I did OK. Nothing special but OK. They rolled by in a haze. I took no notice of them but let my robot soul take over. Pamela's funeral was the following Saturday, and I went with Shanna and Linda. Miss Swett came too. It was in a church with the coffin at the front so that you had to look at it and keep thinking about her body inside. Her family looked hard. There was a man with a pig-pug face, a faded woman with artificial brows and a quivering overbite, some surly lads and a miscellany of tough-looking others. The pig-pug man was her dad, I think, and the woman was her mum. I imagined her standing there with them and yeah, I thought, she fits in well, and wondered who was looking after Bobby. Someone, usually her, always had to stay with him because he hated being alone, she said. Who'd look after him now? They could have brought him to church. They could have; you could, couldn't you? If not, you *should* be able to. Didn't seem fair. Had they just left him? All on his own? That made me want to cry. The thought became so tormenting I thought about going and asking someone about Bobby when the service was over, but I didn't in the end because they were just so unapproachable with their sad red faces and best clothes.

After that, everything just carried on as if nothing had happened, except that now I sat alongside Shanna and Linda and I was always watching Sylvia with questions racing round and round in circles in my mind. Life was duller without Pamela. On Friday I bunked off Games on my own but it was no fun. I went down to Shude Hill and wandered round the bookstalls, looking for books on doppelgängers, but couldn't find anything, so I went to Forsyth's and bought a guitar strap for Robin's seventeenth birthday which was in a couple of weeks. He was going to have a party. That night after tea I waited till everyone was out of the room except Dad.

'Can a person be in two places at the same time?' I asked him.

Dad's feet were on the coffee table. He didn't take his eyes off the TV. 'So they say,' he said, surprising me, 'it happens apparently. Why?'

'I was just thinking about it. Someone was talking about it at school.'

'Well, they do say it happens with some people but it's rare. Saints and people. That sort of thing.' He went into one of his info spiels from his readings, told me all the various names for it, double, doppelgänger, fetch. Fetch was the scariest word.

'It must be horrible,' I said, 'to see yourself.'

He grinned. 'Did I ever tell you about my dad's Auntie Miriam who met herself coming back?'

'No!'

'Yeah, she was going to post a letter and on the way to the post box she saw herself walking towards herself on the way back. So she ran home instead of posting the letter and she died not long after.'

'Really? Is that true?'

He laughed. 'Well, it's one of those things everyone used to say. It's just a story.'

★

'You know,' Linda said one day, 'Margaret Slack's dad says this place is closing down.'

Closing down? This place had been here for all times, before any of us existed. How? She couldn't say. They were going to blend it with another school, she'd heard, and we'd all have to go somewhere else. I'd have to get another bus and it would take forever to get home. But no one heard any more about it after that and I forgot and nothing happened apart from time rolling on implacably, and every now and then I'd look at the dark corner where the small wooden stairs went up to the greenhouse and I'd want to go and sit on the roof where the air was clear and you could hear the hum of the city. Sometimes I got as far as the foot of the greenhouse stairs but then no further.

The place was unsettled. They started talking again about the two shadows in the room across the way, and at lunchtime we cornered Gail's kid sister to ask her what she'd really seen. She started crying and thought we were calling her a liar. Then in 4 Alpha someone suddenly screamed and said she'd seen a hand coming through the wall, and no one else saw a thing but they all screamed too and the door was flung open and everyone ran out into the corridor. We could hear it all because our classroom door was open because of the heat. Such a commotion, voices going up and down, clacking footsteps, Mr Justin sallying on with his deadpan account of the Duke of Wellington and the Battle of Waterloo. There was more after that – a whispering outside the sick room, a clicking in the lecture theatre, a music stand collapsing all by itself, and pretty soon just about everybody was scuttling about looking over their shoulders and putting off going to the toilet unless someone else was going at the same time. In the end Miss Demery gave the whole school a thorough dressing down at Assembly, telling us we were gutless and gullible, behaving like medieval peasants, how ashamed it made her feel that the girls of any school of which she was headmistress could succumb to such mindless superstition. It must stop immediately. Those few girls, and they knew who they were, who thought it clever to scare children younger than themselves and ferment fear would be dealt with forcefully. So it all stopped, and I waited for summer.

It's just a story, I thought, it's just a story, everything is just a story, silhouettes, ghosts, Pamela stepping off the roof.

Shanna said, 'We're having a séance in the Biology lab. Do you want to come? We thought we might see if we could get in touch with Pamela.'

I looked at her. How could she? How could they? But then I thought: so? Why not? Was it bad? I thought it was a horrible thing to do. I thought it was a horrible thing to die. I laughed, a sort of laugh. 'OK,' I said.

'Good,' said Shanna. 'She's more likely to come if you're there.'

Anyway, I couldn't stay away.

'You know,' said Susan Grech as we gathered in the lab, 'it'd be really nice to talk to Pamela again.'

'Yeah,' said Linda, 'I still can't get over it. It's weird, isn't it?'

I was there with my finger on the glass with all the rest.

'Do you want to say anything?' said Shanna, but I shook

my head. It didn't feel right. *Pamela! Pamela! Are you there? Here I am!*

But they tried: *Is anybody there? If you're there, can you give us a sign?*

Of course not. Think she would? In the silence, though, we all listened hard for the nothing that came, and if by wishing we could have made it happen, it would have come. I thought of her at my shoulder whispering, 'Shall I make them jump?'

'She hated these things,' I said.

'Ssh!'

We didn't get her and we didn't get anyone else. My mind wandered. We do this, I thought. If anything really happened we'd wet ourselves. I stared out of the window at the puffy sky, watching all those little whirly things that inhabit your eyeballs busily speeding about, falling and rising and falling again on a white sky backdrop. It was a relief when I closed my eyes. Next thing I knew they'd given up on Pamela and were asking something if it was true this had been an asylum, and were there soldiers on the canal, and is it true it's closing down. Of course no one answered and everyone was getting bored, and then the door opened and Mrs Kidney came in with Mr Tasker and Mrs Stannard.

'Oh, girls, don't you ever learn?' she said. We should have posted a look-out.

We all got detention, even Sheila and Dotty who never got detentions.

★

Rob's party was horrible. I didn't know anyone. The house was full of lads and girls from his school and he was all over the place with his smile, talking to everyone, cracking open bottles. I wished I'd brought someone with me but Shanna had gone down with a cold and no one had been able to go. It was funny to see him in his element, as easy with all these people as he was with me. I didn't mind that, but he left me on my own standing by the table in the kitchen picking at mini sausage rolls. Now and again someone I'd vaguely met with him once or twice would come into the kitchen and we'd exchange a word or two. He had loads of friends. Once Stewart, the only fanciable one, came in and smiled at me and said, 'Aren't you coming in?'

'Oh yes,' I said, downing my third glass of lager.

In the hall I talked to that girl in a white dress; she was puffing away and I bummed a cigarette and she gave me one without a word, then I asked for a light and she offered me her own cigarette and walked off. I talked to some girls by the door. I went into the front room where the piano was and sat on the end of the settee but no one came and sat next to me. Robin was sitting on the piano stool with his knees up against the back of a chair and there was a girl standing behind him massaging the back of his head. I noticed how long his hair was growing, how much of it there was for her to get her fingers into. She was smaller than me with roly-poly hips and a round doll-like face. Her name was Jane. I'd seen her before at a do at his school when she'd been with a boy.

'Aaah!' he said as if he was in heaven. His eyes were closed.

You know, if I went, I thought, no one would even notice.

She was a very pretty girl, brown eyes, brown curly hair, dimples. Up herself. I thought that, but didn't know her. I just got these impressions from her vain little face and toss of the head. Look how he took care of Sylvia on New Year's Eve, I thought. And he lets me sit here alone. I bought him that nice guitar strap. He doesn't know; his eyes are closed. Well, open your fucking eyes, you stupid bastard.

This was ridiculous. All this 'I love you' stuff stifles me. What did he think, after all? At my age, that I'd make promises? No. Couldn't say, 'I love you', and mean it in any complete way. So why bother? If that's what he wanted, I wouldn't treat him well. She could have him.

But seeing *that*, him and her – oh no, I didn't care for that.

I sloped off home early without saying goodbye. He rang the next morning when I was still in bed. My mother called me down.

'Where did you go?'

'Home.'

'On your own? My dad was going to drive you. Why didn't you wait? What's wrong?'

'Nothing.'

'Oh sure. Come off it, Sal. What's wrong with your voice?'

'I don't know what you're talking about.'

Silence on the line.

'So?' he said.

'What?'

'Oh fuck,' he said under his breath, then, 'Go on then, enlighten me. What am I supposed to have done?'

'You really have no idea, have you?'

'No, I don't.'

'Well, there you go.'

Bewilderment.

'If you don't tell me,' he said, 'how am I supposed to put it right?'

'If I have to tell you, there's really no point.'

'Oh come on! I'm not psychic.'

I said nothing because I couldn't think of anything.

'This is going nowhere,' he said.

'Clearly it isn't.'

'What the hell is wrong with you, Sally?'

We could go round like this forever.

'How about the fact,' I said, 'that you completely ignored me all night.'

'I did not.'

'Of course you did.'

He muttered, then said coldly, 'Please explain.'

'You knew I didn't know anyone. You knew. I was just hanging around by myself like a spare part, I felt horrible, you didn't even notice.' As I spoke I grew tearful but wouldn't let it show in my voice. 'What was I supposed to do? You knew I didn't—'

'You know Barry! You know Mike and Stew and Phil, you know—'

'I don't *know* any of them.'

'Oh, I'm so sorry,' he said, 'I thought you did. I thought you were a big girl now, I didn't know I was supposed to hold your hand all night and never leave your side, I didn't realise you needed babysitting, I didn't realise—'

I put the phone down. Well, that was the end of *him*.

I swiped away the tears. Of anger only. Let him stew, I thought, I'm not calling him back. I am not in the wrong here. If he thought I knew his stupid friends, he didn't know me. Babies. Big sweaty babies. He should have seen me sitting alone. He should have noticed. What was I supposed to do? Follow him round? Tug at his sleeve? I did try. I would not apologise. There was a tight hard feeling in my chest as if a bone was stuck there. I despised the whole situation. There must be more than the same old banalities of tit for tat, who did this, who said that. I didn't want any of it, let him go. Should have finished it before now.

He didn't ring back.

Good.

Didn't ring back Monday, Tuesday, Wednesday.

Not that I really cared, but who, I thought, can I go around with now? I arranged to go to the Oasis with Shanna and Linda on Friday night. Thursday he called.

'OK, Sal?' he said.

'Yeah, course I'm OK.'

'Oh really? You're OK.'

'I'm OK.'

'Well, I'm not.'

'Oh? Why's that then?'

'And you don't know?'

God, I'm a bastard. 'Why should I know?' I said.

He laughed. 'Well,' he said, 'you really do know, don't you? You know I'm mad about you. You really do know, I know you know. I'm sorry. Is that what you want? Of

176

course I'm sorry. Whatever I did I'm sorry. What else can I say? Can I see you tomorrow?'

'Can't,' I said. 'I'm going out with Shanna and Linda.'

'Oh. OK. Saturday. How about I meet you in town? At your bus stop. I'll meet you off the bus. Come on, Sally. Yeah?'

I thought for twenty seconds. 'OK,' I said.

So that was that. If I'd met someone at the Oasis on Friday night, who knows? But I didn't, so I went into town on the bus on Saturday and there he was, leaning on the iron rail with the big smile when he saw me. He was something. Other girls envied me. A nice wide-shouldered boy with an easy grace. We walked into the gardens and sat on a bench and he said Jane was nothing, just a friend, she was going out with Mike, and he couldn't lose me over such a stupid thing. We started kissing and the smell of his hair was a comfort, like laying your head on a familiar pillow. What's wrong with me? I thought. Why isn't he enough? We wandered around town in our old rambling way, all around the cathedral, arms round each other's waists, and I forgave him, we forgave each other, we stopped in a random place and laughed and smelt each other's necks, and it was enough, more than enough for now. We ended up in Forsyth's because he wanted some new strings and a plectrum, and oh God, who should be there in the realms of classical music but Sylvia and her dad? Oh joy! She looked like a frump. And her dad was just some posh old buffer, out of our league, polite enough to acknowledge us with a kindly greeting before he wandered browsing away, leaving

Sylvia, curdling with awkwardness, to deal with us. She just stood there like a lump, blushing and looking down.

'Hi, Sylvia,' I said.

'Hi,' she whispered.

And he didn't stay, Robin, he sauntered away with a vague smile on his face, far away to the end of the store, leaving us to negotiate the distance between us.

'OK, Sylvia?' I said.

'Yes,' she replied in a surprised tone.

'That's good,' I said. 'What are you buying?'

'My father's buying some sheet music,' she said.

'Oh. Classical?'

'Yes.'

It would be.

So we stood with nothing at all between us to exchange. Why bother? I could have said – you fancy him, don't you? He'd never go for you, you know. Never mind. Dare say it'll all work out in the end, but hey! All for one and one for all. You're a nasty piece of work after all. Why should I care? Look at you, biting your lip, swivelling your eyes, God, what a mess! What a waste of a young girl. Why be like this? I know, I know exactly how you feel but I can't sink down there with you, it'll kill me. So sorry for your awkwardness, I know it – God help me, I do – but you're on your own. Why should I help? No one ever helped me. So there we stood looking in opposite directions while the thought came to me that I wanted to tell her what I saw on the roof, how she was there when Pamela stepped over the edge. Did you know? Somehow? And even after her dad came back, and Robin too, after they'd left and Rob had bought his strings and plectrum and we were walking along Deansgate, I wanted to tell her because who else could I tell? Not Rob. Not anyone. Where to begin? Every time I tried my throat clammed up.

Monday, late afternoon, no more lessons as end of term loomed. Sylvia was playing Pick-up Sticks on her own in the hall, away from everyone else. Funny, she's always so neat but now look at her, the badly cut hair, irregular tufts on her neck. You're slipping, Sylvia. She was always sullen these days, always a frown line between her eyes. There was no happiness in her at all. I felt sorry for her. Did she have any idea about that thing on the roof? I didn't think so. What if she met it? Would she die? Till Pamela I never really thought people died. I knew they did, of course, but it wasn't real. People's pets died, occasionally a grandparent, that's all. It had made me numb, but the thing on the roof though, that's what was driving me mad. Doing my head in, I would have said to Pamela if she'd been there.

I had to tell her. After all, it was *her*.

'Sylvia,' I said, sitting down next to her on the floor.

She glanced sideways.

'Sylvia,' I said.

'I'm concentrating.' She was trying to hook a blue with a red. Her hand trembled. The blue rose promisingly but just before she could flick it free, the black underneath shivered and rolled and dislodged a couple more. My fault.

'Sorry,' I said.

She sat back with a sigh that was meant to be heard. 'What?' she said grudgingly.

I hadn't rehearsed, hadn't even known I was going to sit down till I did. 'It's all been a bit weird, hasn't it?' I said.

'What has?'

'Everything. Don't you think?'

She looked at me then with deep, miserable eyes. I felt small and stupid. 'We shouldn't be enemies,' I said.

'Oh. *Are* we?'

Still a stuck-up cow.

'Sylvia, tell me honestly,' I said, 'have you ever been up on the roof?'

'The roof?'

'The roof. You know. Up there.' Pointing. 'You know what the roof is, Sylvia.'

'Of course I haven't been up on the roof!' She was livid now. 'Why would I want to go up there? I don't want to go up on the roof, I never *have* been up on the roof and I never will. Now will you stop asking me stupid questions.'

'There's no need to get angry. I'm only trying to talk to you.'

'No, you're not,' she said, 'you're accusing me of something.'

'I'm not, I'm just trying to get something clear in my head.'

'Well, I can't help you with that.' She looked down at her game, dismissing me.

'I have seen you on the roof,' I said, 'twice.'

She picked up the hooked stick with all the colours and twirled it between her fingers. I think she wanted to stab me with it.

'You were sitting on the ledge under the big turret. I saw you.'

'I have no idea what you're talking about.'

'I know. I don't understand it either. I really did see you but when I went downstairs you were there too. And you couldn't have got there.'

She breathed in so sharply that her nostrils flattened. 'You can't possibly have seen me.'

I raised my hands, hopeless. Her game was ruined. Methodically she began picking up each stick separately, putting them neatly together in their round cardboard cylinder. I had never noticed before how small and childish her hands were. 'There's no one else I can tell,' I said, 'it's in my mind all the time. I'm sorry if we were horrible to you. I'm sorry. But I did see you. I was in the greenhouse. I saw you. You scared me.'

A giggle of first-formers ran past, their voices grating. Around us the warm hubbub rose and fell.

'What do you mean?' she said.

'I saw you. But it wasn't you. It was different. You were smiling.'

She looked at me as if I was an idiot. I shouldn't have opened my mouth. 'Why are you doing this?' she said.

'OK, OK,' I said, 'I won't say anything else.'

'You're trying to scare me. What's the matter with you?'

'I don't know. I'm just telling you what I saw.'

'It wasn't me.'

'I know it wasn't you. But it looked like you.'

'That's horrible!' she said. 'What a horrible thing to tell me.' Her cheeks were flushed.

'I wouldn't tell you if it wasn't true.'

'You shouldn't say horrible things like that.' Surely she wasn't going to cry? It was awful. I could have cried myself. I didn't dislike her at all at that moment.

'So obviously you've been on the roof?' she said.

'Yes.'

'We're not supposed to go up there.'

'I know.'

'Why?'

'I don't know,' I said, 'I suppose they think it's dangerous.'

'No, I mean why did you go up?'

'It's nice. It's clear. You're on top of everything. You can see it all differently.'

'But it *is* dangerous,' she said. 'Someone died. They were right, we *shouldn't* go up there.'

'Didn't you ever want to do something wrong, ever,' I said, 'just once in your life? Just once?' I really was trying to talk to her.

She said, 'Why would I—'

'Oh, for God's sake, Sylvia! Just once!'

'What's that got to do with anything?' She was angry again. 'What's that got to do with that horrible stuff you just told me? You're trying to frighten me. You're mean. You're as bad as *she* was. You make things up to scare people just to be nasty. There's something wrong with you. There must be to make you like that. I feel sorry for you. I tried to make friends with you once but it was no good. You're just not a nice person.'

That made my eyes sting. 'OK,' I said, 'OK,' and I got up and left her sitting there clutching her cardboard tube of

Pick-up Sticks, walked out into the long wide corridor that still held the lingering smell of school dinner gravy and meat, went up and up the nearest staircase till I reached the top floor. Drip drip, went the tap in the Biology lab. The cold green smell of the tanks seeped out into the hall and the area under the stairs was as it ever was, dark, forbidden, strangely comforting. I went up to the greenhouse. It was lovely to be up there again. Nothing had changed, same old scraggy plants and mysterious growing things, the mess, the chimneys, the ledges, the proud grey turret. Bright in the middle of it, five pots of showy white flowers against the back wall delicately scented the woody air. Three pigeons sat on the red-brick rim of the turret, evenly spaced about six inches from one another, heads sunk fatly into soft grey necks. I tried the door to the roof but it was locked of course. Always had been since Pamela's death. So I just sat in the peace and quiet on one of the benches looking at the sky and listening to the babyish cooing of the fat-headed pigeons. I had a little cry for Pamela. After about ten minutes I heard footsteps, furtive, not wanting to be heard. They stopped at the foot of the wooden stairs. Someone was standing there not moving.

But then—

Creak, creak. Someone doesn't want to be heard.

'Sally?'

Only Sylvia. Which one?

'Yes,' I said.

She came up, her anxious face appearing first, followed by the rest of her. She walked heavily in, sat down on the bench opposite me. Over her head I could see the turret and the brick wall where she'd sat like Joan-the-Wad. 'What were you talking about?' she said, and as soon as she opened her mouth and that plummy voice came out I knew that this was just the ordinary everyday Sylvia, the one who played Pick-up Sticks alone downstairs. 'About me on the roof.'

'Only what I told you.'

She gave a brief cluck of annoyance. 'I want to know why you're saying these things about me.'

'I've not said anything to anyone else. I've only told you.'

'Even so. Why are you saying them?'

'I'm sorry, I just wanted to tell someone.'

'I was never on the roof,' she said.

'I know.'

Up high, two birds wheeling about each other. Not a cloud in that gorgeous summer sky.

'Best forget it,' I said. 'Let's stop, I don't like talking about it while we're up here.'

But then her face changed and she was furious again, pressing her hands between her knees, hunching her shoulders, blinking crazily. 'You know, you really are unpleasant,' she said. 'For some reason you want me to be scared.'

She was right, I was horrible, nasty, mean, a bully. Oh, the cruel cold depths of me. 'No, no, no,' I said wearily, unable to fathom an explanation. I imagined it all, I wanted to say, but that really would have been a lie. It was very bright up there and she wavered before my eyes, a mess of a girl, awkward and stiff, a girl who made those around her feel bad. Whose fault was that? Not mine.

She bowed her head. Behind her on the other side of the glass was the other one. My hands jittered at my side on the bench. 'It's there,' I said, but I'm not sure that my voice came out. It smiled as if it couldn't keep from laughing. When she raised her head, it looked over her shoulder at me as if there was such a funny secret between us. I don't know how I got from where I was to where I found myself, on the small wooden landing at the top of the steps looking in at the open door of the greenhouse where the two Sylvias stared at one another through the glass pane. Real Sylvia screamed, an unearthly thing I never could have imagined coming out of her, prolonged and self-renewing. It curdled my gut. The other, looking in, laughed.

I almost fell going down. There was no one around on the science floor. The Biology lab door was open. I could see the desk where we had the séance, smell the green algae from the sides of the tanks. By the door a small wet creature with a mythical hybrid body and a strange wise face sat on a black rock, baby hands clutching the surface of a rock. The stairs flew by, a long corridor, somnolent classrooms where girls lay daydreaming with their heads on their arms, waiting for hometime, the bell, the shuffling exodus. Further down, to the echoey voices of girls murmuring like pigeons, the smell, *still* lingering, of school dinners. I stood on the ground floor facing towards the faraway open doors of the hall. Still me. My school uniform, the bit on the hem of my jumper my mother darned. And they're up there, screaming and laughing in one another's faces. The bell went.

The collective sound of chairs moving, sudden murmurs, a trickle of girls issuing from the opening doors all along the corridor, a thickening of them at the foot of the stairs at each end. The din began and grew, someone laughing, someone singing, *Stop! In the name of love.* Sweeping black robes and greengirly giggles.

I was a little faint. Thought of descending still further, to the cloakrooms, the toilets, the double row of porcelain sinks, the sound of water swooshing in pipes constantly running away somewhere in the background, as if some girl in one of the cubicles was always peeing steadily and ruminatively. It'd be OK. Go down now while there's lots of people around, put on your coat and go home and have the weekend that's coming, see Rob tomorrow, come back Monday morning, find everything back to normal.

Girls surged around me. 'Sally,' someone said. It was Miss Frith, long-necked and bright-eyed. 'Are you feeling all right, Sally?'

'I was upstairs,' I said. 'I got scared. I thought I heard somebody scream.'

Miss Frith's face was very serious. 'Where?'

'The greenhouse, I think. It sounded like.'

'Stay there,' Miss Frith said quietly, tight-mouthed, marching away. She went up those stairs at a rush, scrawnily upright, and I did as I was told, clusters, dribs and drabs of girls sifting by as if I wasn't there. A black fluttering of teachers emerged from the staff room at the end of the corridor, blocking my view of the hall, its doors and its interior. I might be ill. Yes, I must be, because it was as if I was having a dream right there standing up with everything going on around me. I thought I was out in the park. Three floaty leafy things glided companionably along the grey path that cut through the green, one turning every now and then its small white face in my direction as if looking out for me.

I was hiding in the trees. Then I was back in the corridor, all noise. So now it all made sense, I was ill, that's what it was, all this not-making-sense. Mrs Stannard and Mr Phelps and Miss Oliver ran upstairs. *Running*. Miss Oliver! Running. Not *quite* running but kind of walk-running. It was all very odd. Anyway, it was hometime, now I could go home. But then there was another bell and Miss Demery herself with her bull-like haunches came out and stood in the centre of it all, orange-red spirals of hair sparsely framing her pink powdery face. Her presence struck silence.

'Perhaps some of you know,' she said, and her voice carried all the way down to where I stood, 'that a girl has been taken quite seriously ill. Please now will you all gather your belongings as quickly as you can and leave as silently as possible and in an orderly fashion. Dismiss.' She swept away.

A hushed bubble of sound swelled. Someone hissed: *Ssh! Ssh!* Miss Frith said to wait here. Miss Demery told us to go. I went upstairs and got my bag. Surely she'd be down any minute, Sylvia, she's pulled herself together, sensible girl after all. Now I'd just go home very quietly, the back way through the yard and up towards the bus station. Weekend, home. But then the face looking over Sylvia's shoulder jumped up in my mind and I went cold as if someone had thrown worms in my direction. The Sylvia-thing might come down from the roof, walk into the middle of us. I went downstairs, would have got my coat and gone but I was collared by Miss Frith and marched to that dark brown room with the smell, of polish and richness and power and Miss Demery's face powder, and the big mountain of Miss Demery herself looming behind the desk, leaning on her blotter. The rest of the school was quickly quietening down, and I still had to go into the basement and get my coat. It would be silent and dark down there and there'd just be my own coat hanging limply on its own in a big empty cloakroom.

'What did you see, Sally?'

Standing there, as if I've done something wrong. What have I done? What have I said? What have I said to Miss Frith?

'I didn't see anything. I heard screaming.'

'And where were *you*?'

'In the Biology lab.'

'Why were you in the Biology lab?'

I rested my eyes on an ink pad and the stamper with its shiny black handle.

'I was looking at the tadpoles.'

'Why were you looking at the tadpoles at a time of the day when you should have been somewhere else?'

'I wanted to see how they were getting on. Some of them were getting their front legs.' The thought of those tiny tadpole hands feeling the bit of rock for the first time made me want to cry.

'Hm.'

She looked at me sternly as if expecting more, and I, dumb, looked back with nothing to say.

'And you saw no one? Either on the way up or on the way down?'

'No.'

Miss Demery thought visibly, looking over my head. 'Well, you may go,' she said in a slightly grudging tone, 'and if you do remember anything, anything at all, you must come and see me immediately.' She stood and ushered me to the door. 'There are no tadpoles,' she said, 'they turned into frogs about three weeks ago.'

I didn't argue. I still had to go down to the basement for my coat. It was starkly lit in the middle with its farthest reaches deep in shade; everyone had gone. Down in the farthest shade, the matron woman and two others I didn't recognise were in hushed conference, heads inwardly inclined. The voices of the matron woman and those others moved away and whispered after they were out of sight. A door stood open far along on the left and a pale light threw itself across the floor from there.

I am a most horrible girl, who would sell anyone else's soul to the devil if I thought it would save my own skin. I'm always there, aren't I? The common factor – Pamela, Sylvia, the greenhouse – one dead, one screaming up there like that kind of girl never did. Have they noticed? Always me in the background.

Am I a curse? I needed a wee but there was no way I was ever going to face the long row of toilets, some with doors open, some closed, and the long double row of sinks, facing each other. I got my coat and dashed, school bag hanging off one shoulder by one strap, tears starting. I ran all the way to my bus stop in the smoke-smelling early evening, stood in the rough hot stench of the engines of the buses all lined up in Piccadilly. As long as I live, I thought, getting in at the end of a queue, catching my breath, I will never go up there again.

No one ever told us what happened to Sylvia. She just never

came back. Eventually word got round that she'd had a nervous breakdown, but we never knew for certain. Once she'd gone and I knew she wasn't coming back I thought it would be possible to forget the whole thing, or if not forget, at least pack it away in a chest in some mental lumber room. I didn't understand and never would, and anyway it was over. It wouldn't stay down, though. I kept wanting to blurt it out, the way I'd blurted it out to Sylvia when I ruined her game of Pick-up Sticks. One night in Lando's it got too much and I told Rob about the Sylvia-thing. I gave him every detail. A voice in the back of my mind said: well look, it'll be OK, after all you're only telling the truth, but I should have known that counted for nothing. He took it very seriously, of course he did. 'OK, let's look at this,' he said after I'd poured out my fears and wondering, and then he talked. He recounted the conditions, the location, the relative isolation, the possibly heightened emotional state of all three of us.

'I'm not making this up,' I said.

'I know you're not. But that doesn't mean that you really saw what you think you saw. I mean, the Northern Lights. They're not really a big curtain flapping about in the sky, they just look like that. Shadows. Electricity. You agree with that, don't you? Things aren't always visible, things aren't always what they seem.'

'Yes, of course.'

I wish he'd taken me seriously. He only thought he did.

'So what do I do,' I said, 'when it's in my head and I can't get rid of it?'

'You don't have to do anything,' he said. 'It's over. It'll

just fade away. Like a nightmare. Or like when you have a pain but then it's gone.'

'But it happened.'

'You experienced it,' he said, 'that's for sure.' He half smiled, put his chin in his curled fist. I could see the cogs turning in his brain. 'Occam's Razor,' he said, 'now that's an interesting one. Doesn't really hold up actually.'

I didn't even know what Occam's Razor was and was damned if I was going to ask.

He gazed out at the street. There was a skin on my coffee and it was too milky.

'The brain's an incredible organ,' he said.

'But if what I saw isn't real,' I said, 'how do I know that anything is? This place. Me. You.'

'Good point.' He laughed. He was off again, talking about Buddhism and psychoanalysing me, saying what an awful year it had been and how it was taking a toll.

'What am I supposed to do,' I interrupted, 'when I'm sitting on the bus and all of a sudden I get this awful feeling of terror – yes – terror – and I see it again in my mind?'

He looked at me with fond eyes and a sneer so slight it may have been just my paranoia. 'Just say, it's natural. Something like the Northern Lights or an optical illusion.'

'You didn't experience it. It was nasty. It was – it made the air feel different.'

'Hm,' he said, 'it's physiological changes, like when people have panic attacks. Are you going to drink that?'

'No,' I said, 'it's yucky.'

He drained my cup with one quick movement, took my hand and pulled it under his arm as we got outside. It was a warm evening with an after-work sleepiness. On the corner by the lights we stood for a moment before going our separate ways. Both of us were in our school uniform, him minus the tie, me with free-flowing hair and sagging school bag pulling my shoulder down.

'Why does everything get reduced to a syndrome?' I said.

We had our arms around each other. He touched his brow to mine and said, 'Are you using that word in quite the right sense?'

'Probably not.'

Then he started kissing me with those big lips which I realised had started to repulse me. I wanted to bite them viciously and hurt him for repulsing me. Instead I went through with it. He left my mouth wet.

'Bye, love,' he said.

'Bye.'

You know, I've tried and tried, I thought as I walked to my bus stop, and there's just no magic. Someone else could really appreciate him. It's not fair. I'd have to leave him. I dreaded it. I worried so much about him being upset, night after night after night, put it off as too hard and waited for him to go to university.

He'd put Liverpool at the top of his list because it was good for architecture. He wanted me to put Liverpool on my form next year so we could be together. That made me feel depressed. I said I would. I knew I wouldn't, though. His going loomed and loomed and he said he'd come home at weekends, it would be easy, it's only Liverpool, and I could go and stay with him too. Then he was gone, only not really, he was home a lot on the weekends and anyway it was easy enough to pop over for the afternoon. I went and stayed once. We slept together in a bed for the first time in his hall of residence, but we didn't do anything. I still wasn't sure and he never pushed for it. Whenever we met up he grabbed me and swung me about as if we were in an advert or something, while I hovered outside us, miles away, thinking, this can't be it, it can't be it. I had no idea what to do. In the end I applied for anthropology at Kent and went to live in Canterbury, miles and miles away down south. Said I really liked the course and it was a shame it was far away but we'd stay in touch, of course, we'd be fine. We wrote and called. And on a rainy Monday night in the first Christmas break back home, while we were sitting in old Lando's with the same old Formica tables and the coffee machine making a racket, he smiled across the table with his eyes as fond as ever and said, 'I suppose we may as well come clean.'

'What?' I said, but I knew.

'Well, I don't know about you,' he said, 'but it seems to me obvious that we have to make a change.'

'I know.'

'I know you know. I mean, it doesn't have to be a big thing, and it's not as if I don't still get shivers looking at you and when you come into a room you just...'

'I know.'

'There's just been this feeling, like it can't be like this forever, and I really do love you, you know.'

An awful surge of tears came up my throat even though it was happening just as I wanted it too. 'So what shall we do?' I said.

'I don't know. I suppose we should just not see each other for a while.'

'We don't really anyway, do we?' I said lightly. 'We hardly see each other as it is.'

'I know. But – what do you really want, Sal?'

'I don't know,' I said truthfully. 'Not this.'

We didn't speak for a while.

'If you want,' he said, 'we don't have to do this.'

'I think we do.'

'I really wish you'd say what you mean.'

'You know,' I said, 'once you have a conversation like this, that's that really, isn't it?' I just wanted to go home.

'Yeah,' he said, and his eyes grew fonder still and a bit wet. 'So are you sure you're OK with this?'

'Oh, for God's sake, Rob, let's get this over with!'

'OK then,' he said, 'if that's what you really want. God forbid we stick together just because.'

He squared his shoulders, took a deep breath and looked out of the rain-stippled window, covering his mouth with his hand and closing his eyes. He looked quite beautiful at that moment. I could have stopped it then, but he raised his head and smiled. 'OK then,' he said again, and we gathered up our things and walked to the lights side by side but no longer touching. When we got there we kissed for the last time, a quick awkward nudge. I didn't look back. On the bus I sat at the back and started to cry. It seemed to me that he wasn't upset enough. All that soppiness and then just to harden up like that and go all stiff upper lip. I got home and found no refuge even in my old room. Since I'd been gone everyone had started putting things in there. I'd go in and find a pile of the brats' laundry on my bed. They didn't treat it like my room any more, and I lay on the bed feeling just as alien as I did in Canterbury.

I lost touch with him after that. It was strangely easy and gradual.

I didn't go home much any more. My virginity was lost to a hippy called Mike in a tent somewhere in the dunes atop a shingle beach on the south coast. There was nothing marvellous about it. I liked the course, made friends, did work experience in a museum archive and a National Trust place and scraped a 2:2. I could have done better but didn't want to work that hard. I met a boy called Dave, who was small and clever and rough around the edges, moved to Cambridge with him and lived there through the red-hot summer of '76. There were jobs – this and that – and a couple of other boys after Dave, a spell in Leeds, one in Halifax, but then, hardly knowing why, I drifted back home.

No way was I going back to live in the old house, though. Whenever I'd stayed a night or two it was just too peculiar, being in my old room with my childhood books and the trains rattling by as if all the years between had never existed. The young twins were both still at home, now with incipient facial hair and bathroom-hogging tendencies (suppose I have to stop calling them brats, I thought) but the big ones had gone. Jo had married a fire engineer and had a baby, an odd little niece with a gappy grin and slanting eyes. Tony was living with his girlfriend and doing some posh thing with money, wearing a grey suit for work. Mum and Dad of course were just Mum and Dad and always the same. I was still in touch with Shanna Glassman and

Linda Corey and went over for a weekend from Halifax and just kind of stayed. We had such a good time eating out and drinking home-made tequila sunrises in the back garden of their house-share near East Didsbury Station, and I'd just broken up with someone and was sick of my job doing market research, so when the room came up while I was there I moved straight in and got my stuff over from Halifax the following weekend.

I hadn't seen them for a while and they'd both changed. Linda worked for the electricity board. She'd turned into a tall woman with a handsome masculine face, and her hair was exactly the same as before, lank and fair and full of straight edges. Shanna was a nurse. She'd cut her lovely black curls so close that they were no longer extraordinary. Susan Grech called round sometimes. She worked in some kind of office and was in touch with Gail Turnbull.

It was OK for a while. I got a job in a nice old library a short bus ride away, with a portico at the front and a red-brick arch. It was a bright friendly place with a sweet children's corner and a record library corner with posters on the wall. I liked making sure all the tickets were neat and regimented, wheeling round my slope-shelved trolley, getting lunch from the chippy round the corner that was always full of schoolgirls. They made me feel old, though I was only twenty-six.

Were we ever this tall? This loud, this confident? All dipping their fingers into their hot vinegary chips and stuffing their crowded fistfuls into their mouths.

I still had no idea what I really wanted to do with my life.

Part Three

Antumbra

IT WAS A WINDY DAY, LATE afternoon, and I had my collar up and was hurrying down the approach to Piccadilly Station when the voice said, 'Sal!'

No one else called me Sal.

'Oh my God,' I said, 'it's you.'

It had been nine years. His face was thinner, that was the first thing I noticed. Thinner and wiser and sharper, more mobile. His eyes older, deeper. I couldn't see him at all, he was too familiar and too different all at once. At first there was a ghost in his face but soon it morphed into a weird hybrid of what he'd been and what he was. I'd thought about him of course over the years, the way you do. I wonder what happened to old so-and-so? We were both going in different directions, my train was due. He was on his way to see his mum and dad; he said they'd moved and lived near Altrincham now. That was a step up. He'd been in Liverpool for most of the intervening time but came back a year ago for a job.

'What about you?'

'I'm working in a library,' I said.

'Oh, great.'

I was late and dashing to meet Shanna from work; we were having a bite to eat and going late-night shopping. 'Oh shit, the time!' I said, and laughed. He was dashing too, train to catch.

'Look,' he said. 'Peveril of the Peak, Sunday. Three. Yeah?'

'Of course.'

I ran down the hill grinning, running over his new face in my mind. Something funny was going on inside me. My stomach fluttered. It was physical but it wasn't love in the way you could marry someone, it was just a familiarity so deep it cut. Sunday. Peveril of the Peak. I'd never been there before and didn't know the layout. If I arrived early I could case the joint, have a drink before he got there. When I told Shanna she said, 'You'll go back with him.'

'I don't know. I have no idea what to expect. It's not as if I've been pining all these years, is it?'

'No, but it's fate, isn't it? Of all the gin joints, et cetera.'

We were heading for Chinatown. I laughed. 'Who knows?' All through the meal and while we wandered around town I felt light. Looking at myself in a mirror in Lewis's I wondered about my face. He was still the kind of boy it was good to be seen with, but me? No idea, it was just my old taken-for-granted face looking back. I never thought about it much. He always liked it anyway.

Back home we opened a bottle of wine in my room, Shanna tried on her new top, and Linda came in yawning. I might as well have been sharing a room with Linda, the walls were so flimsy. We pretty much had to go to bed at the same time if one of us didn't want to end up creeping about trying not to wake up the other. On my days off, I'd lie in bed with the covers over my head and listen to her getting up for work at the last minute, gulping down her tea in fits and starts as she got dressed. Thinking, ha ha ha, I can go back to sleep and she's got to go out in the cold. Even better if the rain lashed the window and the wind gusted.

'You'll never guess who I met.'

'Who?'

'Robin Callan. Do you remember?'

'Oh, I remember Robin,' she said, 'we used to look at him through the window. Sitting on his bench waiting for you.'

'Fate,' Shanna said.

'No. It was on the Piccadilly approach. Everyone meets there.'

'I saw Mr Tasker there once,' said Linda.

'Did you say hello to him?'

'God no. He didn't see me, thank God.'

'I said I'd go for a drink with him in town,' I said.

'Mr Tasker?'

'Robin!'

'Aha!' Linda poured more wine. 'Well, we all know what's going to happen now, don't we?'

This house had an impersonal air, the labelled food, the beige bathroom tiles, the abundance of pebbled-glass interior windows, the complete forgettableness of the frontage, so that I had to be very careful not to go in at the wrong gate. Once, some large pale yellow roses had briefly bloomed on an austere but graceful bush by the front door. I sniffed them each day of their reign but they never had any perfume. Linda and I were on one side of the downstairs hall, Shanna on the other with a boy called Phil. Upstairs was a shy Indian boy who got drunk every night, and a tall bossy woman who strode about checking the rotas were kept to. The rotas were stuck on a corkboard in the kitchen and changed every Sunday. She'd tap on your door if you were having a lie-in and say very pleasantly, 'You know you're on bins today, don't you, Sally?' The kitchen was the only communal room but you could only fit three people in there with any comfort and it was always hogged by a plump smiley woman called Nyree who spent all the time when she wasn't frying cheese and garlic standing at the back door with a water pistol waiting to shoot next door's cats if they dared so much as stick the tip of a nose through the foliage. The landlord was creepy and dropped by too often. Once he opened my room door with his key while I was still in bed and dashed across to look out of my window to check up on who'd just gone out the front door. We weren't allowed to have anyone stay the night. I asked him about that once, suggesting that it may not be entirely legal as we were paying our rent, but he gave me a nasty look and said, 'Well, I can't have just anyone staying in my house, can I?' I told a bloke at work about it and he'd said, 'I bet he comes in when you're not there and buries his face in your underwear drawer.' I'd been queasy ever since.

The Peveril was a lovely old pub, green and yellow tiles on the outside, stained glass and old wood inside. I arrived early, made sure he wasn't there and bought a double vodka and tonic with ice and lemon at the bar. It wasn't too packed. I took my drink into the loo with me and placed it on the side of the sink. What the hell are you nervous for? I asked my face in the mirror. It's only dear old Rob. I looked at myself closely, conscious of being a disappointment to myself. This place was very old, supposed to be haunted. It was dark behind me and the light flickered. I grabbed my drink and glugged. I didn't think I looked too different. My hair was the same. Bit more makeup possibly, not much. If I couldn't talk to him I couldn't talk to anyone. I drank some more. How long should I wait? Nearly three. I walked out and slipped my empty glass back on the bar. He was right down at the other end with a pint in his hand. I waved, he grinned and came towards me. 'So that's where you were hiding,' he said. 'What you having?'

We sat under a window and light streamed in over our heads and lit on the stained glass over the bar. A packet of cheese and onion crisps lay torn down the middle and spread out on the table, and we shovelled them down.

'Well, here we are,' I said.

'We are indeed.'

'So what are you up to now then?'

'I'm an architect,' he said. 'You're a librarian, right?'

'Yes,' I said, though I was not a qualified one. Still, let him think. I had to try and make it all sound better than it was, the house, the library, everything. I had to explain it in a way that would sound interesting. I was doing well, happy, great.

'I think that's amazing,' I said. 'You always said you were going to be an architect and now you are one.'

'Yeah, look at us – all grown up.'

'I don't *feel* grown up.'

'Me neither.'

'Perhaps no one ever does.'

'You look great,' he said.

'So do you.'

'No, really, you look fantastic, you haven't changed at all. Honestly, when I saw you it was so weird, it was like going down a time tunnel.'

I laughed. 'It's not been *that* long.'

'It has! Aeons.'

'You've not changed much either.'

He was twenty-eight and had just become a qualified architect. He worked in an office on King Street. We did all the usual – how's so-and-so, how's your mum and dad, how are the twins? Said he couldn't imagine Jo married with a child, spoke of my family with smiling remembrance, as if they were good old friends. We talked for ages but never asked each other if we were with anyone else. He'd have mentioned, surely, I thought. It shouldn't have mattered, I still had no spark for him but I did feel some possessiveness.

'You'll never guess where I'm living,' he said, grinning.

'Where?'

'Your old school.'

'You're kidding me! Those flats?'

'Yeah. You know they turned it into flats?'

'Oh yes, I knew that.'

Hadn't thought about that place in a long time. At least I hadn't thought that I'd thought about it. I went to the bar for more drinks. Suppose it's significant that I hadn't got round to looking at it. Town centre flat, must be expensive.

Must be doing pretty well. Poor old school, gone. Good riddance. I was getting a nice woozy feeling. 'This flat of yours,' I said, putting his drink down in front of him. 'I've just got to see it.' He didn't say yeah, right now, which was ridiculous, because it was easily within walking distance. I felt it pulling me.

'Definitely,' he said after the slightest pause, 'how about next week? You could come round now, only I've got to go straight after this drink. I have to meet someone.'

Meet someone?

'OK,' I said, then he said, 'Hey, d'you fancy going to see Iggy Pop? Next Sunday? I can get tickets.'

'Can you?'

'Yeah. Guy at work's got some and he can't go. Broken up with his girlfriend and – complicated story – anyway, if you...'

'Oh yes,' I said, 'definitely, yes, I would.'

'Brilliant.'

Did I sound too keen?

'I know it's all different and funny now,' he said, 'no big thing if you don't want to go, I just thought I'd ask.'

'No, no, that's fine.'

'Tell you what,' he said, 'let me make sure I can get the tickets and I'll give you a ring. That OK?'

'Sure.'

So we exchanged phone numbers. It was no big thing.

'You could come over before the show and we could get something to eat and have a drink first and you could have a good look at your old school. You won't recognise it.'

We had one for the road and left together. The daylight

was bright and made my head spin as we stood on the pavement with the buses snuffling past, just like in the old days. I laughed. 'I know what you mean about a time tunnel,' I said. We started walking with our hands in our pockets because of the cold.

'It's weird, isn't it?' he said. 'Are you walking up to Piccadilly?'

'Not yet. One or two things to get.'

'Oh, OK. Well, I go this way so...' It was suddenly awkward and we just stood there smiling stupidly till it started to get embarrassing.

'See you then,' I said.

'Yeah. I'll give you a call.'

I turned once and glanced back. He was walking quickly in the direction of Piccadilly, broader in the shoulders, more of a man. He started to turn so I looked away and pretended to be concentrating on crossing the road.

I'd said I'd go to his flat, we'd have a drink before the concert. He hadn't mentioned anything about food on the phone so I had a toasted cheese sandwich before I went and a glass of red wine from the box in the fridge. It was too cold. I drank it too quickly and it froze me up inside. I had to wait ages on the platform at East Didsbury and got still colder and on the train I got a fit of nerves. My teeth chattered. I was wearing my very best, a subtle brown-gold-fawn dress that fitted perfectly and ended just above the knee, with gold-brown tights and dark brown boots, and my thick black coat that came nearly to my feet but still didn't keep me warm because it had lost its buttons and couldn't be fastened up. My hair was like it always was; I never changed it in my whole life. Brown, straight, simple, parted in the middle.

When a place has got inside you over – what? – seven years, it comes back when you dream. This was no dream but it felt like it. Coming down from Piccadilly, passing the spot where once, without my school hat, hair free-flowing, I encountered Mrs Stannard and pretended not to, walked straight past, the corner of my eye noting how she stopped and deliberately stared at me. I just walked on, brazen, hoping she'd let it go. I was right back there. The familiar road, the very sounds and smells, then the blank brick wall I walked alongside a million times. It had painted itself on my mind over all those years. Where our old back gate used to be there was a big new one, spiky and painted silver with a sign: Massey House. It was open. Someone had just driven in in a big black car and was parking in one of the bays that covered the yard. The building was exactly the same, except that down under, beyond the railings (also painted silver), the area where Pamela landed was now an underground car park. It was Sunday, a September sky. If this was still school we'd have been back a while already. Tomorrow would have been another dreaded school Monday morning. Dammit all, Chemistry first thing. Mr Tasker.

It had been so long since I'd thought about what happened here. I'd put it so far out of my mind that it was like a far memory of a film seen ages and ages ago. But when I crossed the yard and stood by the back door looking up, I was suddenly surrounded by a crowd of green girls all standing with their necks cricked. I shook myself, rang his buzzer and heard his voice crackle through the intercom. He buzzed me up. My God, they'd done a good job, or at least a thorough one, in erasing whatever they could according to the regulations; in some way, because of the renewed bright lighting and spotlessness and slightly off-putting hotel-like ambience, they had done right by the grand old building. It lived anew.

Ah, but the ghost of it.

They hadn't put in lifts. You walked up exactly the same stairs. There were flashes that were exactly the same, sudden corners, things they hadn't been allowed to get rid of because of its listed status. He was at his door on the first floor, my head going round thinking which was that, 4B? What was over there? He was smiling and lounging at ease, a bottle of beer dangling from his fingers. 'Bet this feels weird,' he said. I smiled and made a helpless gesture, said, 'You would not believe.'

'Come on in and have a drink, love.' He'd obviously already had a couple. He drank from the bottle neck. 'Take a look around.'

The flat smelt of curry. I walked straight over to the window and looked out onto the park. There was the path I used to walk along when I bunked off Games on a Friday afternoon. There was the bench where he used to sit and wait. This side of the building was more expensive than the one overlooking the car park. He'd done well. Great place to live, fantastic central location.

'Do you want a beer,' he said, 'or some wine? I've only got red.'

'Wine. You made curry.'

'Yes.'

The toasted cheese sandwich lay heavy in my stomach. 'Don't give me too much,' I said, 'I'm not that hungry.'

'That's OK.' He looked bigger than before. How could that be? We weren't such children, were we? 'It's better next day anyway.'

'If I'd known you were making something...'

'Well, anyway...'

We stood with our drinks. Something played in the background, a thumping beat.

'Did I not mention I was making food?' he said.

'You may have said something but I don't think it was that specific.'

'This is unreal.'

'Isn't it?'

'You for real, in the flesh.'

'Yes,' I said and laughed, 'it's me, all right.'

He swayed forwards and his brow nearly touched mine. His breath was familiar. It's true that I hadn't spent the last nine years pining. It's true that I'd gone for weeks at a time without a single thought of him entering my mind. When I *had* remembered him it had been with fondness only. Still, there was a feeling of something clicking into place. We sat down either end of the settee and did all the catch-up talk all over again. He swigged from the bottle.

'Aren't you going to eat anything?' I said.

'Oh no. I'm not eating garlic if you're not.'

'Don't be silly.'

'Aah,' he said, 'I'll have something later.'

'Are you sure?'

'Oh yeah, sure, look, what do you wanna do? Shall we walk or get a cab?'

'Oh, walk,' I said. 'It's not that far.'

He jumped up and looked out of the window. It was still light. 'Is this really funny for you?' he said. 'I mean being here. In this building, after everything... Is it freaking you out a bit?'

'I don't think so.'

In fact I felt strangely enlivened. Though everything about the place was momentous, I wasn't scared. I wanted to explore. It felt like wanting to climb a big tree when you were little, knowing it was dangerous but knowing you could get to the top. I wanted to go down under and aloft, beneath the basement, up onto the roof, see what they'd made of the science labs and cloakrooms and the big hall. But that was for later.

We walked up to the Apollo and had to queue for ages even though we had tickets. I put my hand in his pocket as we shuffled forwards. It was warm and there was nothing in it but a couple of screwed-up bus tickets. By the time we reached the foyer I was walking in front of him and he was breathing on the back of my head. He'd got us good seats about eight or nine rows back on the left-hand side and when the band came on Iggy reminded me of the somnambulist in *The Cabinet of Dr. Caligari*. Everyone was standing up, the music rolled over and over us in huge waves and it was all wild and sweaty and roaring. We stood in the throb of the crowd, from time to time turning to each other and kissing in a way we never had before, a way that was edged with brutality on my part and on his a swooning seriousness. It was obvious I was going back to his place. No way was I waiting on the platform for my train and going back to that boring house, to Shanna and Linda, poor old Jeet throwing up in the bare flower bed, Melinda poking about in the kitchen sticking her big nose in everything, Nyree shooting cats. I was going back with him. We'd drink some more and play music and talk and of course it would all happen. It was happening already, unstoppably.

It was all too quick. It should have worried me more.

We didn't have to discuss it, we just floated home when the show was over. Home was not the building with its memories, it was him. He was more home than my mum and dad's old house with the railway line, the house in Didsbury with its rotas. Home was the thing you had and knew you'd leave one day.

I knew it was rash when I moved in with him. Because I never thought of living with him forever without a shrinking. But this thing between us was a strong and gluey thing; on meeting again our past affairs floated away as if they'd never existed and all that remained, overpoweringly, was our old friendship, strong as ever. Of course it had to be different this time. Before, no matter how much we'd nuzzled and kissed and occasionally slept side by side with our clothes on, we'd been as innocent as Adam and Eve before the snake slithered in. Living together of course meant sleeping every night in the bed from his old bedroom, the one he'd brought over from his mum and dad's house.

I knew it well, as I knew the shelving unit and bookcase, and the rug on the floor, a ridiculous threadbare thing with a faded pattern of footballs. I brought my stuff from the Didsbury house and more from the old house, my wardrobe with the stuck-on cut-outs of the Stones and David Bowie, which I couldn't get off so they stayed as wallpaper; all my books, even my kids' books, and my records and tapes, and some posters – Narcissus, Ophelia, Salome and the Black Cat – and soon had them all dispersed about the place so that it didn't feel as if I was just visiting.

But I never really did get past that feeling. And though the companionship was if anything even better than before, the sex for me always had a slight tinge of incest because I knew him so well. It just didn't feel quite proper. But it was so compelling, the flesh. And though I never reached passion, his body was fascinating and beautiful, and to see him rise naked from his bath with water running off him was a glorious thing. It was warm, his arm across me in bed as we slept, and sometimes, less so, mine across him. A hundred times I questioned myself: what is wrong with you? Why can't you be satisfied?

At first, for a while, it seemed ideal, a big new place in the middle of town that I never could have afforded on my own, closer to work. We were going halves on everything, though he took on more of the bills because he made more money than me. The flat was large and elegant with its high ceiling, a huge living area and decent kitchen, and a doorway leading into a small enclosed area with a *Taxi Driver* poster on one side and, on the other, one for *Attack of the Fifty Foot Woman*. From here two further doors led to the bedroom and bathroom. It seemed impossible that we should not be together after everything we'd gone through, though when I thought about it, it really wasn't as if we'd climbed mountains or penetrated rain forests. We'd hitch-hiked in the rain, kept warm in a bus shelter, wandered the back streets of town and fooled around in the porticos of churches. Still, it felt that we had been through something profound. When I'd first told her I was leaving, Shanna had given a little shudder and said, 'Ooh, I don't think I'd like the idea of living there.'

'Have you been inside?' I said. 'They're really nice flats. It's *so* different.'

'I don't know,' she said, 'it just would feel weird. As if it hadn't let go. The place. I just wouldn't like it.'

It's true, it was strange being in the old haunt. Long ago I'd rationalised all of those things that had happened or seemed to happen here. Not that I'd doubted what I'd seen but somehow I could put it away in a separate place where it existed in the same way that a recalled nightmare exists, in a time and space that had been superseded. Living on its remains was a big two fingers up to fear, a metaphorical holding up of the head. And it was also a dare to myself.

I was often alone there because he worked ridiculous hours, long late nights and sometimes weekends. Once or twice after I got home from the library I wandered around the old building, along the corridors and up and down the two staircases, still there just the same at either end. It was maddeningly confusing. The entrance and exits were still somehow the same, and so was that small square of space outside where the old school office used to be. The office lady – what was her name? – used to sit up so high looking down, and in the memories that came pouring in I was always very small like Alice, shrinking down and down till I could almost feel my chin hitting the floor. But I couldn't work out which classroom had gone where. Our flat took in, I think, 5 Alpha and part of 4 Beta, but it was very hard to say. Sometimes I felt as if, under its veneer of fresh paint and clean-cut corners, the place began to rearrange itself. I couldn't swear to where anything had been, not the music theatre, the gym, even the science labs, because the very dimensions had changed. Up there, where I'd have sworn there was a dark little side-step into the corner where wooden steps rose up to the greenhouse, there was now nothing but a pale yellow wall.

There *was* a roof garden, though, but that was half way along the corridor and accessed through a frosted glass door. It was nice up there; someone was obviously looking after it, tending to the potted plants, wiping down the green metal chairs. They'd put railings round to stop people falling off, and round the base of the big tower in the middle of the roof someone was raising mint and parsley. There was a friendly sign saying *Please use considerately.* Don't be a pig, in other words. Later I found out there was a rota for watering. I liked that, going up and watering the plants. The roof landscape felt subtly different. After a while I realised it was because a three-foot-long skylight that in my day had always been covered up had now been revealed. It was shaped like a Toblerone bar and you could look down and see the landing right underneath. I thought it was the top floor one facing the stairs that went down to where the Physics lab used to be but I wasn't sure. Mr Tufton, my God, a picture of him sprang into my mind, his humourless stodgy face saying something dry and sarcastic as he stood in his white coat in front of the blackboard. The view from the garden, a majestic old cityscape, cried out for the camera lens. Often when I was up there I found myself aware of the exact spot where Pamela went over, even when it was out of my sight, and sometimes it bothered me so much that I had to go back downstairs.

Here and there in the old building, because of its age and listed status, the parts they were not allowed to disturb broke through like ruins in Rome: a stretch of dark green and brown tiles, an old wooden board listing the names of old boys from the time it had been a boys' school, cornices, mouldings, high windows in which grey turrets towered against blue sky. Everywhere was now bright and light, the flats on either side of the wide corridors quietly vibrating with the hum of lives, even the murmur of babybabble, behind numbered doors painted different colours. Ours was maroon. Number 8 on the first floor.

I didn't see many people as I wandered about, and Robin didn't really know the neighbours because he wasn't there much in the day. Then one day, my afternoon off, there was an almighty crash in the corridor right outside our door, and I ran out and so did the woman two doors down on the other side, a ginger freckly woman with long ringletty hair, a good six foot I'd guess, in a three-tiered gypsy skirt and tight red top. 'Oh Jesus Mary and Joseph!' she cried, throwing her hands round her face in an overdramatic gesture, 'What was that?'

'I've no idea.'

We dithered, turned this way and that. She walked to the top of the stairs at the end of the corridor, looked up one flight, down the other. 'There's nothing!' she said, aggrieved.

'Nothing at all.' I started towards the other set of stairs but stopped. What was the point? The crash still lingered in my head. It had been right here, outside my door. I turned back and met her at the half-way point. 'We both heard that, didn't we?' I said.

'Damn well did.'

We stood still, listening to muffled sounds, traffic, faint voices, a radio DJ heartily burbling on in her flat, then we burst out laughing, both at the same time. 'Look, I'm shook,' she said, 'I've got to get back to my baby, d'you fancy a coffee?'

'God yeah,' I said, 'let me get my keys.'

Her flat was a big mess, with peach décor and a sunburst clock. A fake coal fire blasted out tropical heat, and the long-haired beige carpet was strewn with toys and books and crayons. A dark curly-haired girl of about two sat on a cushioned settee mauling a doughnut, bare plump legs sticking straight out in front of her, face all covered in jam. 'Gettel, Mum,' she said, pointing. Under the bookshelf was an enormous hamster, almost a guinea-pig.

'Oh my God,' said the big woman.

It sat frozen with one paw raised, stiff and in shock, staring beady-eyed. Its eyes looked as if they'd been blown up unbearably tight and were about to burst at any moment. 'Oh Gretel,' the woman said, 'my poor little baby,' and for a moment I thought about her saying she had to get back to her baby and wondered if she'd meant her daughter or her hamster.

'Is it OK?' I asked.

She got down on her hands and knees and reached under the bookcase, lifting the creature to her chest and kissing it between the ears. Her round freckled arms bulged under the short sleeves of her top. 'And I left the door open!' Her hair was a similar colour to its back.

'I remember when a hamster got down into the basement from the top floor,' I said. 'The bowels of the building. I used to go to school here, you know.'

'You never!'

'I did. It's really funny seeing it like this. Oh, she's moving.'

'Gettel,' said the child.

'Yes, Gretel.' The woman's voice was shouty. 'She's all right now. That was funny, wasn't it?'

'This was 4 Alpha,' I said, and she laughed. Her flat was, I realised blindingly, the classroom where we went for Geography, with the big pull-down screen at one end. My God, on this very spot. Where that silly girl saw shadows. The room where Gail embarrassed Mr Phelps by talking about her period, and where the whole class had once orchestrated a long continuous hum to disorient a podgy prefect.

'This was 4 Alpha,' I said again.

'There,' she said, stroking the hamster, 'there,' then she looked at me. 'I wouldn't like to go back to my school, ah no. It was OK, I suppose, but ah no. Do you want to look after her, Chlo?' She dumped the hamster in the little girl's lap. 'Give her a nice stroke? Nice and gentle now.' Gretel twitched her tight pink nose. The girl chewed stolidly, running her jammy hand all over the poor thing's back.

'Come in here,' said the woman, and I followed her into a kitchenette. 'It was right outside the door,' she said, putting the kettle on. 'I thought it was someone breaking the door down.' She reached up for the coffee jar.

'Really?' All the time I was gazing around me like someone at an exhibition. Is that where the cupboard was where they kept the chalk and dusters? Surely there was a window where the cooker stands? 'I thought it was outside *my* door,' I said.

'I'm shook,' she kept saying but I shrugged and smiled. 'Things like that happen.'

'I just like to know what a thing is, that's all.' She got mugs from a mug tree and started spooning Nescafé into them. 'I don't like it when there's no explanation.'

'I'm sure there is one.' I leaned on the counter. Funny, I wasn't rattled at all but I had a funny feeling, slightly faint, and could hear my voice saying inane things from a distance. 'I'm Sally,' I said.

'Oh, I'm Maggie.'

'Nice to meet you.'

'Your old school, eh?' she said. The kettle boiled. She made the coffee, blowing out her cheeks. 'And you came back? You're insane.'

'Yeah.'

She laughed. 'You're a braver man than me, Gunga Din,' she said. 'I wouldn't go back, oh no, no, no, no, no...' handing me a mug. We went through to the messy room. Maggie kneeled on the rug and I sat on the other end of the settee from the little girl, who fortunately ignored me completely. I couldn't talk to kids. This was one of those implacable ones that doesn't even want to look at you, thank God. Maggie had made the coffee very strong. The radio was on, golden oldies in the afternoon. Gretel the hamster ran about all over the room, into everything, here and there, up and down, over everyone and everything constantly like a wind-up toy, flashing her snow-white underbelly.

'Well, *she's* recovered anyway,' I said.

A daytime DJ droned lightly on. It was boiling hot in here. I was looking at the matted carpet with its toys and jam stains and suddenly it seemed as if this big Irish woman and her sombre little girl and the carpet and heat were all in my head and really I was in 4 Alpha. Gretel ran in front of me, stopped right there and got on her hind legs and looked up at me curiously. What eyes. Never blinked. I looked right into them and they were scarily unfathomable. I was sweating. 'You want to be careful,' I said, 'she *will* get out if you leave the door open, you know. Wouldn't it be best to keep her to one room?'

'Oh no!' Maggie was shocked. 'She has to have the run. It's her life too.'

That was a shame. I'd been planning on getting a little cat. I didn't want to have to worry about a hamster running up and down the corridor.

'But was that weird or was that weird?' said Maggie. She swallowed, and her thick milky neck rose and fell like a swelling breast.

'That was weird,' I said.

The next record was 'Monday Monday', which only

added to the sense of being out of time. Funny, this music in this building – it brought back a memory so long buried it had all but ceased to exist, yet here it was, immediate, fully formed. Here we all are sitting around in the cloakroom (how had we had so much time just to sit around?), me and Linda and Shanna and someone else. Gail? Susan Grech? Linda had started it, trying to get us all singing the harmonies.

Fa da, fa-da-da-da

They took me off the fa-da's because I was putting everybody off, but it was even worse when I was supposed to sing the opening:

Monday, Monday, so good to me

It was just awful.

They tried several ways, and every time I came in with my part they all stopped and sighed and looked at me, and in the end they told me to shut up because I was putting everyone else off. They weren't amused, they were annoyed. 'Don't mess around, Sally,' Shanna said in a disappointed voice.

'I'm not.'

'Yes, you are.'

'She's doing it on purpose,' Linda said to whoever the other person was.

I wasn't, though, that was the thing. That was just me trying to sing along.

Back in my own flat I wondered if I was coming down with something. I lay down for a bit then spent the evening watching TV, sometimes kneeling on the settee and looking out of the window at the park. After dark I liked to watch the glow of lamplight on the leaves and the sparse and sporadic flow of people cutting through from one place to another. It was getting too cold for anyone to linger very long. I had to have some background noise always, if not TV, then music or the radio because it masked the sounds the building made, the most bothersome of which was a constant high-pitched humming that came and went. Sometimes it took over for so long that you forgot about it altogether till it stopped, then you realised your head had been vibrating in time with it for the past couple of hours. I'd be glad to get back to work tomorrow. I didn't have to be in till ten, which was good because I wasn't remotely tired enough for a sensible bedtime. Rob got back about half past nine with a bottle of red wine. It had been a suit day. I couldn't get used to him in a suit. He pulled off the tie, took the jacket off and slung it over the back of a chair.

'I had coffee with the woman across the way,' I said. 'Maggie,' when he returned from the kitchen with glasses and a corkscrew.

'The big one with red hair?'

'She's in 4 Alpha.' I laughed and told him about the crash on the landing, the hamster, the heat.

'Sonic boom,' he said, rolling up the sleeves of his blue shirt and pulling at the cork.

'Ah, that's a good idea. Of course it was, I must tell her. She was really freaked out by it. Sounded like it was just outside.'

'It would sound like that, I suppose. Far more likely than a ghostie-ghoulie.'

'I didn't *think* it was a ghostie-ghoulie.'

The cork popped out and he poured. 'Bet you did.' He sat down on the settee, kicked his shoes away, took a long drink and sighed happily, threw back his head, displaying his throat as if baring it to the knife. The change in him I had thought subtle now glared. If I met him for the first time and had never seen him before, what would I see? Another suit home from work, wine, feet up. What did you expect? Would you rather be in Mangle Street snogging in the cold? It was one of those moments when I disliked myself intensely. Oh you, my mother said, you'll never be satisfied.

'Why don't you get changed?' I said.

'Not worth the bother.'

The wine was bitter and I pulled a face.

'Don't you like it?'

'It's OK. It's nice. Have you had anything to eat?'

'Kebab,' he said.

'You eat crap.'

He yawned hugely. 'Is the window open? Feels cold.'

'I'll close it,' I said. 'I like it open so I can hear the streets.'

'You like that?'

'Yeah.' I got up with my glass of wine and stood looking out for a moment. The park was empty but there were people coming out from the pub on the far corner.

'Oh, close it, love,' he said.

I pushed the window down. 'I was thinking about getting a cat,' I said.

'A cat?' He smiled, rolled his head to one side. 'A pussy cat?'

'A pussy cat.'

'Mm.' He thought. His eyes slid sideways and he yawned. 'How would we let it out?'

'The window?'

He laughed. 'A Heath Robinson contraption.'

'I dunno. We could have cat litter.'

'Oh God, not cat litter!'

'I wish you didn't get home so late every night,' I said.

'So do I. It's a pain. It's not all the time, though, is it?'

Then a whole lot of words came out of my mouth that I hadn't known were there. 'It's peculiar,' I said, 'it's not your fault, nothing's your fault, you mustn't think that but it feels like I'm just living in your flat, as if it's not my own place, like when I want to invite someone round it's not just me inviting someone round to my place, I'm inviting them into someone else's flat and it feels weird.'

'Oh Sal, you don't have to feel like that. You know it, Sal. Surely you know that? You can ask anyone you want round. That's you, not me.'

'It's like I can't just go out and get a cat like I could if I lived in my own place. I feel like I have to ask.'

'You don't have to *ask*. It's not like I'm your dad, this is just what it's like when you're living with someone. You negotiate.'

I watched the patterns of light on the leaves in the park.

'We're living together,' he said. 'We work these things out. I mean, what if it turned out I was allergic?'

'You're not.'

'I know, I'm just saying what if...'

'It's not just that.' I started feeling panicky, as if making him understand what I was trying to say was paramount. 'It's more than that. I wish you didn't have to work so late all the time.'

'It's just work,' he said, getting up and coming over. He thought a hug sorted everything out but I wasn't in the mood.

'What's the matter, love?' he said. 'What can we do? What can *I* do? It's only this thing at work, it's a phase, it should ease off after Christmas. You can do what you want with this place, you really can, I wish you would, I really do.'

My glass was empty. I looked around for the bottle. 'This place is starting to get to me,' I said. 'It's just peculiar, all the memories. I keep having dreams.' I went from the window and filled up my glass. He followed me.

'Do you ever get those dreams?' I said. 'Where you're back in your old school but you can't find your classroom? Or you find your classroom but you can't find your desk. Or...'

'Everyone has those,' he said.

'Yes, but this is for real. That's what it feels like. In the evenings if I don't have background music or the TV I start to get such strange feelings, as if outside the door it's all just the way it was, and I have these dreams where I go out the door and it's all gone back, and I start walking about but I get lost and can't find my way back into...'

But he started talking about his own dreams, how in *his* he had an exam but he hadn't revised for any of the questions.

In mine I walked for hours up and down the stairs and along the corridors, lost in a place I know – knowing and not knowing it's a dream, stuck hopelessly and unable to get out. When I woke up from those dreams, I was exhausted.

'It's bound to feel strange,' he said. 'Don't worry, my love, it'll wear off.' He put out his hand, smiling. 'Sit with me, love, I don't want you feeling bad.' So I did. 'You don't really feel you can't invite your friends round, do you?' he said. 'That's awful. How can I convince you it's OK? Bring anyone you want round. I mean it. Anytime. It's your place as much as mine now.' He shook the bottle. 'Gone,' he said.

In bed, after we'd made love, he leaned up on his elbow and looked down at me. 'I know,' he said, 'why don't we have a party?'

Not a big thing, we decided, just a few people, drinks and crisps and things. Shanna and Linda, Susan Grech and Gail Turnbull, Stewart and Michael, his old friends from way back, Maggie and Rami from down the hall, someone from his work called Vic, someone from mine called Marsha. Plus any extraneous boy- or girlfriends. I kept planning it after he'd gone to sleep, little sausages, cheese, falafels, olives, maybe a trifle. Booze. He slept so well, so effortlessly. I was awake, open-eyed, watching the light in the window, the shadow of leaves, the smudgy darkness, listening to the peculiar night-time hum of the old building and hearing a door close somewhere above, sometimes a voice, sometimes a sound I couldn't define. Running water on another floor perhaps, or conversation, distant and monotonous.

★

So we had a few people round, Saturday night two or three weeks later. It was coming up to Christmas so I'd put up lights and got us a tree that stood by the big window. It was only about three feet high. He wouldn't have bothered. I bought baubles for the tree and a big gold star to put on the top and all he could say was, oh let's just shove a bit of tinsel here and there, but when it was all done he had to admit that it did look nice. We pushed the big table back against the wall and had wine and punch at one end, food all over the rest of it, crisps and nuts and chocolate and savoury things from M&S. There was beer in the fridge.

I'd say it went OK. Everyone seemed to have a good time. There was smoke in the air and the window was open a bit so you could hear the gentle hum of traffic, murmuring on like a river. Elvis Costello was on the sound system. Linda and Shanna were the first to arrive and ran about all over the building, squeaking with recognition and exclaiming at the changes. Then Gail Turnbull turned up without Susan Grech but with a skinny boy called Gavin in a studded leather jacket. Susan was sick, she said. Gail had put on weight and looked a bit like Miss Piggy with her long black eyelashes and full blonde hair. She'd taken on a bit of Miss Piggy's manner as well and insisted on being shown around immediately, wanted to see *everything, now*, so I ended up trailing round with her. We started on the roof.

'This is nice,' she said, rubbing her plump pink arms in the cold.

'Everyone comes up on the roof on New Year's Eve,' I said proudly, 'to watch the fireworks. And everyone brings up a bottle and something to eat.'

'Wow!'

We worked our way down the school with her gasping and sighing and constantly stopping and looking around as if she couldn't get her bearings.

'Strange, isn't it?' I said.

'Right!' she said wonderingly, walking with her goosebumped arms folded before her.

'So what are you up to these days, Gail?'

'I'm training to be a hairdresser.' She laughed breathily. 'I'm starting at the bottom, washing hair and sweeping up and all that.'

'Fantastic,' I said. 'I've always wanted a friend who was a hairdresser. You'll have to come and do something with my hair. I'm sick of it.'

'I love cutting hair,' she said, and I had a quick vision of her upside-down face saying, 'Is that temperature about right for you?' as you broke your neck bending it backwards over the sink.

'God,' she said, 'it's so funny, I've forgotten where everything was!'

'It comes back to you.'

By the time we got back to the flat Maggie and Rami had arrived. I'd met Rami by this time, he was the one who kept the roof nice. Maggie had brought a beautiful pineapple upside-down cake, all shiny on top, and I made room for it on the table. By nine everyone had arrived. People moved backwards and forwards between the table and the cosy area where beanbags and chairs had been strategically placed within reach of the coffee table. I drank a lot of strong, fruity punch and ended up on the settee with Linda and Shanna, Shanna in the middle. I kept nibbling away at the halva squares brought by Linda, the Turkish Delight, the nuts in bowls. Vic from Rob's office, who'd come all the way from Miles Platting, was sitting on the floor to my left. His lips were unpleasantly wet and red. He'd taken on himself an American accent and was telling Maggie's Rami a convoluted story about his travels in America.

'So – what was this room?' asked Linda. 'Must get my bearings.'

'5B,' I said.

'Apparently,' said Maggie, whose hair must have just been washed because it stuck out around her like a fuzzy pyramid, '*we're* in 4 Alpha.'

'They don't correspond exactly,' I said. 'They overlap. We've got a bit of 4B as well, I think.'

Under the big Aubrey Beardsley poster of Salome, Marsha from the library was sitting on the dragged-out futon next to Rob's old friend Stewart. I remembered him years ago at some do at Rob's school, walking across the hall looking moody and pretty. He was still pretty. Marsha was just sitting chain-smoking with her arms folded, while he talked to a couple I didn't know. I thought I'd better go over and sit with her as she didn't really know anyone, but when I tried I didn't seem to be able to get up. It was a strange feeling, as if I'd retreated into a little room inside my forehead and was looking out through a window. Above Marsha, blood from John the Baptist's head drooled down from a plate in a straight line into the precise middle of her centre parting. I think I stopped hearing for a few seconds. When I tuned back in Gail was saying from the beanbag into which she'd sunk with her boyfriend, 'Oh, I remember that. My silly sister.'

Linda and Shanna had been telling Maggie about how Gail's sister had seen something scary in her flat.

'Oh stop,' said Maggie, 'I really don't want to know.'

'Oh, it wasn't anything,' Gail said, 'my sister's an idiot.'

I remembered a podgy scared little girl with terrified eyes. How we cornered her for interrogation and she burst into tears. What was her name?

'Does she still remember it?' I asked. I could move now.

'Oh, does she! Of course she does. She'll still bang on about it if you let her.'

'What's she doing now?'

'Can never remember. Some pointless job in Reading.'

How we scatter. I went to the table, ladled myself another glass of punch.

'Oh but,' said Maggie, 'there *was* a funny thing. Wasn't there, Sally?'

I smiled, saying nothing. The Christmas lights twinkled in the tree. Through the window more shined from across the park.

'Sonic boom,' Rami called across from the other side of the room. 'Yeah, Rob?'

'Most likely.'

The two of them were sitting at the little round table next to the tree. I'd put a Christmas cactus there in a pot and Rami was using its water dish as an ashtray.

'Go on then,' Shanna said. 'What happened?'

'We heard this very loud, like *huge*, crash out in the corridor, you know, like something ginormous like, I don't know, a lorry or bigger than that falling from a great height, or no, it wasn't really like that because it was just like one big loud bang, know what I mean?'

'It was just a big bang,' I said, now completely back to normal.

'And we went rushing out, the both of us...'

'Yeah.'

'Nothing there.'

'Nothing there.'

'Sonic boom,' said Rami.

'He hates anything like that,' Maggie said, pulling her chair closer to our settee and lowering her voice a bit.

'It probably was a sonic boom, though,' I said.

Maggie pulled a maybe/maybe not face. 'We used to get sonic booms over the west coast of Ireland,' she said, 'that's where they cross the sound barrier going to America. It was just a bit freaky-deaky, that's all.'

'Oh well, this is a freaky-deaky place,' said Shanna. 'Remember how we all used to sit upstairs in the Biology lab telling scary stories?'

'And the séances.'

'And Mrs Kidney coming in and saying—'

'Mrs Kidney?' said Stewart, who must have been listening. 'You had a teacher called Mrs *Kidney*?'

'We did. She taught Biology.'

Laughter.

So we were off. It must have been awful for everyone else with me and Shanna and Linda on the settee and Gail joining in from her beanbag, the four of us babbling on about school, giggling, talking over each other, outdoing each other with our remembrances. Throwing our hats in the canal and them all floating away like green balloons. The school mag, pumps, white ankle socks, ugly shoes. School photographs, in summer the horizontal stripes strobing too brightly in the sun. The bouffants of the girls standing on chairs on the back row billowed up by the wind. When so-and-so drew a cartoon of poor old Miss Oliver on the board and she sat in front of it for twenty minutes without noticing. Oh, that was horrible. And Miss Swett coming in and—

'You had a Miss Sweat too?' Stewart spluttered. 'A Mrs Kidney and a Miss Sweat? You're making this up.'

'Mrs Stannard told me I looked like a street walker because of my hair,' said Gail wistfully.

'D'you remember when your plait fell in the custard?'

We shrieked with laughter.

'Yeah,' said Gail, 'I was just looking to see if it was lumpy or smooth and my hair fell over my shoulder and the end of my plait went in the custard and Miss Frith was walking through and saw and was furious and made me take the jug away and get a new one as if my hair was really filthy and full of nits or something. *What* are *you doing? Do you expect people to want to eat that after you've been hanging over it like that with your nose?*'

'With your nose!'

Lumpy custard, gravy, trays of meat pie cut in squares, balls of mash.

'Do you remember *Caesar and Cleopatra*?' I said.

'It was awful.'

'Yeah,' said Shanna, 'Hilary Brogan in that Cleopatra

wig. Made her look like Max Wall. Kept going: *I look like Sandie Shaw in this, don't I?*'

'Sandie Shaw! Didn't look anything like Sandie Shaw.'

'And the second form did a sort of a sand dance—'

'We were killing ourselves—'

'—only it was supposed to be serious!'

'Oh my giddy aunt!'

'I don't know why they didn't just make it an out and out comedy and have done with it,' said Gail.

'*Twelfth Night* was a laugh.'

'Oh Brave New World!' cried Shanna. 'A few first-formers with knobbly knees doing ballet, looking as if they'd cacked themselves.'

I'd eaten too much of the warm squashy halva. 'This must be incredibly boring for everyone,' I said, getting up and crossing the room to sit with Marsha out of my sense of duty. It was mean of Stewart to ignore her and rattle on with that anonymous couple on the other beanbag.

'Not at all,' said Rami. 'On the contrary, I'm fascinated.'

'It did have a reputation, though,' Linda said, 'this building. There were all these stories, kind of handed down.'

'Like the man in the basement,' said Gail.

I remembered: bare feet walking along next to the row of toilets, visible under the partition.

'It was a lunatic asylum.' Shanna leaned forwards and scooped a handful of pistachios.

'It wasn't!'

'Oh, that's just a myth.'

'Well, it's an old building,' Gail said, 'it's bound to have a history.'

'All old places feel like that.' Marsha spoke for the first time to the room in general. 'I hate being the last one at work and having to lock up.'

'Don't let's talk creepy stuff,' I said, 'I have to live here.'

'Me too,' said Maggie.

'Doesn't feel creepy now,' said Rob.

'The lecture theatre always had a reputation.' Linda flicked her lighter with a big double-jointed thumb. 'I was in the choir for a bit and we used to practise in there. I can see it now, poor Mr Phelps standing with his wand at the front.'

'His baton,' said Gail. 'I was in the choir too.'

'You know what I always really loved? Those Christmas services we had in St Anne's. We sang "Ave Maria" once and it was sublime. The acoustics. Much better than when we sang it at school. Oh, Sylvia Rose's voice!'

A terrible feeling came over me, much worse than before. I was looking at Linda's face through the smoke she was blowing out of her nostrils, and it went into sudden supersharp focus, the prominent diamond-shaped bone in the middle of her nose, the creases high up in her forehead; it felt as if I was fading away as the world out there sharpened.

'Oh yes!' I heard my voice say. 'She was in her element.' I could see her in the centre of the front row singing her heart out into the echoing church. I picked up my glass. 'I was never in the choir,' I said to Marsha. 'Terrible voice.'

'Oh, me too,' she replied. 'Can't sing for toffee.'

I started counting the people, one, two, three, four—

I had certainly eaten too much halva. Too sweet. I wished I hadn't.

'Have you had any of the halva?' I said. 'It's really nice.'

'Oh yes,' said Marsha.

People kept moving around and I counted and the number came out different each time. This scared me. I wondered if someone had slipped something into my drink – but how ridiculous. I could have sworn someone was in the kitchen but couldn't work out who was missing, so I started counting again.

'Do you remember,' said Gail, looking at me, 'all that awful stuff with Pamela and Sylvia Rose? Wasn't it terrible when you think about it? You and Pamela were pally, weren't you?'

'We were,' I said. 'I always felt sorry for Pamela.'

'Smoke?' Marsha was shoving a cigarette at me so I took it.

'Poor Pamela!' Shanna said.

Marsha flicked her lighter and I realised as soon as the smoke hit the back of my throat that I might possibly be sick before the night was through, so I leaned back and closed my eyes. I saw the old greenhouse, pink and blue hyacinths, Pamela blowing her smoke out of the window. I still hadn't been able to locate it.

'People really didn't like her, you know,' Linda said.

'I know.' I opened my eyes. 'I always thought it wasn't fair. I can understand why, I suppose, but she was OK when you got to know her.'

Then Gail said, 'It was horrible what she did to Sylvia, though.'

Robin pricked his ears up. 'What did she do to Sylvia?'

So then of course it all had to be explained to those who didn't know.

'It was so embarrassing. This girl Sylvia, you see, she had such a lovely voice...'

'I remember her singing at your party, Shanna,' Rob said.

I didn't like thinking about Sylvia.

'And it was the Arts Festival and she was going up to sing – what was she singing?'

'"The Trout",' I said.

'"The Trout". And just before she went up on stage, Pamela put pepper in her hankie...'

Rami and Vic from Rob's office burst out laughing.

'It wasn't funny.'

'Well, it does *sound* funny,' I said, 'but it wasn't.'

'It was terrible, she must have got a real noseful of it right up there and she starts choking and sneezing and her eyes gushing, standing there in front of the whole school. I thought she was having some sort of seizure.'

'Awful,' Shanna said.

'Awful.'

'Nobody knows for sure that it was Pamela,' I said.

'Oh it was,' they chorused.

'See what I mean?' I looked at Rob and he smiled at me. 'Whatever it was, if in doubt, blame Pamela.'

'You told me about this,' he said, 'at the time.'

'My God, how long have you two known each other?' Vic asked.

'Years.'

'Donkey's years.'

'Yes, we met in 1965.'

'True.'

'That's so nice,' said the girl I didn't know.

'Well, we had a few years apart as well,' I said. Christ's sake, what are we? Darby and Joan?

'Still,' said Linda, 'that's a thoroughly nasty thing to do.'

'*If* she did it.'

'You really think she didn't?'

'Well, I never knew anything about it,' I lied brazenly, determined to defend her, poor dead girl, 'and I'm sure she would have said something if it was true.'

'Well, she was your friend,' Shanna said. 'She wasn't so bad.'

After this I started feeling seriously sick, and I got scared, not just scared of standing up in case I couldn't make it to the bathroom but outrageously, cosmically scared, ridiculous considering the fact that I was sitting in a crowded room in my own flat with my boyfriend and some old friends. The music had become brassier and louder and my forehead pounded to its rhythm.

'I wonder what became of Sylvia,' Linda said.

'I wonder.' Shanna leaned forwards. Red wine went glug-glug-glug into her glass. Marsha passed me another cigarette and my gorge rose.

'No thanks.' I got up and went to the bathroom. Got two doors between me and them. How horrible to be sick at your own party. Everyone would know when I didn't come back. Rob would come looking for me. He had to go into work tomorrow afternoon to look at a building site or something. God knows why on a Sunday, ridiculous, but fortunately he was a good riser and never got hangovers. Not like me. Bloody typical. Tomorrow would be deathly. Over the sink, nothing coming, then a rush of stinky horror spattered everywhere over the porcelain. Couldn't stay here, someone might want to go to the toilet. Halva. Red wine. I sank to my knees and rested my clammy forehead against the nice cold pedestal, and the peculiar fear that had fallen like a sword as I sat on the futon next to Marsha rode on the nauseous waves, waxing and waning.

At some point Rob came and tapped on the door and asked if I was OK.

'No,' I called back.

He tried the door. 'Can you let me in, please?' he said.

I got to my feet as if I'd been knocked out, two steps to the door, pushed back the bolt and he stepped in, lifted me quickly in his arms and swung me through the open door of our bedroom to deposit me on my side on the bed. 'You're OK,' he said, 'you're OK, you old drunkard. I'll get you a bowl. Try and hold it.'

No one would ever love me as he loved me then. He got me a bowl and put his hand on my head. 'Just lie still, love, you're OK.'

'I'm sorry,' I said.

'No need to be.'

He went out. The room was spinning. I was sick again and felt proud that I got it all in the bowl at the side of the bed. But it happened again and again and I cried with dread and boredom, holding my pillow tight as can be. A long time passed till I was hearing voices.

'Is she OK? Is she OK?'

'Yeah, yeah, just had a bit too much to drink.'

'Oh, don't we all at some time.'

Doors closing.

★

I was lying on the bed, the room whirling, a bowl, emptied and newly rinsed, at the side of the bed. I saw the ceiling of 4B.

Someone called, 'Night-night, Sally. Hope you feel better soon.'

Not long after, he came to bed. I lay on my side, away from him so he didn't have to smell my breath. I was disgusting. I was standing in shame in front of the big brown desk. Miss Demery said with withering scorn, 'Well, you have made perfect fools of yourselves, haven't you,' and a crescendo of fear welled up and I blacked out.

Every time I came home to the empty flat on a dark winter night I'd open the door and turn on the light and find myself, against my own advice, swiftly checking every room because I felt as if someone was there. Sometimes it was Robin unexpectedly home, lying on the settee eating an apple or coming out of the shower, but usually there was no one at all. Then the feeling would fade away, and I'd think how nice it would be to have a little cat, black and white I thought, running to meet me, getting on my knee when I sat down, purring, allowing strokes. I'd never had a cat but always wanted one. I didn't see how I could easily let one out here, there was no easy way down, and I didn't want to keep the poor thing in all the time.

These homecomings were unpleasant. Since moving in I'd been subtly worried, unable to get into a book or anything on the telly, and once I'd eaten, I'd feel wide awake and jiggly and roam around the room aimlessly, stopping occasionally to look out of the window at the odd soul crossing the park. I couldn't look at anything around here without a memory popping up. Me in my uniform walking diagonally towards the pub on the corner with my school bag and white ankle socks, trying to be invisible under the hostile windows. Often on a night like this I'd wander around the old building. It fascinated me; you could say it obsessed me. Once a woman I met at the turn of the stairs gave me the fright of my life, a huge woman in drab grey clothes, with a wide coarse face the colour of raw meat. She was soaking wet. Not just a bit of sweat standing out on her face, this was as if someone had emptied a bucket of water over her head, and it was unnatural so it scared me. She was coming up and I was going down and I never heard her approach, and I jumped and gasped. 'Oh my God, sorry,' I said, laughing, but the woman chattered her teeth at me and did an odd little dance backwards on the half-landing, staring at me as if I was a ghost. The peculiar moment gave me a chill. The way she looked, soaking wet, the way she moved, standing back into the corner as I hurried past, foolishly grinning, 'Sorry, sorry,' cheerful and hearty but with a nasty cringing feeling as if I was trying to get past a dog of uncertain temperament. What a fool, jumpy as hell. I told myself: she was wet, so what? And it wasn't raining. Can't go freaking out over every little thing. Just a woman from one of the other flats, not my floor, and indeed I saw her a few days later from a window getting into the driver's seat of a car in the yard, one thick leg with an ugly shoe on the end of it sticking out onto the concrete till she got it in and slammed the door.

So there I was scolding myself for my imagination, chastising the prickles on my skin and the clammy cold of my temples, till one night between Christmas and New Year, having just got in and drawn the curtains against the night I became aware of something like the humming of a mosquito or a gnat somewhere in the room, going up and down, up and down on the far edge of hearing, fading and increasing as if the thing was flying here and there invisibly, as they do. Not a gnat, I thought, after it had irritated me for quarter of an hour or so while I was getting changed and combing out my hair, there are more shades in it. Perhaps several gnats. At this time of year? Don't be stupid—

Someone shaving in another flat, a distant hairdryer, a pipe.

People always say it's pipes. If all the pipes suddenly sang in harmony. Because it was starting to sound a bit like singing, maybe even on the other side of the park, tuneful, but then a gnat or a mosquito can also be tuneful in its own way. Then I thought it was singing on a radio far away, tuning in and out as if the reception was coming and going. So annoying. Nagging. So I turned on the radio and heard the traffic news and the weather, then put the TV on with the sound down low and went behind the curtain and pushed the window up.

It wasn't coming from out there. The park was empty. The cool air felt nice. I closed the window then turned off the telly in a spirit of defiance because there was nothing on worth watching and I wanted to see if the sound was still there. It was.

This would drive me potty. It was like having something stuck in your tooth, or a piece of loose skin or something, or trying to go to sleep with a bunged-up nose. I stood still and listened to the up and down lilt, very clear now.

I went to the door, opened it and looked out into the long corridor, stretching empty and wide either way. The sound had gone completely, as if my opening of the front door and putting out my head had turned it off like the flick of a switch.

I was stepping back with relief when it rose again, closer, sounding definitely like voices now, voices but different. Under water. With muffled ears.

I can tell you this right now: I'm not going to do that stupid thing like they do in films, that stupid thing where they go out and wander about in creepy places: oh yes, I'll just take a look in the basement, no particular reason, oh dear the light's gone, well, it would, wouldn't it, better take a candle, wait for the jump scare. At which point all the jump scares I ever saw crammed into my head, all right up there in my face, the *Exorcist* girl, the demon, the ghost of Peter Quint at the window, let me in let me in, don't look in the mirror. Oh yes, I know all the tricks.

No way was I falling for all that.

I stood listening for a while and it faded to a drone then whisked away, only to relocate somewhere far above. I walked to the stairwell and looked up. From there it was impossible to say if it was coming from above or below. The stairwell was a distorting void.

Someone was coming down.

Got myself all fight or flight but it was only Maggie with Chloe on one arm.

'Oh hello, Sally.' She beamed. 'Wait'll you see what Ram's doing on the roof.'

'What's he doing?'

All good normal life going on, Maggie with her big presence. 'He's made a thing for a little fire up there when we go up for the fireworks. I'll give him this much: he's not useless. A whatchercallit.'

I couldn't imagine anything more bizarre than a bunch of adults drinking round a fire on the roof of my school, fireworks exploding in the sky.

'Was he making a noise?' I said. 'I keep hearing a noise.'

'There wasn't much noise. I'd say it was fairly simple, I don't know. Go and have a look.'

'He's up there now?'

'He is. Be sure to praise him like mad.'

Couldn't hear the noise now anyway. 'I'll go up,' I said.

'We're going in to get nice and warm, aren't we, Chlo? Oh Sally, while I've got you, I don't suppose you could maybe keep an eye on Chloe for me, could you, only for about an hour and a half next Thursday? I've got the dentist, I hate the dentist, and Rami was supposed to be here only he can't...'

'Yeah, sure,' I said.

It was OK now. Rami had been making a noise on the roof so that explained it all. I went up and there he was, all wrapped up in a thick woolly scarf and leather gloves, smoking a cigarette over a big iron pot and a heap of stones.

'OK there?' he said. 'Like my fire pit?'

'Fantastic. It looks like a witch's cauldron.'

'Does, doesn't it?' He banged his hands together. 'I want to put bricks round it but it's getting the buggers up the stairs.'

'Few at a time,' I said.

'Has to be. How are you, Sally?'

'I'm fine.' I looked over the railings down to the yard, or should I say the car park. There were only three or four cars, as most people put theirs underground. 'Were you using any power tools,' I said, 'a drill or something?'

'Oh no,' he said, 'nothing like that. There's nothing to it really.'

It was bloody freezing up there.

'We'll need it,' I said. 'Great idea, Rami.'

I couldn't see any point in saying anything about the funny noise. He thought I was daft as it was, me and Maggie getting bothered by the Big Bang and all that.

'Well,' he said, 'so long as it doesn't rain,' then chucked his dog-end down and shoved his hands in his pockets. 'By, it's chill up here, it is,' he said, clapping his gloved hands again, and we walked down together and parted at my door. I didn't want to go back into my empty flat. It was like living on my own really, I thought, Robin's never here. And if he was I'd probably be wishing he wasn't. God knows what I should do. I hit myself on the head. What is wrong with you? Oh you, you're a hard one to please. I made sure the door was locked, then unlocked it again because it was ridiculous. I listened. I didn't know what I was listening for.

Whatever it was it had stopped.

Robin didn't get back till after ten.

'Sorry, love,' he said. He had a great wad of work under his arm.

'These hours are ridiculous,' I said.

'Yeah. It should ease off in a couple of weeks.'

'You said that before. You said it'd get better after Christmas. Well, it didn't, did it?'

So he'd be stuck at his table with a load of diagrams all weekend.

'You know, Rob,' I said when he'd settled down, 'I'm beginning to have doubts about this flat.'

'Oh, Sal!' His face closed up. 'I thought you liked these flats.'

I babbled. 'I know, I know, I do, but I'm just not sure, it's too much my old school still, it makes me feel funny, I never liked school, you know.'

He grabbed my hand, oddly tense for him. 'Is that what you really mean?' he said with pained eyes. 'Or is it something to do with me? Maybe it's not the flat, maybe it's *me*.'

'It's not you.'

I didn't even know whether or not I was lying.

'Sal, it's not your old school any more. It's not. Is it really that bad? Can't you just see it as a nice old block of flats? I really like living here. I was so pleased when I got this place, I felt really lucky. Oh really, Sal! Honest, is it as bad as all that?'

'I get scared,' I said, getting to the crux of it.

'Scared,' he repeated flatly, shaking his head. 'What can I do? Tell me and I'll do it.' He put his arm round me and gave me a squeeze. 'There's nothing to be scared of. I've lived here – what? – months before you arrived, and I know there's nothing to be scared of. It's not the place, love, it's you. What can we do about it? What can we do about it, eh?'

I could have thumped him. I pulled away. 'You're not taking me seriously,' I said, 'you're patronising.'

'No, Sal, I'm...'

'Yes, you are. I got scared tonight, I don't know why. I kept hearing a funny sound.'

'What funny sound?'

'Something in the background. Like a gnat singing, you know the way they do? Only it wasn't a gnat singing because it was outside, out there in the building as well. I couldn't tell where it was coming from.'

'It could have been anything,' he said. 'It's an old building, old buildings make funny noises. Look – what can we do? Why don't we get a cat?'

'There's no way to let it out.'

'I'm trying to help here. You're doing that thing.'

'What thing?'

'That thing where everything I say to help, you'll find a way around it. A dog then. You could take it out for walks.'

I thought about that. 'Are we allowed dogs?'

'Bloke on the ground floor's got one.'

'A dog,' I said sadly. I'd never had a dog.

'They're great company.'

'But it was like singing.'

'Singing?'

'I'm not sure. It wasn't clear. It sounded funny.'

'That's probably exactly what it was,' he said, 'singing.

Someone singing in one of the other flats. People are allowed to sing, you know.'

'But it was funny, the way it moved. The way it changed.'

'Sound can be deceptive.'

Poor old Robin. Get a cat, get a dog, he'd do anything. Look at his worried face. He was OK before I moved in. Lived happily in his tip – he'd tidied up for me, I realised, the night we went to see Iggy Pop.

'Oh, I'm sorry,' I said, 'I don't really want to move, it's just these long winter nights. Have you eaten?'

I walked to the kitchen and he followed. 'Grabbed a pizza.'

'One of these days,' I said, 'it would be nice if we could eat together.'

He loomed, unsure of himself. 'We did that two nights ago.'

'Did we?'

'I made you one of my omelettes.'

I don't like omelettes. I'd eaten it and forgotten.

'Please talk to me, Sal,' he said. 'Are you regretting this? Moving in with me?'

'Not *you*. It's the place.'

'Really, Sal' – he came round in front of me and clutched my arm. Looking at his eyes made me hate myself – 'if anything's wrong you have to tell me.'

'There's nothing wrong with *you*.'

I should give him a cuddle, a kiss. After a hesitation that echoed like the void, I put my arms round him. 'I'm so tired, I have to go to bed. Please believe me, it's not you.'

Little voice, saying, 'Liar, liar.'

'Give it a little bit longer,' he said, 'it'd be such an enormous hassle to move.'

'I know.'

'Think of it, Sal. It makes me wilt just to think of it. Give it a little bit longer, please. Then see how you feel.'

'OK.' I didn't want to argue. He started kissing me then, and the old shrinking surged back in me like a curse. I drew away when I reasonably could, smiling my deceitful smile, went to the bedroom and started brushing my hair. He came in and stood behind me and I wanted him to go away. 'What are you doing?' I said. 'Are you coming to bed or staying up for a bit?'

'I think I'll stay up for a bit.'

But he still stood there.

'OK.' I went in the bathroom and closed the door. I sensed him outside. You're not just going to stand there outside the door while I have a pee and clean my teeth and pick the specks of black out of the corners of my eyes, are you? But when I opened the door he'd already gone back into the living room and I could hear the telly blathering on, and a burst of music.

I couldn't sleep that night. He came to bed at one. I was still awake and we had sex as if we weren't really there. At least I wasn't, I can't speak for him. It was OK. Then he kissed me tenderly and yawned an awful loud full-mouthed yawn that sounded like a lion in the jungle, and fell asleep immediately. My mind was wide awake but my body and brain were comatose. Next to me was this sleeping innocent, oblivious, an animal, a lump, a child, gently snoring from time to time.

How dare he?

I gave him a push and he turned over.

The dark hours passed while I lay wide awake, back in that classroom of bored endurance, idling time away, tracing the juts and curves of the moulding round the wooden blackboard surround. Drifting into sleep – a sound came, a gnat singing, high, far, far away.

There were small things.

A knock at the door, opening it, finding no one there.

The phone ringing, no one there.

It rang again.

'Hello?'

No one. But there was a sound, *the* sound, I could have sworn, only this time it was buried in the bowels of the telephone system.

'Go away,' I said pettishly and dropped the receiver onto its hold. After that I went out and walked round town in the dark for a couple of hours. Town was always crowded, it was good – whatever happened I could just run outside and there'd be lights and bustle and the sweet ordinary sounds of people, cars, buses huffing and snuffing like big beasts. But this was a ridiculous way to live, I thought, marching through Piccadilly. Scared of my own flat. I went to Lando's Snacks but it had gone. Felt like death to stand there in front of the brash new hairdresser's that had replaced it. Heads in the window, smiling or sultry. Everything goes. Only a matter of time. I thought of me and Rob sitting in there at our table, the awful coffee with too much milk, the weirdo regulars, the paper boy throwing the evening news through the door and the little Italian boy coming out to get it and take it to his father.

It started to rain. I found another place for a coffee but a bloke came and started talking to me. I wanted to say fuck off but didn't. I just answered him in monosyllables then left. There was my bus, the one I used to catch going home. I actually stopped and stood still, watching the people getting on, the doors closing, the driver looking back as it moved out into the traffic.

I had to go back. I hadn't brought an umbrella with me and my hair was straggling ratty down my back and dripping water down the sides of my neck. Now if it had been raining like this when I saw that wet woman on the stairs – but that was nothing.

What was wrong with me? Scared at every little thing. Just the world telling me I was on the wrong track, that moving in was the stupidest possible thing I could do. I must have known it deep down all along, even when it had seemed like the easiest, most natural thing in the world. Even when the small voice was whispering inside: this will end.

I must go. I didn't love Robin. Go where? Not back to that shared house, no. How to tell him? His old familiar face appeared in my mind. How could I say I didn't love him? Of course I did, always would. Why should I have to lose him? He'd still be there, my eternal friend. We could go out now and then, have a meal, go see a film.

He was there when I got back. 'Bloody Nora,' he said, coming towards me with a toothy grin, 'state of you. You're soaking wet! Where've you been?'

'I went for a walk.'

'In the rain?'

'It wasn't raining when I went out.'

'You must have been gone ages.'

'I told you.' He followed me to the bathroom. 'I don't like being here on my own at night. I go out and walk around.'

'Not getting any better?'

'Not really.'

He put his arms round me from behind as I was trying to rub my hair with a towel. 'Might not be a bad idea to go and see the doctor,' he whispered in my ear as if it was an endearment.

I hadn't re-registered since moving out of the old house. I'd have to traipse all the way over to Didsbury.

'And tell him what?'

'Everything. How you're feeling. You might just need some kind of an anti-anxiety thing, just while you're getting used to being here. It's probably raising all sorts of old baggage about what happened – after all, it was pretty extreme, wasn't it? Your friend Pamela and all that – it's all churned up again for you...'

'I know.'

He kissed my fingers as they rubbed my head. 'It'll be all right, I promise. If it's really that bad, we'll move, of course we will. I'd never make you stay somewhere you were really unhappy...'

'I know.'

His arms tightened in a squeeze. What could I do? 'I'll make an appointment,' I said.

'Tomorrow,' he said. 'First thing.'

★

We all piled up onto the roof on New Year's Eve: us, Maggie and Rami and about twelve other neighbours that I didn't know. It was the night I made a huge fool of myself.

Rami's fire pit was a great success. We all stood around it with our plastic cups of wine, politely jostling for positions closest to the flames. He was a clever sod, Rami, I'll say that for him. He'd got those bricks up there somehow – 'one by one,' he said – and everyone was having fun, *I* was having fun, and Rob was getting to know the neighbours he'd been saying hello to on the stairs for months.

But all the time I was looking to identify the exact spot where Pamela went over. Honestly, I just couldn't stop. It was making a nightmare of the night.

A jolly man with a bald head and shaggy eyebrows distributed sparklers, and we all lit up at midnight, and the fireworks went off all over town, and on the roof in the middle of the city with other voices in other streets joining in and a roar in the air to welcome the New Year in, that was the only place in the world to be. I'd drunk far too much. Rob grabbed me and pulled me in hard and kissed me, saying, 'Mmwah! Mwah! Happy New Year, my love.' We swung our sparklers about, writing on the air, making figure eights and squiggles. My eyes made the lights crackle, and the fireworks high up were those magical colours of past Christmases when everything was new.

I wandered along out of our own little patch of party, into the shade of the next chimney along, to the place where they'd uncovered the long skylight shaped like a

Toblerone. A silvery light shone up from below so I drifted over and looked down. Below was a harshly lit half-landing. I couldn't work out where it was. By my calculations it should have been over where the cookery room was, but why could I see a stairwell tilting down to the left? Where did it go to? It was too hard to work out so I returned to the fire and the people. They'd opened the bubbly. I filled my glass. Everyone was laughing about something and it was the first of January. Rob was in a little group of people I didn't know. I knew exactly where she went over now, it had computed. There. Just where the man with the balding head and shaggy eyebrows was having a real good gummy laugh with a woman from the ground floor. Funny that a spot like that could host this scene, what happened erased. Gone.

I went back down early. It was wrong, laughing and drinking and doing the small talk up there, thinking about Pamela going off the roof.

I opened another bottle of wine when I got downstairs. I felt ridiculously bright-eyed and wide awake. You couldn't hear the party from here. I poured wine, swayed out into the living room with it spilling over my fingers, put on one of Robin's mix-tapes and danced about in front of the mirror, smiling at myself. They do say that if you look yourself in the eyes in a mirror long enough, your face changes. I've tried it and it's true, but as soon as it starts to change I blink and run away. I wouldn't push it. You never know, do you? I started scolding myself. It *is* a nice flat. What are you fussing about? You'll not get a better one, you'll end up in some poky little hole. You're never satisfied, you. Why am

I down here? Am I scared? Scared to look up and see the Sylvia-thing smiling down at me from the turret?

There. I'd not thought of that, not *really* thought of it – her, it, whatever – not in ever such a long time. Back of the mind, maybe. But not like this, full in the face. Suddenly it was worse being alone down here than up there with them, so I drifted back up, daring the corridors and stairs. Trouble is, when you've seen a few horror films you're always waiting for the jump scare.

I couldn't see Rob. Fewer people than before. It was getting cold.

'Seen Rob?' I asked Maggie.

'He was here a second ago.'

I walked along past the turret. There was nothing up there. Robin was standing by himself gazing into the long skylight.

'You can see right down to the landing,' I said, coming up to him.

'I know.'

The light on the landing and on the stairs and in the corridors was always so bright. Everything was clean and clear-cut. 'Do you know,' I said, 'I really can't make out what I'm looking at.'

'It's a landing,' he said.

'But *which* landing? Where? I can't get it to fit.'

'Sally,' he said, 'are you OK?'

'OK how?'

'I don't know, just OK.'

'I'm fine.' I smiled. 'Tired, that's all.'

'Sure?'

'Course I'm sure.' I looked down again. It was that funny old pale blue on the walls, must be an old part of the building.

'Rob!' someone called. 'Come and get some of this cake!'

'Cake?' I said. 'Wow, who brought that?'

'Someone,' he said, standing back and gazing at me with a vague worried look.

'I'm fine!' I said.

'Come on.' He took my hand.

'In a minute,' I said, 'you go on, I just want to get another angle on this,' and I gave his hand a quick kiss to show how absolutely great everything was, before I pushed him gently away and walked the length of the skylight to see the landing from a different perspective. 'Save me a piece of cake,' I called as his shadow faded away beyond the turret and I took another swig from the drink I'd brought with me. I was sloshed beyond recall. Watch yourself, I told myself severely, don't want to fall down the bloody stairs.

I looked down and found myself staring at the top of someone's head. Brown hair with a parting in the middle, a girl in our old school uniform, green blazer, orange collar, grey socks, limp skirt, standing stock still a room's length below.

I ran, spilled what was left of my wine, emerged into the light where about eight people remained on the roof finishing off the wine and eating slices of chocolate cake from a massive plate resting on a flowerpot.

'Here,' said Robin.

My heart hammered.

The cake was luscious and I concentrated all my senses on it, gorging. It was wrong. Standing so still. What was it? Some more wine, sparkling rosé, refreshing. Soft chocolate, thick cream, cherries, consolation. Get fat. Who was it? A glimpse. I ran. The faces around me were homely, red with cold.

'Sally!'

It was Robin. I won't stay here, I thought. It's too much, it's sending me off my head, and I went to him smiling. How many times in life would I find a sweetheart like him?

I got very drunk that night, horribly so, woke up crying in bed at some lost dark hour, with Rob putting a sick bowl down. 'Oh, my poor love,' he said, 'why do you do this to yourself?'

Sick as a dog in the night.

'It's all right,' he said, hand on my soaking brow. 'You'll be all right in the morning.'

Morning was savage and strange and stupid, with horrible dreamlike flashes of memory sparking randomly in my brain. Did I say all sorts of shaming things in front of all those neighbours? I could vaguely remember stumbling over my words and knowing it, dying inside, brazening the moment, rambling to a woman I didn't know about when Pamela went off the roof, how weird to be there then and now, it really was very strange, and her going, yes, oh yes, that sounds awful, oh what a terrible thing, it must be strange for you, strange, strange, strange.

I couldn't remember how I'd got down. I was fragile for two days, and the next day, when Rob went back to work,

I went into Maggie's, just for the diversion. Rami was there. Chloe was sitting at the table eating some goo from a bowl with a spoon that was too big for her. Gretel scuttled.

'Coffee?' said Maggie.

'Only if you're making one.'

'I'll have one, babe,' Rami said. I hadn't thought he'd be there. He nodded but did not smile at me. I'm one of those awful neighbours, I thought, that's always knocking on your door. Surely not. Or is it because I made an absolute fool of myself the other night? God, what a nightmare.

'Hello, Gretel,' I said as she ran over my foot.

Chloe banged the top of the goo with her spoon and it flattened like quicksand. What did I say? What did I say? Rami looked at me in a funny way. When I smiled, he smiled back but not easily.

'Did I make a fool of myself on New Year's Eve?' I asked.

'God no,' he said, laughing. 'We were all at it. New Year's Eve, for crying out loud. Don't worry.'

'I know but...'

'All fine,' he said, 'all fine. All fine, all fine...'

He disapproves of me. I know.

'Here you go.' Maggie, marching in with a big mug in either hand. 'Is that strong enough for you?'

'Oh lovely!' I said.

'When are you back at work, Sally?'

'Got another week,' I said.

'Not bad.'

'I have time owing.'

She plonked herself down next to the child. 'And are you still all right for Thursday, Sally?'

'Of course.' I hadn't got a clue what she was talking about.

'Eat the bloody stuff, Chlo,' she said.

It came back to me. Dentist, babysitting.

'What time do you want me?'

Buggered if I could remember.

'Could you come over about twenty to?'

'Twenty to two?'

'Twenty to two.'

'Sure, that's fine.'

Pity Rami was there. I don't know what it was I'd imagined. Some conversation, maybe a connection with this big friendly woman. I realised I'd wanted to tell her something of the peculiar way this place was making me feel but it had probably always been a stupid idea. 'Coffee's nice,' I said.

'She won't be any trouble,' said Maggie. 'You won't be any trouble, will you, Coco?'

'Coco the Clown,' I said, for no reason.

'You know,' said Maggie, 'my brother once had a job lighting Coco the Clown's sparklers.'

Me and Rami laughed.

'He never,' said Rami.

'He did. In the circus. Which circus was it? I can't remember. It was in London. You know, in a Big Top and all that, on a common somewhere. Coco the Clown was supposed to run on with a sparkler in each hand and run round the side of the ring or whatever it was he did, and Brian's job was to stand there and light the two sparklers at the right moment, and he said it was terrible because sometimes they didn't catch or the match fizzled out or whatever and Coco the Clown'd be swearing and cursing and missing his cue.'

'What a great job,' I said.

'Ain't run o' the mill,' said Rami. He was sitting, I now saw, right where that silly girl, Gail's sister, had seen whatever she saw. I can see where the desks would have been, so clear, two by two. Pity if you got to share with someone you didn't like. I could see the rows of two-by-two desks across this room, vanishing through the wall beyond the kitchen and into there where the bedrooms must have been. The little girl ate her goo sideways on to the blackboard.

'This place is doing me in,' I said.

'How'd you mean?' asked Rami.

'Too familiar.'

I couldn't remember whether I'd told them or not, there was a huge stretch of time I couldn't remember at all. I could have said anything. Had I already rambled it stupidly, over and over? That look of his again, still friendly but wary.

'It is silly,' I said. I'd say no more.

'She's making a right mess of that, love,' Rami said to Maggie. The kid's bowl, slop.

The shadows would have been just where the line of the rug meets the edge of the table. I wonder if I ever told them about the shadows in their flat?

'Freak me out, it would.' Maggie got up and swiped the bowl.

'What?' asked Rami, looking at me. 'Bad associations?'

'Well – there were some.'

'I hated school.' Maggie went into the kitchen.

'I quite liked my school.' Rami smiled.

'You need an exorcist.' Maggie returned, stooped and picked up Gretel. 'I'm not serious.'

We laughed.

I had to go back. It was quarter past four by my watch, which always ran a bit slow. The sky in the windows was dull, already drained of the light of day. How long it seemed since I'd smelt spring and warmth. Rob should be back by seven. I was supposed to be making spaghetti bolognese but there was bags of time so I thought I'd have a lie-down, not sleep exactly, just zone out for a while under the covers, so I went in the bedroom and found that no one had pulled back the curtains since this morning and the room was dark and fuzzy with shadows, the bed unmade. I turned on the light and met myself in the mirror of the open door of the wardrobe. Made me jump. It didn't look like me. It looked old and weary, red around the eyes, but when I blinked, it was me again. May as well leave the curtains closed, how terrible, a whole day without opening them, lazy slob. But I left the light on and the door ajar so I'd hear if he got back early. You never could tell. It's a good job I don't have a lover, I thought, him dropping in and out of the place any old time. It *is* his flat. A lover, huh – chance'd be a fine thing. I closed the wardrobe door and lay down under the covers without undressing as it opened again, closed my eyes but they wouldn't stay that way. The clock by my head said twenty-five to five. I could see a couple of his shirts sticking out of the wardrobe and the sleeve of a tweedy kind of jacket that I'd never seen him wear. These days he wore a red checked shirt most

259

of the time when he was home. And jeans. His socks were full of holes.

There was a sound somewhere like a slow metronome or an old ticking clock. Can't be in here, I thought, we don't have a clock like that, the kind that used to sit on the mantelpiece when I was a kid and tick away the day and in the night, still audible, tock away the hours in the dark distant land of downstairs. The sound was next door. I closed my eyes. I was opening and closing them like a strobe till I think I must have fallen asleep, because I woke in a vivid thing like reality that I knew was a dream because of the fact that I had tunnel vision. I was walking down a city street at night wearing blinkers, and all I could see was the bit directly before my eyes, but that bit was clearer than anything normally is, the faces of people randomly passing, cracks in the pavement, the flattened grey blobs of chewing gum like an abstract painting. It was raining. Someone shook water from a shutter. Then a face came towards me, blurry but made of brightly clashing colours, pink, snot green and an odd light purple. I didn't want to see it close up because no face should be those colours, so I turned and ran, and the next thing, I was awake for real and the old clock was silent. There was a noise in the living room. It sounded as if someone was slowly tearing up paper.

'Rob!' I called, and the sound stopped. I sat up. The flat was quiet.

'Hi, Rob!' I yelled.

I got up and went into the living room. Everything was normal. I heard footsteps, someone coming up the stairs, a couple of muffled voices, one of them Rob's, then his key in the door.

'That was weird,' I said.

'What was?' He was taking off his coat, hanging it in the hanging place near the door, tired, a bit frowny.

'A funny noise.'

He looked at me, annoyed. 'There's always funny noises,' he said, 'that's what the world is. A big mess of funny noises. What do you want me to do about it?'

I'd slept for over an hour. 'Jesus Christ,' I said, 'is that the time?' I should be making spaghetti bolognese. The thought of it depressed me. 'I think we've got mice.'

'We haven't got mice.'

'No, really, you know that noise like when you've got a hamster. You had a hamster once, didn't you? You know when it's tearing up paper for its nest? Like that.'

He threw himself down. 'Fine,' he said, 'I'm all for a hamster. Get one. Are you putting the kettle on? I'm knackered.'

I went into the kitchen, put the kettle on, started chopping an onion. My eyes watered. Perhaps Gretel followed me, I thought. How silly. A hamster doesn't follow you like a dog.

'You never made that appointment, did you?' he said, standing in the doorway.

'What appointment?' I got the mince out of the fridge.

'See? You're not trying. You promised me you'd make an appointment to see the doctor.'

'All right,' I said, 'no need to go on about it, I'll do it.'

'You should, you know.'

'I will.'

'I don't know, get a tonic or something.'

'Yeah, yeah. I just haven't got round to it.'

'Seriously, love,' he said, 'I worry about you.'

Here we go.

'It's this place,' I said.

Round and round.

'OK!' He nearly shouted. 'If you really want to move, we'll move.'

'Really?'

'Really.'

But I could see how disappointed he was.

Next morning I woke up early. The curtains were closed but a fair amount of light came in over the top and the room had that soft morning dimness. The door stood open. I could see the wall in the alcove with its *Attack of the Fifty Foot Woman* poster. Robin was asleep, breathing deeply.

I lay looking at the ceiling for a while, realised I was hardly likely to get back to sleep now, turned over on my right side to look at the clock and just about made out the time: 7:11. There was a coat hanging on the wall between the window and the back wall. Funny. Why did he hang it there? Too small to be his. Not mine.

It was getting lighter all the time. At first I couldn't make out the colour but soon I saw that it was green. It hung limp with one sleeve towards me, the end of it disappearing into a pocket.

I closed and opened my eyes, drifted. The green coat was always on the wall when I opened my eyes.

The sleeve moved. It came out of the pocket very slowly.

'Rob,' I said, but it was less than a whisper.

It may have hesitated briefly at the no-sound of my voice but I'm not sure. Anyway, it came on steadily out of the pocket.

'Rob,' I said with no voice, 'Rob,' and would have shaken him if I could have moved. Didn't want to attract its attention. I know how stupid that sounds but that's how it was.

There was a hand at the end of the sleeve – coming and coming out of the pocket.

The alarm went off.

I jerked and grabbed Rob. 'Wake up, wake up,' shaking him, 'there's something there.'

He came blinking into the world, saying, 'Wha—'

I burrowed down.

'What's up? Sally, Sally, what's up?'

'A coat.'

'Tell me.'

'A coat. On the wall. With a hand.'

'Only a dream,' he said. 'Oh sweetheart, it's OK. It's all right, it's all right, it was only a dream, a dream, love, everything's OK. Look,' and he turned the lamp on next to the bed. 'Get up from under there, love, it's OK, it's morning now.'

He jumped up and crossed the room, threw back the curtains and let daylight in, so bright I could feel it under the covers. I came out like a snail, slowly, and he put his arms round me, sitting on the edge of the bed wearing only the T-shirt he wore to sleep in. 'See?' he said. 'Nothing there.'

Nothing at all. No coat, only blank wall.

'Do you want a cup of tea,' he said, 'or d'you want to sleep some more?'

'Tea,' I said.

I sat up in bed, letting the world return to normal, watching him pull his underpants on. That's it, I thought, I have to go. It's getting worse.

'I'll be glad when I'm back at work,' I said when he came in with the tea.

'So will I.' He smiled.

'Awful nightmare,' I said.

'Don't tell me about it. Let it go.'

'I will.'

The tea went down warm and soothing. Rob sat next to me on the bed, arm around me, mouth resting in my hair.

'Why don't you get Shanna over,' he said, 'or someone? Or go and see someone. Or – it's not as if you really are on your own – I mean, there's people in all these flats.'

'They're all at work,' I said.

'Maggie isn't.'

'I can't keep going round there.'

'I don't know what to do,' he said, so bleak I could have cried. 'I have to get ready.'

'It's OK,' I said, rallying, 'I just had a horrible dream and it upset me, that's all. I'm OK, honest.'

He stood up.

'I promise,' he said, turning at the door, 'we'll start looking for somewhere else. I promise. I can't see you like this. You never used to be like this.'

*

I spent most of the day out. In the morning I went to see my mum and dad, and in the afternoon went back to town and wandered around the shops. I still had the Christmas money they'd given me, so decided to cheer myself up by spending it. I bought chocolate and wine and a new hairbrush, then saw some shoes I liked in a window, cloggy-looking ones with ox blood and black leather and a platform heel. I wished I hadn't got the other stuff now because I couldn't quite afford them, but then I thought: oh why not, it's been a rotten few days, I shouldn't, oh but I should, oh but what on earth is wrong with me, I must pull myself together. I hadn't really seen that thing, I was half asleep. What a fool to go creeping back to Shanna and Linda's. I could even go back and live at home, watch telly in the evening with Mum and Dad. Shudder.

I went in the shop and they had them in my size. It was amazing – I can never get a pair of shoes to fit, always slipping up at the back or tight in the toe or some damn thing, but these were perfect. I walked up and down, springy on my platforms. It wasn't hard to walk in them at all even though they were higher than I'd thought. I suppose they were three inches.

'I'll keep them on,' I said. 'Can you put these in a bag for me, please?'

'Of course,' said the girl, then she started trying to sell me all kinds of stuff, polish and such, but I was probably already in the red so I said no and paid and walked out into Market Street in my nice new shoes and walked home feeling so much better.

I wore them a lot after that, indoors and out. They made me taller and stronger. Rob liked them too. We went to Chinatown and had a fantastic meal and Stewart came round in the evening and we played Scrabble and I don't know what was so funny but we were all laughing a lot. Next day I wore them to Maggie's when I went to babysit.

'I wondered what it was,' she said. 'You're taller, so you are. They look nice. I can't wear platforms, they kill me.'

'They're surprisingly comfortable,' I said, though in truth I was just becoming aware of a nasty little sharpness in the back of my left ankle.

'There's biscuits in the tin,' she said, 'and you know where the tea and coffee is. She shouldn't need anything, I've just filled her cup. Won't be long, Coco. Kiss kiss! There's my good girl.' And off she went leaving me wondering how to talk to this child playing with her bricks on the floor and doing her best to ignore me. I kneeled beside her. Her mother had rolled the fluffy rug back to give her a flat surface to build on. She'd made quite a sophisticated edifice with big letter blocks for the base and smaller coloured ones on top. The colours, like the fireworks of New Year's Eve, reminded me of a Christmas morning once when I got just such a set for a present, how they'd spilled out of the box shining with impossible brightness.

'That's nice, Chloe,' I said, taking my shoe off. She was a plain child but her neck was sweet and graceful. The back of my ankle was getting ready to blister. I'd need a plaster.

'Boom! Boom!' Chloe slapped her podgy hands on top of the tower and brought it crashing down.

'Oh dear,' I said.

She started building it all back up again. I got up, took the other shoe off and made myself comfortable on the settee. 'Where's Gretel?' I asked her but she didn't answer.

Asleep in the cage, I suppose.

I leaned back. A fat brown teddy the size of a large baby sat stoically at the other end of the settee. 'Hello, Brown Teddy,' I said.

It was terribly hot in here. I started thinking about that girl I'd seen through the skylight. I could have sworn it was our school uniform she was wearing. Nothing wrong with that, nothing at all, why shouldn't a girl stand there, a girl in an old uniform of the school that used to be here – who knows, maybe it was some woman that lives here now, that went to school here, and – why would she be parading around in her old school uniform? Why would you keep it? Chuck it in the canal, along with the horrible hats on the last day of the last year of school, breathing freedom. Perhaps she's sentimental? Schooldays, golden schooldays, best days of your life, what madness. Couldn't wait to get out of the place. Why am I here? Who'd want to hang around in their old school?

Chloe said something.

'What?'

She pointed with a short stubby finger.

'What? Do you want Teddy?'

She shook her head. I couldn't make out what she was pointing at, just looked like a patch of wall. 'Would you like a biscuit?' I said, but she turned away and set about demolishing the latest tower. Boom-boom, slap-slap. A shadow passed across the wall and flickered in the corner of my eye, sunlight, traffic. I felt tired and lay down with my head next to Brown Teddy's. Very carefully, humming softly, she began putting brick by brick, B, H, T, then brick on brick upwards. I closed my eyes. She's so good I could have a little nap and I don't think she'd even notice. Not sleep of course, just doze.

I think I must have dropped off, hardly any time at all I'm sure, but when I woke up she was singing tunelessly and I hadn't even noticed when she started. She was singing: *Iya tella OX-a, Iya tella OX-a...* and the bricks were rising up and up. It had started raining, the sky loured. The drumming noise was Gretel galloping round her wheel. I sat up. *Iya goa gazy la la la la...*

'My goodness, what a big tower,' I said.

'Boom!'

Down it went.

'Why don't you leave it up this time,' I said as she once more laid the foundations, 'so your mummy can see it when she gets back.'

A vague tune was emerging from the muddle of her voice. *Iya tella OX-a* went up the scale and when she got to *OX*, she shouted.

'Goodness me,' I said. I only say things like that and in that tone when I'm talking to a child. They see right through me, as animals pick up on your nerves.

He-e-ey, she said, *h-o-o-o, ho-ho-ho-ho-ho...*

I know that. She's singing—

'I know that song,' I said, sitting up as she started it again, 'we used to sing it.' I sang along:
I have twelve oxen, they be fair and brown, they go a-grazing down by the town, with hey, with ho, with...
Maggie's key turned in the lock.
'Did your mummy teach you that song?'
'Did you miss me?' cried Maggie, flinging off her coat and scarf.
Chloe said something incomprehensible.
'We were having a sing-song,' I said.
'Well, *I've* had a filling,' she said, as if it was a rare treat, her mouth one-sided. 'Don't you just hate it? Can't talk, can't eat.'
'We were singing "I Have Twelve Oxen", weren't we, Chlo,' I said, trying to sound as if we were best friends.
'Lovely,' Maggie said. 'Don't know that one, sing it for me, Coke, go on.'
Chloe stood up with a little jump to attention, hands behind her back, and sang the whole thing through in her pidgin tongue and there was no doubt, no doubt at all that this was our old song and that it would go round and round in my head now for the rest of the night.
'Hooray!'
We clapped and cheered and Chloe sat down again and picked up another brick.
'Well, that's lovely, that's a beautiful palace or what is it you're making there, Chlo? Aren't you the clever one?'
'Where's she got that from?' I said.
'What? The song?'
'It's a really old song.'

'Must've picked it up at playgroup. She goes to playgroup Monday mornings.'

'I haven't heard that song in years,' I said.

'Boom!' went Chloe, bashing away.

'Aw, you're such a wrecker,' said Maggie.

Next day when I was getting up, the gnat-like sound returned. I walked into the bathroom where Rob, wearing only a T-shirt, was cleaning his teeth. 'Can you hear that?' I said.

He rinsed his mouth and spat. 'What?'

'A kind of humming.'

He listened for about ten seconds.

'I can't hear anything.'

'Maybe the fridge.'

I went through the living room where the curtains were still closed, to the kitchen where I filled the kettle at the tap. It wasn't the fridge.

These were dark mornings. While the kettle boiled I went to open the curtains and just for a second, when the dull light emerged, the corner of my eye did that flickery thing so that something rippled on the edge of vision. It was starting to rain. Rob came out with his hair all over the place. I liked him tousled, bare-arsed in the mornings. 'Toast,' he said, making for the kitchen.

'It's not the fridge.' I followed him in.

'Are you making tea, love?' he said, then his eyes slid to the window. 'It's the rain,' he said. 'You're hearing the rain.'

After I'd watched him walk across the park, not hurrying

in the light rain, I decided I'd spend the day sorting out my clothes. I was running out of things to wear, things needed mending, ironing, chucking out, so I went into the bedroom and started randomly pulling things out of the wardrobe. The rain whispered at the window but it didn't hide the sound. 'Load of crap,' I said aloud, took a pile of stuff into the living room, flung it on the settee and went in search of needles and cotton. There was a top with a burst seam which would be OK for work, and thank God I was back in the morning. Searched high and low and there wasn't any; own fault, I thought, should have got some, couldn't expect *him* to have that sort of thing. And he needn't think I'm doing his sewing for him either – not that he'd asked. I'd have to borrow from Maggie.

I opened the door and put my head out. You couldn't hear the rain in the corridor. And no sound. I didn't want to bother Maggie, but it was that or go out in the rain so I put the latch on and was stepping out when, as if a door had opened, the sound of singing came from an upper floor. You couldn't make out words but singing it undoubtedly was, and it had been all along. All those midge-mumblings and fridgy hummings now resolved into the real sound of girls' voices.

The door must have closed, because the sound was once more faint, but now that I knew what it was it was easy to hear and I wondered why I hadn't recognised it much sooner.

I don't know how long I stood there like a fool, straining my ears towards the sound as the morning light slanted across the stairwell. It was enchanting. I went to the stairwell, looked up. Half way up the stairs I stopped and listened. The upper landing was flooded with bright light.

Marianina...

I caught the faintest hint of piano. Still in my dressing gown, barefoot, with sleep in my eyes and uncombed hair, I went higher. The tune went down in staggered cascades, I knew it well – *Marianina, little friend, whither whither do you wend...* girls' voices tripping along as I ascended, till I reached the next floor, the next empty corridor, where it stopped abruptly. I walked right along the middle of the corridor. It was all too light and early and normal to be scary, but there was a pitter-patter in my heart and I watched my bare feet closely as they strode along looking quite biblical under the stripy hem of my dressing gown.

The music started again but now, in that maddening way that sound can move, it seemed to come from the other end of the building –

Marianina, do not roam, whither, whither is your home, come and turn us into foam

– and when I got to the top of the stairs it had muffled itself under a blanket.

I chased it along the top floor but by the time I reached the other end it had already moved up to the roof. It was very close. I stood still. I got the urge to go up on the roof in the pouring rain just because I could. Me and Pamela would have done. Not because I really thought I'd find three rows of girls in green jumpers and yellow blouses singing their hearts out in the rain, but just because it would be nice to be up there with it all hammering down on my head. By the time I got up there, though, the sound would have moved again, and I wasn't going to chase it round all day, so I defied it and went down instead and only realised when I got back that I hadn't gone to Maggie's for the needle and thread and now I couldn't be bothered.

It was still going on. Only now it sounded as if it was under water.

This school's too full of its old self, I thought. Twelve oxen, Marianina, the madwoman in her old school uniform still hanging around the place. But then what was *I* doing? Hanging round in my old school, pathetic.

I got dressed quickly, pulled my fingers through my hair, put on my new shoes and went out. As I was going down to the back door I heard footsteps coming down from a flight or so behind me, scuffling on the stone stairs. At the foot of the stairs I looked back. I could have sworn someone pulled back out of sight.

I didn't wait. I pulled my hood up and over my head and hurried across the yard in the old familiar diagonal to the gate.

So lovely to walk out into the wet street and see the world going its sane old normal way. I breathed in the fumes and rain, and a food smell from somewhere, like school dinners. Gravy from a ladle. I looked in my purse. Enough for food. I wasn't going back till much later. Might give Shanna a ring, no, she'll be at work, no good. I found a place to sit and drink coffee in a window watching the people go by with their hoods and umbrellas. I got a second cup with a tuna sandwich and a slice of Bakewell tart; after I'd wolfed it down a sick feeling came into my throat, and I was suddenly terrified.

It was real, I heard it. *Ma-a-a-arianina, Ma-a-a-arianina.*
And if it was real, what did that mean?

I managed to stay out till four. I went to see a film, then I
bought plasters to protect my heel and walked all over the
place in the rain, even as far as the docks, at which point I
realised I was getting lost and turned back.

It was lovely and warm in the flat. Robin was home.

'You're early,' I said.

'I am indeed.' He was sprawled on my clothes pile on the
settee, eating an apple. 'Your shoe's bleeding,' he said.

'Actually,' I sat down and eased it off, 'it's my foot.'

'So it is.'

'You back for the day?'

'Yeah. Dead quiet at work. Sneaked off.'

'Not like you.'

'My love,' he said facetiously, 'I wanted to be with you.
You're soaking wet.'

In the bathroom I grabbed a towel and rubbed my
hair. Getting changed in the bedroom I heard it again, far
away, downstairs this time, I thought, but it could have
been anywhere. 'That's it,' I said, zipped up my jeans and
marched out. 'Listen!' I dragged Robin up from the settee.
'Come and listen to this.'

'What?'

'Come on, come on.' To the door and out. I made him
stand still in the corridor and we both listened.

'I can't hear anything,' he said.

'Ssh!'

It was upstairs and growing louder, fading in on an
unknown wave length.

'I really can't—'

'Ssh!'

'I'm trying.'

I took his hand and we walked to the stairwell. We looked up at the big window, getting dark now, and there was no doubting it. The singers were reaching the end – *come and turn us into rain* – and, 'Can you hear it now?' I said.

'Yeah.' He grinned, looking a bit sheepish.

'Above or below?'

'It is funny,' he said, 'the way sound can travel in these old buildings.'

A door closed above.

'It's just some singing,' he said.

'It's "Marianina". We used to sing it.'

'Ah! Creepy!' He laughed.

'Listen though.'

Because it was fading away.

'OK,' he said.

'Listen!'

'I know.'

'Why is it doing that?'

Because it was beginning again, but the words were no longer even slightly decipherable, and it was under our feet.

'Doing what?'

'*That*. You know. You *know*. As if it's under the water.'

'It's the acoustics.'

'You know that's not right. Sound doesn't move like that.'

'*I* don't know, I'm not a sound technician,' he said. 'Look, Sally, I'm not getting into all that other stuff. It's just singing. I'm not interested in where it's coming from. Do you want me to go door to door demanding to know what music everyone's playing?'

'Don't be ridiculous.'

'Well, I don't know where it's coming from and neither do you. What's the big deal? Don't try and make something out of it. You don't have to. We'll move, it's sorted, OK?'

When I brought up the move again he said, 'It's not so bad here, is it, Sal? Might be a good idea to leave it till spring, it's not that far off, and honestly we're both so busy now.' I was back at work so wasn't on my own there so much, and I just let things roll on when I should have insisted. I still kept hearing it, though, the singing, fainter and fainter, sometimes in the middle of the night, and when that happened there was no chance of getting to sleep again so I'd just lie there straining my ears, and all day long that tune would go through and through my mind like a record on repeat.

It must have been around this time that I started imagining I was going to meet the Sylvia-thing. I'd go out and be sure it'd be just round the next turn of the stairs, or I'd come in and think the footsteps coming down towards me were its footsteps. My heart would go into mad overdrive. But it was just the people in other flats.

The trouble is, once you start thinking of things in this way it's very hard to stop. I started feeling as if it wasn't finished, the past, the whole thing, as if all that stuff with Pamela and Sylvia had just happened yesterday. I'd catch things in the corner of my eye and look around to find nothing. It's like opening the third eye, I suppose, that's what I thought. Only I thought that was supposed to be a good thing, but this didn't feel good. Everything about the place reminded me, and a creeping feeling grew that if I stayed here I was going to have to face it all again even though that made no sense at all.

Then one day I came home and realised I hadn't heard the singing for ages but by that time it didn't matter, I just had to go. It fell upon me suddenly sitting on the settee in the silence, a terrible urge just short of panic, leave now before it's too late.

I rang Shanna to see if I could go there, not for long, I said, only till—

'Oh no!' she cried. 'You're breaking up with Rob! No!'

'No, no, it's just complicated...'

She was flustered, apologising, her boyfriend had moved in for good, she'd have to see, listen, let me get back to you...

'Not at all,' I said as she floundered, 'no problem, honestly, really, it's OK, it's not important.'

Linda, I thought, but no, she'd moved far out to some place near Bury; getting to work from there would be a nightmare. Mum and Dad. *God* no. That street, the twins, the nosy old neighbours, the sheer stifling tedium. The failure returns. So I sat and sat with it all chasing round in my head and it was like a dream from which I couldn't wake up. I was still sitting there when he came in an hour later. He took one look at me and said, 'What?'

'I can't live here.'

His eyes glazed.

'Go on then, go on,' he said. 'I know what you're going to say.'

'You're always saying we can move but you never do anything about it.'

'Me? Couldn't you?'

'It's *much* easier for you.'

'Why is it? You think I'm not busy?'

'You like doing all that stuff.'

'Oh yeah, love it. Don't be stupid.'

'It's not you,' I said, 'it's the place.'

He glared at me and said, 'Yamma, yamma, yamma,' and I burst into tears.

'You just don't care,' I said.

'Don't you dare say that. It's you that doesn't care, you haven't cared about me for ages. Do you think I don't notice anything?' I was scared of his anger. He never got angry. 'You've not been happy since you moved in. All this crap about the place is just an excuse, I think it's me. You don't want to be with me. And I don't want to fuck around any more, I want the truth.'

'That's what I'm trying to tell you. It's not you. It's not. But I can't stay here.'

'You're cold to me,' he said. 'Don't you realise how cold you are to me?'

Was I? I couldn't be any different.

'You only use people.' He swiped at his face. 'That's all you've ever done. As long as I was useful to you, it was fine. Now it's not. I'm expendable. So go.'

He went into the bathroom, slamming the door.

How can that be true, I thought. I'm not like that, I'm not

a nasty person. Me, use him till it's not working? Everything was collapsing. The world beneath me felt like rubble turning to dust and I had nowhere to go.

'So we'll move,' he said, reappearing. 'I don't think there's any other way.'

'You really think that's what I'm like?'

'Don't cry,' he said. 'All I'm asking for is honesty.'

But then he started crying too and I couldn't bear that. I did love him. I went to him and tried to put my arms round him but he wasn't having it. 'I can't imagine you not being in my life, Rob,' I said, 'honestly, it just doesn't figure.'

This whole part of my life was an aberration, no more.

'It's *her*,' I said.

'What are you talking about?' He walked away, stood looking aimless and sulky as if wondering where he'd put his keys.

'I'm scared,' I said. 'I can't help it.' An edge of panic crept into my voice. 'I don't want us to break up, I don't. I'm scared.' I shivered. I felt weak and sat down, grabbed my head with both hands because it felt as if it was about to fly off. 'I just can't live in this place. It's eating me.'

'Sally, you sound weird.'

'I know.'

'I don't know what to do.'

'Neither do I.' I laughed.

He sat down next to me but I didn't look at him. 'Who's *her*?' he asked.

How explain? Too hard. 'I told you before. Sylvia Rose. When Pamela died, how it all went weird at school, when I saw Sylvia on the roof?'

'Who?'

'Oh, for God's sake, Rob! You never took it seriously. It's her. I keep thinking she's still here.'

'I don't understand this at all.'

'That's the trouble.'

He made a fist and gritted his teeth. 'Make me understand it then. I'm trying.'

But everything I could find to say sounded stupid. I tried. I sounded mad.

'I'm trying,' he said, 'I really am. Sylvia? That girl who fell down? I remember Sylvia.'

'It's not her,' I said. 'It looks like her but I don't know what it is.'

The scared look he gave me then turned my blood cold. 'Do you know what that sounds like?' he said.

'I do.'

'You never rang the doctor, did you? You said you would.'

'I was going to. But I think if I could just get out of here…'

He was gazing somewhere far away, like a child seriously trying to work out something much too hard for him. '*That* Sylvia?' he said. 'She's not even dead. I don't even understand what you're saying, are you saying she's a ghost?'

'Dead? I didn't say she was dead. I didn't say it was her.'

He put his head in his hands.

'That poor girl,' he said gently. 'She was so shy. How can you be scared of her?'

I jumped up. 'What do you think it's like to be scared like this, day after day?' I cried. 'And you expect me to stay here?'

'Don't cry.' He looked up.

'You're safe enough,' I said, 'that's why you never notice anything. It's not about you. It's me. She peeps round corners. Every time I close my eyes I can see her.'

'I don't know what to do, sweetheart. I'm—' He shrugged and looked up at the ceiling. 'I'm glad it's come to a head. We can sort this out.'

'Are you listening?'

'I am. We can sort this out, you and me. We'll start looking for another place tomorrow. First thing. And you have to ring the doctor. Just go and talk to someone, please. We're sorting things out.' He took both my hands. 'It's OK, I'll *make* it OK.'

I couldn't stand this any more. We put our arms round each other and made up but it was embarrassing rather than cathartic and I wanted to get away. The burden of him was too much.

'You will, won't you?' he said. 'Make an appointment with the doctor?'

'All right,' I said to put him at ease.

'There's nothing to be scared of. I won't leave you alone if that would help. I'll get time off. It won't take long. Find a place. Couple of months. You can manage that, yeah? Couple of months and I can get time off. Can you manage that? Sally?'

This would drive me mad. Poor Sally! What a shame. Gone bonkers.

'Yes,' I said, but all my pulses were pounding. We went to bed and I felt shy, as if I hardly knew him. He treated me like an invalid, I half expected him to bring me a bowl. For a long time I lay on my side pretending to be asleep, heard his breathing change to the sleep rhythm and lay wide awake still, listening to my fractured thoughts gabbling at one another as if I wasn't there. Three o'clock came. He snored peacefully. Goes both ways, I thought, getting angry, not just me to blame. I try but what am I supposed to do? Why should I stay? What about all I've given up so he won't be hurt? Doesn't that count?

It was so horribly sad and unstoppable. I did drift off for a while towards morning. He got up carefully, kissed my cheek before he left. Then my eyes opened wide and I had the strangest feeling, as if the place would never let me go. I got up and called the doctor and made an appointment for next week, then I went to work. He was there when I got home, with a bunch of flowers, a sheaf of estate agents' leaflets and a young cat. He got her from a shelter so I suppose she must have had a rough upbringing, and she didn't want anything to do with us. She ran under the settee and I put down a saucer of tuna to try and coax her out, because of course he hadn't thought to get food and bowls and cat litter and all that stuff. I put newspaper down under the window.

'Leave her,' I said, 'she'll come out when she's ready.' We looked through the leaflets and none of them were as nice as this place.

He made such an effort, getting home by seven every night, bringing treats, chocolates, Oolong tea from Chinatown, milky Indian sweets. I didn't hear the singing any more.

I called my cat Mabel. She was small and black and lithe

and when she emerged from her two days under the settee she wouldn't use the litter tray I bought her. It was awful: every time I came home from work I'd find neat little piles of shit on the newspaper all around the tray but never in it, and it stank the place out. I'd imagined a dear little friend who'd sit next to me in the evening and sleep on the bed at night but she kept well clear of us, and every time I looked at her I felt sad for her. No life for a cat, kept in all the time. The doctor told me it was good to have a pet. He said I could have tranquillisers if I wanted to (I'd hardly told him a thing, just that I felt nervous in the flat) but to be honest, he said, he didn't think I was too bad; I'd be just fine in the long run. Come back if you're not feeling better in two or three weeks.

Rob was outraged. 'Doesn't know what he's talking about,' he said. 'You should have taken the prescription, Sal.'

And I was almost thinking that we'd roll along like this indefinitely when something happened.

I had a time-slip on a bank holiday Monday morning, about eleven o'clock. It wasn't unpleasant and not so much scary as interesting. It was a lovely day, the first we'd had that carried a tinge of spring. Robin was off work too, having a good lie-in, something he hardly ever did. I hadn't for the life of me been able to sleep since six o'clock so I got up and kicked about the flat. Mabel sat on top of the record player, staring at me in an accusing way. By the time I'd cleaned up round the litter box and had a shower and eaten some toast the sunlight streaming in was so brilliant I decided to go for a wander round town, see what was open.

I got as far as the stairwell. I don't know what made me turn and look back.

On either side of the long corridor were high glass windows coming half way to the floor. The ceiling was too high, yet shadowy and oppressive at the same time. It was so quiet I could hear the blood in my ears. I wasn't surprised. I moved back along the corridor, stood on tiptoe and peered through a window. 4 Alpha. Miss Oliver was speaking to a class. Rows of girls, the backs of their heads. Miss Oliver wore a bottle-green dress underneath her black gown and was sitting behind the front desk, smiling timidly. She spoke but no sound came out of her mouth.

I walked further along. Behind all the closed doors were classes at their desks but I couldn't find our class. The stairs went up to a bright arch of window. The smell of school dinners rose rich and heavy. I saw with huge exactitude the likeness of a pale blue jug with a round belly and curvaceous spout, in the top of it an uneasy queasiness of pallid custard that was beginning to solidify. Now I could hear the voices of girls, downstairs I thought, but I didn't trust sound in this place. It was too real. Everything. The shaky school feeling in my stomach. I needed to start coming round. One of those lucid dreams you can control, keep hold of the destination, which is to wake up.

I found myself by the back door as if I'd just left my flat and was on my way out for a walk. My hand was on the door handle, and I was about to turn it when I realised someone was standing near the top of the basement stairs. It was the wet woman, standing still and looking at me with no expression and water dripping down her face.

I ran back upstairs. I don't know why I was so scared of her, but it struck me as a very bad thing to see her.

At the end, opposite the stairs, was the Gym, its door open. Empty, wall bars, ropes, the horse, the buck, the box, mats. An echo rose from the silence, a murmur of limp gym shirts, grey skirts, navy blue knickers. Someone in one of the classrooms was singing a silly song in a silly voice. It involved a chorus of: *Boo-hoo! Boo-hoo!* In a crude raucous Widow Twanky voice that the whole class joined in with.

It should surely be going away now, the hum of girls like sleepy bees in a hive, and an upper level of sound, the shrieky ones, the clowns, the strident. Pamela had been a bit like that, only her voice wasn't shrieks, it was deep and tough and not to be messed with. Had I dreamt the last twelve years and was I really still here, still wanting, wanting always to be somewhere else *with* someone else, somewhere where the air did not smell heavy with gravy, where the light was less dim and flat and blank. Brown tiles, grey underfoot, the boredom, the tiredness, the stairs I walked up every day, year after year, with tears in my chest, wanting out of it all. What a way to live. Sometimes I was so unhappy here.

And yet – it was also beautiful, perversely – these girls with their silliness and nastiness and unreadiness, all of them unaware of the ocean before them. I wished I could have seen them this way at the time. But all I'd known then was the boredom and fear, the feeling of ice shifting beneath my feet.

I had to get back to now. I closed my eyes.

Ma-a-a-arianina! Ma-a-a-arianina! Come, oh come, and turn us into foam.

It had all gone when I opened my eyes.

Robin was up and in the bath. I went in. He lay full length, fringed with suds. 'Oh, there you are,' he said.

'Here I am,' I said, as if nothing had happened. 'I was going out for a walk but I changed my mind.'

'Lovely day. Why did you change your mind?'

'Suddenly very tired,' I said, which was true. 'I've been up since six. Going for a nap.'

That's all I wanted to do. Lie down. Let me sleep. Let my mind go to mush. Let me go.

But when he was dry and dressed he came and sat on the side of the bed and stroked my hair. He sat so thoughtfully that time passed, keeping me from sleep.

'I was thinking,' he said, with his dear face, 'do you think if you could talk to Sylvia – the actual Sylvia – and hear what she has to say, that might help?'

I was horrified. I couldn't speak.

'Well, I mean,' he said, 'you're still thinking about it, I know you are, making it into something weird in your head, I don't know, it's some kind of fixation and it's making you unhappy, love.'

I felt as if I had to answer for something but didn't know what. 'I haven't said anything,' I said.

'But I know. I know you.'

'I don't want to see Sylvia.'

'That's OK,' he said kindly, 'just an idea. Just thought if

you could talk about whatever it was that happened back then, the two of you, and see how it had all looked to her – I mean, it involved her, didn't it? – and if she remembers things differently, whether it would make you realise that—'

'No.'

'It was just a thought.'

'No.'

'OK.' He got up, smiling and conciliatory. 'OK, OK, you have a nice sleep,' and went out, closing the door softly.

I saw him as if from a great distance, as if aeons had passed and I was another me in another life looking into a magic scrying glass and seeing this nice boy so far back, one I never truly appreciated. The first I loved. Only at the time I didn't call it that, I called it going out with Robin. And somehow I'd ended up here with him, and the constant inner strain of not wanting to be in this place and not wanting to hurt him was wearing me out.

However could I have thought it was a good idea to come back to this place? All the dreams over the years when I'd been back here – I'd walked the stairs and corridors so many times in endless repetition like a ghost, not quite understanding the rules of the place, and woken in relief, saying, oh thank God, it was a dream!

I'd drifted through the weekend, staying in bed a lot, in and out, his presence both comforting and irritating, coming and going beside me in the bed. Woke early on Sunday, found him gone. Went for a walk around all my favourite back streets, still trying to shake the remnants of a certain detachment I'd been feeling since Friday morning. In a funny sort of way I felt as if I hadn't woken up since then. It had been a dream, I thought, and what I'd thought had been the waking, when I'd gone in and found Robin in the bath and he'd come in and told me to go to sleep, had probably just been another bit of the dream. I wasn't sure which bits were in and which were out. Of course I knew I was awake now, these streets I'd always known. But some dreams were very convincing. It shocked you when you woke.

Another nice day. I loved town on a quiet Sunday. The bells rang from the cathedral. Hardly anyone was about. I stood for a long time in tall narrow Mangle Street where me and Rob used to snog, and in spite of the pissy smell and the litter, it seemed, with its weary closed shutters and black windows, like the most beautiful place on earth. I was quite serene by the time I floated back, in my red platform shoes now more broken in but still a little sore on one toe, to the dread building.

That was quiet too. My own footsteps on the stairs were the only sound. I couldn't even hear a radio anywhere.

As I opened the door, I heard voices in my flat, Rob and a woman.

I stood in the hall trying to place the voice.

They were speaking in low confidential tones as if bending towards one another, and at one point he said something and chuckled and she laughed too, a fast, polite laugh.

I opened the door. They were drinking coffee, him on the

settee, she in the armchair. A tall pale young woman with a pleasant, haunted face and shy demeanour.

She smiled with a show of warmth. 'Hello, Sally,' she said.

I felt dizzy. I wanted a drink desperately, something that had never happened at this time of day before. 'Hello,' I said, trying to make sense of her face, never seen her before in my life but something was there, a trace.

She had a fringe and long straight hair hanging down to her waist.

'Don't you recognise her?' Rob said, grinning.

Sylvia Rose.

I wanted to kill him.

'You look really different, Sylvia,' I said, 'took me a while to recognise you.'

'Oh, I recognised you, Sally, straight away.' She cradled her mug with ringed fingers. Her nails were clear varnished and looked very pink and healthy. 'I'd have recognised you anywhere. You haven't changed a bit.' Her eyes were prominent, far more so than I remembered, and her voice was different, lower and less plummy, more confident.

'Well,' I said, 'this is – amazing,' and we all laughed.

'So, how did—'

'I looked her up,' said Rob. 'Easy. You work in a library, you know that. You just look on the electoral register.'

'Well, of course.'

I could just walk out again. Say nothing.

'So, you're a librarian now,' she said.

'A library assistant. Not quite the same.'

'Oh.'

'I have to take an exam to be a proper librarian.'

'Oh, I see. Will you, do you think?'

What had they been laughing about, talking so cosy? Talking about me.

'I might,' I said. 'Probably. Yes, why not? I enjoy working there.'

My face was hot. What had he said? *Oh Sylvia, poor Sally's in an awful state, can't cope, all sorts of funny ideas she has, I wondered if*, talk, talk, talk – How dare he? I tried to tell him with my look, but he dropped his eyes and glanced at Sylvia. 'So look,' he said, 'I think it'd be really good if, you know, you two had a good chat about things' – a quick swivel of the eyes to me, a grin – 'I just think, you two you know, look, I'm just nipping out for one or two things. So I'll leave you two together, yeah?'

Oh, for God's sake, just go, you fool, I wanted to shout, and at the same time, no, no, don't leave me alone with her. But he went, cheerfully pulling on his jacket and practically walking backwards, darting his anxious glances. After the door had closed and his footsteps had died away down the stairs we just sat and looked at one another, me one end of the coffee table, she, vaguely smiling, the other. I looked her up and down. Her face was thinner than before. She wore jeans and a denim jacket and a plain peacock-blue silk top.

'What did he say to you?' I asked her.

'Oh, not very much.' I couldn't get over all those rings she wore. I wouldn't have thought she'd be the type. They were sensible and understated but there were so many of them that they reminded me of neck rings and gave her a faint touch of austere exotica. 'He said he thought you were still traumatised from when Pamela jumped off the roof,' she said frankly, 'and that talking about it might help.'

My cat Mabel walked in and stared crossly at the two of us. I said nothing. I'll kill him, I thought. 'Oh, I don't think I'm unreasonably traumatised,' I said, 'he's a worrier.'

'He did say something rather odd.' She put her mug down with deliberation.

'Oh. Did he?'

What a fucking cheek. I couldn't remember her hair being that straight and she'd never had a fringe like that before, dark and straight and a bit straggly. She peered up through it with serious, muted eyes, none of that troubled frown between the eyes, none of the veiled anger she once had. 'He said you had a strange idea about me,' she said.

'Oh well' – I walked into the kitchen with a great air of not caring – 'he's got that all wrong.'

I came back with a bottle of wine and two glasses and plonked them down.

'Wanna drink?'

'Thank you,' she said.

I just had to brazen this thing out, whatever it was. I was surprised she'd accepted a drink so I poured her a large one.

'Thank you,' she said again, sipping. Mabel had approached and was cautiously sniffing her jeans.

'He does get some very silly ideas,' I said.

'So you're OK, are you?' Sylvia looked down into her drink.

'Pretty much.' I wasn't going to perform. 'Or I will be when we're out of here. Too many memories. Should have realised.'

She looked around, taking everything in. 'I can imagine,' she said.

'It just doesn't suit me to live here, that's all. We're moving, you know.'

'Oh, where to?' Smiling, with politely clasped hands.

'We don't know yet.'

Sylvia put her hand down to the cat. Mabel flicked her tail and sidled under the chair. The sunlight coming in shone very brightly on Sylvia, showing her milk-pale skin and the paleness of her watery eyes. She had a dreamy short-sighted look. We sat for a while in awkward silence, and I don't think she had any more idea what to say than I did. He'd put us in an awful bind.

'How about you?' I said. 'What are you up to these days?'

'I work with fabrics,' she said. Turned out she measured out bolts of cloth for customers in a store on Deansgate.

'Do you still sing?'

She looked sideways. Her eyes darkened but maintained their serenity. 'I don't sing any more,' she said as if it was nothing, 'not for years.'

'You're joking!'

She gave a little laugh as if embarrassed. 'I just stopped, you know. Funny, isn't it?'

I had not been prepared for how this would hit me. 'I can't believe it. It was your *thing*.'

'Oh, I know...' a small shrug, raised eyebrows.

'But that's what you did!' To me this was more dreadful than anything, that someone so incredibly talented could give up, that this was nothing to her and she was stable and calm and existing without her genius. She saw my reaction and smiled. 'You know I had that panic attack in the greenhouse?' she said. 'I think this might be what we're expected to talk about,' and she leaned towards me in an intimate way so that I automatically drew in also.

'I just lost interest,' she said, 'after the panic attack. So I just stopped.'

I was expected to comment.

'You gave up altogether? All of it? Music and singing?'

'Yes,' she said without remorse.

It would be wrong to say I'd pictured her in a posh dress at the Royal Festival Hall, because I'd never pictured her at all. But if I had, that's where I'd have seen her, in a concert hall at a tall microphone with a pianist accompanying, the polite ripple of an audience subsiding into reverent expectation before she opened her mouth and sang.

'What did you see up there, Sylvia?'

'Nothing,' she said.

'What happened?'

She blinked. 'I hardly remember. They said it was a panic attack. It's not a nice thing. It was a breakdown of sorts, which is why I didn't come back to school.'

'They didn't tell us anything,' I said, 'just, Sylvia's not coming back.'

'It was a very odd experience.' She looked sideways and down, with the stillness in her face of a Madonna in an old painting. 'The thing that really bothers me,' she said, 'is that I can't remember going up there in the first place. And I still' – shaking her head – 'after all these years can't imagine why on earth I would have gone there.'

'You don't remember? You don't remember playing Pick-up Sticks in the hall and I was talking to you?'

'Oh goodness, no.'

'You don't remember seeing anything through the greenhouse window?'

'Nothing, Sally.' The way she looked at me, with wry mouth and sympathetic eyes, made me want to thump her. 'I think this is what Robin was talking about,' she said gently.

Oh great. Poor Sally's seeing things.

'You have no memory of looking out onto the roof and...'

'Not a thing.'

I looked at this Sylvia, whoever she was. She solved nothing. There was no need to be afraid of her, her eyes wouldn't change, she wasn't what I'd seen on the roof all those years ago.

'But I got a knock on the head,' she said, 'did you know that?'

'No.'

'It was when I was coming down. I tripped on those very narrow stairs coming down from the greenhouse, if you remember them, and I knocked my head. I was actually out for a while, and I don't know if you ever had the experience but I can tell you, it's extremely disturbing; it's when you're coming round.' Her calm, worried face belittled me. 'Sally,' she said, 'I honestly have no memory whatsoever of seeing anything out of the ordinary while I was in the greenhouse. The only mystery to me is why I was up there in the first place because I honestly don't remember what I'd gone for – it must have been something – I just remember being there and feeling very scared and trying to get down the stairs. I

don't even remember falling. I don't remember anything at
all till I was in Miss Demery's room and my dad was there
and Miss Frith. Miss Demery was so nice to me.'

'You liked Miss Demery?'

'Oh yes! But then after I got home I wasn't very well for
a while. I had a sort of a breakdown.' She gave a small, self-
deprecating laugh and I wondered if she was on some kind
of medication. It was then that I began to suspect of myself
that I truly had no heart. I felt nothing for Sylvia and knew
that I should. It just wasn't there. I thought of Robin setting
all this up and telling her things about me, and I felt nothing
for him either. Inside me was the endless Steppe, lonely and
beautiful, that nothing could ever touch.

'And after that,' she concluded, 'I went home with the
all clear, you know, I had tests and things, and my parents
didn't want me to go back to school so they got someone to
come in and give me lessons.'

'I'd have loved that,' I said, knocking back my wine and
pouring another, 'to have got out of going to school. I hated
it.'

She laughed her quiet laugh. 'I suppose we had that in
common,' she said. 'I wasn't too keen on it either.' She sat
back with a conclusive movement. 'All water under the
bridge,' she said. 'You were OK. Pamela, though, I don't
think she was a very nice person. Not really.'

But that was me, I thought. I did that to you. Not her.
She just got the blame. And that's where we ran out of
things to say. I suppose it's OK, fabrics, I thought. There are
worse things. Not to sing at all, though, that was criminal.
I could never have been Cleopatra, never had what it took.

She, though, she had it and let it go. Posh Sylvia with her music room at home and the big garden. Not university? Something clever and important?

Fabrics.

'And,' I said, 'are you married? Or...'

'No. I live with my parents.'

I can't remember how we spent the rest of the time. Small talk, I suppose.

By the time Rob came back I'd drunk half the bottle and she'd only had one glass. I was heavy, tired and headachey, but she wouldn't go. She sat there, he sat there, very pleased with himself, chatting pointlessly away. Is it still warm out? Not too bad, why don't you have another cup of coffee? No trouble. He kept glancing at me with encouraging smiles: look there, see, didn't that help, don't you feel better now? See, she's just an ordinary girl, nothing weird there.

'Are you all right, love?' he said.

'Got a headache.' I wasn't speaking any more.

'I'll get you some paracetamol.' He jumped up. 'Hang on.'

'Why don't you go and lie down,' said Sylvia, being kind to the inadequate.

'That's a good idea.' He dropped to a loose squat in front of me. 'You go and lie down for a bit and I'll bring you some paracetamol and a cup of tea.'

'I think I will.' I got up, refusing his hand. He came with me anyway, fussing away, hovering, bringing water, searching my eyes for traces of how it had all gone with Sylvia, but I wasn't giving anything away. When he left, I closed my eyes. I didn't think I'd fall asleep but I did, a heavy, deep sleep, just what I needed, though it can't have lasted very long because when I woke up the sky outside had hardly changed and Sylvia was still here. I could hear her voice, then his, going back and forth, very easy with one another. I got up and went into the living room and saw them through the kitchen door.

There was food on the stove, last night's soup being gently heated through. Had he asked her to stay for a bite? I couldn't hear their words but imagined them talking about me with well-meaning condescension. Robin and Sylvia, home in the flat, me listening at the door. I drew closer. Rob was feeding the cat. 'Look at that cat,' he said. 'She's not usually friendly like that.' Mabel sat on the cupboard watching them with unreadable eyes.

'She's a nice cat,' Sylvia said.

'It's cos she knows she's getting fed.' Robin forked mush into the cat's bowl. Sylvia leaned on the counter, looking up at him sideways. Look at them, I thought, you can just about see it pass like a shrill nerve between them. She'll do better by him than me. She was a cold fish really, I imagined him saying to her when they were easy enough to talk that way. And he'd be right. He'd say it kindly. But then I thought: no, he's too honourable to say a thing like that, though who can tell? If you could be a shadow on the wall, who knows what you'd see and hear?

They didn't know I was standing there listening.

I remembered then that this was only a dream. I hadn't actually got up off that bed in there – the one I could sneak back into if I had a mind to – and if I went back in I may even be able to see myself still lying there fast asleep. I wouldn't do that. I felt so peculiar, as if I might be going to faint. It's the place, it's always been the place. I really must get out of here.

I'd go now, just as I was. That would give them something to think about. I saw my shoes lying skew-whiff on the rug and tiptoed over and put them on. They didn't hear me slip out into the corridor, silently closing the door. I can control this, I thought. Step by step, one foot in front of the other in the centre of the corridor, my nice newish red-brown platform shoes walking away from the doorway. I'd go down. Lately it seemed whenever I'd tried to go out something would turn me back, but no – wait – had I not been walking outside just this morning? Or was that yesterday? Or was I dreaming then? I can control this, I thought, if I can just keep calm.

At the head of the stairs the sun was creeping yellow on the windowsills below. I nearly tripped because the lights were giving me shadow caterpillars in my eyes. It was three or four steps down, my left shoe turned on its platform. I staggered and had to grab the wall and it's true what they say, your heart flies out of your mouth and you reel, and the stone steps look cold and brutally hard. But I righted and collected myself, took a cautious step, found my ankle untwisted though crying out, and went on down.

Whew! Could've been nasty.

And on the next bend in the staircase I felt the scene change behind my back, but I didn't look over my shoulder because the floor below had also changed, just like it did before. But it was OK. Still a dream, just a dream, a lucid dream to be handled and controlled. I could make things happen. Anything I wanted.

As if it was pre-ordained I moved down the stairs, not sure that I could feel my feet, though I could still feel a twisted shriek of pain in my left ankle from time to time. I couldn't have said I was floating exactly – it was something other than that and quite compelling, as if I was the eye of a camera speeding up towards the turn of the staircase, zooming in towards the shiny brown tiles. Quite lovely, they were, I suddenly realised, and so too the old building. Legion upon legion of shadowy girls and boys swarmed in layers about the place. I felt them rustling in the air.

I should have gone out; the door to the yard was there but I had no means of opening it so I went down to the basement instead and, oh my heart, it was the same, the eternal same with the long shadows and the toilet block and the cloakrooms yawning at each end. Above, the murmurous school. The door to the nether world was open so I sneaked in. Nothing had changed on the narrow stair. When I reached the bottom it was still there, the place with the boiler and the benches to sit on. Now, though, it was empty and there was nothing but grey concrete all around, and what I remembered as a maze was just two corridors, dingy and dark, one going left and one right.

I was no longer sure I was in control. I thought maybe not. I peeped in our old cloakroom. Coats hung limp in rows, a tap dripped, pale light lit up the high ceiling from the narrow windows. I turned away and walked as far as the main toilet block but didn't go in. There was no need, I knew it all, the sinks and toilets, the unfriendly strip lights,

Izal toilet paper, hard soap, cold water. Why should we have to go through all this at all? You would, wouldn't you? You would if you were her, you'd jump off the roof when the Sylvia-thing came up behind and whispered in your ear on the roof. She stood on the ledge. She let herself go. She was falling still through my mind, falling forever.

I had a feeling it was going to turn into an ordinary dream, one that would just keep doing its thing regardless and making me watch, so I turned to go back upstairs where there was more to look at and more in the way of sound. The first- and second-form cloakrooms were straight ahead with the sick room on the right.

It was always dark down there. Sylvia walked out from the sick room, short-haired and in school uniform, white ankle socks, clumpy shoes. She came towards me. It was the moment to wake up but I didn't wake up. The fear was finely pitched between panic and acceptance, teetering on an edge. She looked idiotic with that smile she'd worn on the roof and her large, wavery-watery eyes. I could have run but wanted to see it up close.

A great pity rose up for the horrid wavering thing, caught seething here forever as it was.

It came up close and smiled at me from a foot away.

There comes a point where you just give in. I gave up trying to name this thing, dream, lucid or not, awake, hypnopompic, whatever. The only thing that mattered was that I couldn't get out of it. I tried with all my might, put my whole mind into it, but it didn't work. Whatever I did I was still here and she was still there, not even the streaky glass panes of the greenhouse between us, only the malevolence of the wronged. We stood looking at each other like boxers getting psyched for a fight, in it together.

Time was unnecessary.

At some point I realised we were the same.

We started walking up the stairs. Through the windows over the stairwells evening was coming down, the sky intense indigo. The lights of the town shone. By the time we reached the middle floor the building was changing again. There was my door. I don't know why this seemed so funny. We both started laughing at the same time and for a while we couldn't stop. We'd try, but then we'd look at one another and start again. We laughed a little madly, the way she'd laughed in at herself through the greenhouse window that day.

We passed by my door but didn't go in. Robin and Sylvia were together in that nice flat. And now we were in the corridor outside 4 Alpha. The door was open. Four rows of empty desks all faced the front. The class hadn't come in yet so we sat down in the back row, side by side. We smiled at each other and there was a certain bond, as if we were forged on the same anvil. We'd probably always been here and all the rest was a dream. I'd be Cleopatra waking up between the paws of the Sphinx to stretch my arms and say, what a curious dream. Where was I? And what is this place? Did I die and was I resurrected? And have I learned kindness yet or will I poison slaves? A woman with orange hair drifted across my view. A man walked up and down with a child in his arms, and it was like watching the TV with the sound turned down. A small brown furry thing ran laps around the room. They were gone and the desks filled up with girls. All around us people came and went and time was still and always unnecessary.

We watch them change, the girls and the others, and all those still to come. As if I wasn't here, they move around me unknowing, and every little once in a while one or another might see from the corner of an eye my shade, a shadow perhaps, an unreadable silhouette, still there after all the years, tattooed onto the fabric of the place.

And one of these nights – who knows? – I might drift along a few doors and cross the corridor, sit by his bed and say –

Hello, it's me –

And he'll have uneasy dreams because I'm not yet all gone.

After

HE KNOWS NOW WHY HE STAYED. It had maddened him not to understand at first, to be forced into a corner saying, I just feel this way, that's all there is to it. But he's older now. Logic said stay, and he was a pragmatic man. He just never again used the back entrance, never would walk up or down the staircase where Sally turned her ankle in her platform shoe, him in the kitchen when it happened, basking in the shy appreciation of Sylvia's eyes. A woman returning in the rain found her.

For a long time he believed staying was purely a matter of convenience and good sense. Six or seven years passed before he realised sentimentality played its part. Now he knows he stays for the bond he has no wish to surrender. Still, the old cliché holds true. Time heals.

He never parks in the yard. Returning, he leaves his car in the underground car park and comes in the front way. He walks up; the flat is light and warm and smells of dinner. He flops onto the settee. Sound hangs in layers like fading smoke; if you just sit and listen you begin to appreciate the levels of it. He does this these days, something he never would have done before. It's times like these, when it's pouring down outside, peaceful within, the sounds of the building and the city overlaid by the pattering of rain, that the thoughts run in: if he'd just looked in on her, just to see if, if, if, if, if... Though mostly now the guilt has subsided, he still gets these times when it rushes back. Don't blame yourself, they all said. But you do, don't you? Then he is overcome with an interior landscape of time-dappled rooms and streets that changed long ago, and closes his eyes because the backs of his eyelids are burning.

Where did she think she was going? Out with no coat in the rain.

Then Sylvia comes, places her cool hand on the back of his neck and sings very softly to him, one of her old songs, making him feel like a child again. Sometimes she just hums with no words and he sinks into the comfort of her voice. Oh sweet content, she sings, and surely this is what he now has. This is what he thinks, opening his eyes to her slow smile.